D0065962

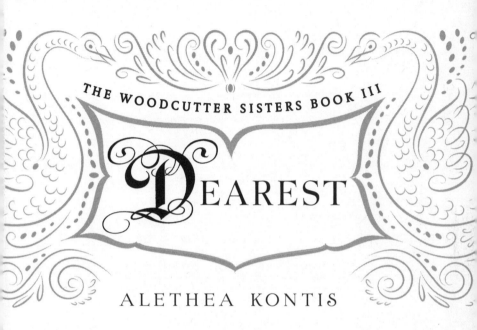

THE WOODCUTTER SISTERS BOOK III

Dearest

ALETHEA KONTIS

Houghton Mifflin Harcourt
Boston | New York

www.hmhco.com

Text set in 12.5 point Perpetua Std.
Book design by Christine Kettner

LIBRARY OF CONGRESS CATALOGING-IN-PUBLICATION DATA
Kontis, Alethea.
Dearest / by Alethea Kontis.
pages cm.—(The Woodcutter sisters ; book 3)
Summary: "When Friday Woodcutter, a kind and loving seamstress,
stumbles upon seven sleeping brothers in her sister Sunday's palace,
she takes one look at Tristan and knows he's her future. But the brothers are cursed
to be swans by day. Can Friday's unique magic somehow break the spell?"
—Provided by publisher.
ISBN 978-0-544-07407-1 (hardback)
[1. Fairy tales. 2. Magic—Fiction. 3. Characters in literature—Fiction.] I. Title.
PZ8.K833De 2015
[Fic]—dc23   2014000737

Manufactured in the United States of America
DOC 10 9 8 7 6 5 4 3 2 1
4500512028

For Jonathan Brandis, Barrett Oliver, Noah Hathaway,
Val Kilmer, Scott Grimes, River Phoenix,
Harrison Ford, and Michael J. Fox,
because an impressionable young girl
needs to fall in love a lot

&

for Murphy,
because a jaded young woman
needs to fall in love only once

1

Some Strange Magic

CONRAD SLOWED his pace, not because he lacked energy, but because the hard calluses on his feet had cracked and started to bleed. It had been a long, dry road from Rose Abbey, part of an even longer road that had begun in the slums of Sandaar. Conrad's battered feet had trod the length of this continent from the fiery south to the frozen north, but his soul had yet to find its destination. Omi had told him his journey would end when he found the place where his heart waited for him. He hoped Omi had not died at the hands of the sultan.

Conrad's stomach growled, distracting him from the wistful sadness that always threatened to overcome him when he thought about Omi, but he knew she would be proud of him, proud of his accomplishments, proud that he had kept his promise to leave the slums and never return.

The tips of his fingers throbbed. Perhaps he should not have declined the offer of food and drink at the Woodcutter house. Omi had advised him to rest where he was welcomed. The breeze picked up and Conrad stopped altogether, closing his eyes and spreading his arms wide so that the gusts might better cool his sweat-damp body. He took a deep breath. There was water on the wind.

The sky had been clear this day, with not so much as a cloud in warning. They were there now, rolling quick and fat and angry up from the west. The gray of rain blurred the horizon and erased the sun. Conrad had never seen clouds behave like this. Had he been in Sandaar, this would have meant a sandstorm. Here, in Arilland, the circumstances were all wrong. The colors were all wrong. The *water* was all wrong. He needed to find shelter.

He turned back to the road and froze mid-stride; a long-eared owl stood before him. The bird stared at him with unblinking yellow eyes. Omi had warned him against being superstitious, but Conrad had seen too many strange things on his travels to take chances. He backed away into the wooded area off the road. The owl's head turned slowly, those flat, yellow eyes never leaving Conrad. The wind kicked up again, lashing Conrad's now-damp hair into his face, but still the owl did not take wing. Conrad bowed low to the owl and eased farther into the brush.

Lightning flashed in the distance and thunder rolled soon

after it — booming, unending thunder that trembled the earth to such a degree that Conrad could feel it through the soles of his shoes. The second tremor knocked him off-balance. The third ripped away the forest on the opposite side of the road completely.

The last things Conrad remembered before losing both his footing and his consciousness were giant waves washing away the trees before him and those solemn eyes of the long-eared owl.

~eelee~

He awoke soaking wet and face-down in the mud. His head throbbed; when he placed his palm to the tender spot behind his right ear, it came away bloody. Conrad spat bark and soil out of his mouth as he slowly rolled over and sat up, leaning back against the trunk of a tree that had no doubt been his unwitting bludgeoner. He blinked once to clear his head, and then again, only to realize that it was not his vision that had erased the sparse woods before him. The landscape had erased itself. Across the empty road now lapped the ceaseless waves of an ocean, ebbing and flowing in the twilight as regularly as the tide from a distant shore. Some strange magic had not removed Conrad to this coastline — it had moved the coastline here, to Arilland.

Carefully he rose to his feet and shuffled to the water's edge. This water, he knew, would not slake his thirst, but it would tend to his wounds until they could be properly addressed. He threw his tattered shoes farther up on the muddy beach and waded into the surf. It was not as cold as it might have been for the climate; Conrad suspected the ocean was still energized from its journey east. If there was any latent magic still crashing with the flotsam in the waves, he hoped that it was good, natural magic. Either way, he would risk it rather than remain caked in mud from bleeding head to bleeding toes.

Once satisfied of his cleanliness and reinvigorated by the salty bath, he retrieved his shoes and walked barefoot along the new coastline as it skirted the main road to the castle. Night fell, the moon rose, and odd sounds erupted from both sides of the road, the moaning and wailing of confused sea creatures and shorebirds against the crickets and locusts of the Wood.

Conrad strained to hear the hoot of an owl, but none came. He concentrated so hard that he did not see the long lump of rags on the beach before him until he tripped over it and fell sprawling into the mud.

Conrad cursed.

The bundle groaned.

Lifting himself onto his hands and knees, he turned back to the bundle and sifted through yards of soaked material until he unearthed a face. Long dark hair was plastered to the face; he brushed it aside with a muddy palm. It was a young woman, he surmised, from what little he could discern in the moonlight. There was no mistaking the curve of her cheek or the softness about her mouth. She might have been of marrying age but there was no jewelry marking her person; at the moment she was simply a very pale, mostly dead girl. And she was now his responsibility. Conrad took a deep breath and let it out slowly and loudly. As if he didn't have enough to do.

He took off his shirt, went deeper into the surf, and collected some water so that he might discover the extent of her wounds before moving her body. It took a few trips to wash the mud from her completely. Like him, she had a rather large bump on the back of her head and a few angry scratches, nothing more. But she did not regain consciousness during his ministrations, and this worried him.

Conrad did not feel comfortable leaving her here alone, but the castle was still a distant shadow on the horizon. He could not carry her — she was almost twice again his scrawny size. He caught the heavy material of her overskirt in his hands. It seemed thick enough — though a good portion of its weight was due to water — and if the waist was a drawstring . . . it was. Conrad fumbled at the knot with shaking cold fingers until he had it undone. He peeled the overskirt away from her petticoat — she was lucky not to have drowned under the weight of so much clothing! — and then pulled the drawstring tight, closing the waist-hole completely. He laid the great circle of fabric out as best he could, and then rolled the girl up into it. With apologies to the girl, he began dragging her down the muddy shore.

Conrad had carried strange parcels and ridden stranger animals, but he had never dragged a body any significant distance. His arms quickly began to tire. Still he pulled and pulled the girl, in shorter and shorter bursts, until his skinny arms shook and his numb fingers could hold the skirt-sack closed no more. Defeated, he fell to his knees beside his charge. The looming shadow of the castle seemed no closer than it had before.

He moved the material away from her face, allowing the unconscious girl to breathe what little air she could. Her pale skin shone out from her dark cocoon. Conrad wondered if he had caught a fallen angel.

Divine or not, he couldn't leave her. There would be no warm bed and hot supper for him this night. He only hoped he'd be able to rest in this mud and regain what little strength he had come sunrise.

"Ho there, friend!" called a voice from the road. Conrad quickly covered the angel's face again.

Conrad rose and walked back to the road, where a round-faced man sat high in the seat of a cart filled with what smelled like sour hay. The cart was pulled by a donkey; Conrad approached the animal first. He could instantly tell the measure of a man by how he treated his animals. This donkey nuzzled Conrad's chest without hesitation, using its nose to lift his arm and sniff for the treats the man undoubtedly kept in his pockets. A good man, then. So good that his animal seemed to retain no memory of the earthbreaking storm that had just passed.

"Did you see it?" Conrad asked the man.

The man shook his head. "Never witnessed anything like it. Hope to never again." The man waved at the donkey. "Bobo here braved it far better than I did. Are you all right?"

Conrad chose his words carefully. "I am, but my companion is not. She hit her head in the storm and will not wake. I was trying to get us to the castle, but . . ." He raised his scrawny arms in illustration.

The man laughed. "Worry not, son. You've still got a ways to grow." He hopped down from the seat of the cart. "Show me to your friend, and I'll help see her safely into the cart. I assume she's somewhere along the shore?"

Conrad hesitated, startled at the sight of the man's eyes, bright and yellow as those of the owl that had saved him. "Thank you," said Conrad.

The man, more than he — did shoveling hay make all men so strong? — carried the girl to the back of the haycart and gently laid her inside. Conrad slipped in beside her, tied up the tailboard with his numb fingers, and let Bobo steadily walk them the remaining distance to the castle gates.

There was already a commotion at the main doors to the palace as guards tried to calm the throng of people desperate to see the king.

"Order!" cried one of the guards. "King Rumbold will hear all of you, each at a time, but not until I have order!" Some of the people obeyed and stepped to the side, but others still clamored to slip by the guards and worm their way through the gates.

"I will let you off here," said Bobo's master. "If you think you can manage it."

The ground seemed level, and there were only a few steps up to the main doors. "I can," said Conrad. "I thank you again."

"Don't mention it," said the man. "We are family now. Family weathers the weather together."

Conrad bowed to the man. "It is my honor." With renewed

strength he pulled the skirt-sack together and lifted the girl out of the cart. If he held some of the hem in each hand, he could distribute her weight across his back and make it up those stairs. He prayed he wouldn't have to carry her much farther. Those prayers were soon answered.

"Ho there, boy." A guard who seemed to be all muscles and no hair barred his path to the door. "You'll have to wait your turn like everyone else." A few people in the crowd behind Conrad rudely jeered their support.

"I have a very important message for the king," Conrad said, almost under his breath. He did not want the crowd to hear anything he had to say.

"Wazzat?" bellowed the guard. "Speak up!"

Conrad did no such thing. He merely closed his eyes and invited a sense of calm into his body. He knew when the guard leaned down to him; Conrad could smell the meat and beer on his breath. Conrad opened his eyes.

"I bear a very important message for their majesties, from Seven Woodcutter," he said, only slightly louder than before. "Please handle this parcel with the utmost care."

The guard shot a glance to the angry crowd, looked at Conrad again, and shook his head. He snapped at another guard by the door — this one full of muscles *and* hair. "Parcel for the king."

Conrad held out the ends of the skirt-sack to the hairy guard. "It's heavy," he warned. The hairy guard nodded, pulling the sack up over his shoulder and lifting the girl with ease, as if she were nothing but potatoes.

You may not be strong, Omi's voice echoed in his mind, *but you are quick. You move mountains in your own way.*

The hairy guard entered the receiving hall only a few steps before him, so Conrad saw everything. He saw the young queen raise her head as they entered and calmly reach over to her husband. The young king stopped mid-sentence at her slight touch and turned to her. They communicated without a word. The king followed his wife's eyes to the hairy guard's burden and his face became stern. He slowly raised a hand and curled his fingers, urging them forward. The queen raised a hand too, putting trembling fingers to her lips.

Conrad knew from experience that the best way to deliver bad news was quickly. "Your Highnesses, I bore a message this day to Seven Woodcutter from Rose Abbey. Tesera Mouton is dead." He turned to the queen. "Your father asked that I deliver the same message to you, in hopes that you would send a carriage to take your mother north."

The young king seemed confused.

The young queen's big blue eyes were anxious and sad. "Of course, but . . ."

Another guard—copper-haired this time—leaned in to the royal couple. "All roads north are blocked at the moment." The guard added no honorific to the sentiment, and neither the king nor the queen admonished him for it.

". . . but what does this have to do with Friday?" the queen finished.

It was Conrad's turn to be confused. "I'm sorry, Your Highness. I don't understand." Was something supposed to happen on Friday? Had the Woodcutters neglected some pertinent information in their message?

A dark, fey gentleman uncurled himself from the chair behind the copper-haired guard. "Everyone out." He casually swept an arm across the room and the assembly turned and left. Conrad, unaffected by the magical influence of the gesture, remained.

"I'll get Monday," the copper-haired guard said, before disappearing himself.

What? Would the guard really not return until Monday?

This did not seem to further upset their royal majesties, who stepped forward as soon as the hall was clear. The hairy guard gently lowered the sack to the floor. The skirt was dull and damp with mud, but the soul of its original colors still shone through. In the dark, Conrad had not noticed the richness of its many fabrics. A unique material, to be sure. The queen had certainly recognized it at once.

Conrad began to realize just how important his delivery truly was. He rushed to the girl's side and uncovered her face.

The queen gave a choked gasp and the king caught her in his arms before her legs gave way completely. The fey man appeared on his knees next to Conrad and placed a pale, long-fingered hand on the girl's equally pale shoulder. His lids fell over eyes the deep indigo of late twilight. After a moment they reopened.

"She is well. The sleep is a healing sleep. She has a bump on the head, nothing more." The fey man backed away, allowing the young queen room to collapse in a billow of golden skirts. She gently cradled the girl's head in her lap. Conrad noticed the family resemblance now. He noticed, too, that the queen's feet were bare. He smiled inwardly at this.

The king was speaking to him. ". . . what happened?"

"I had just left the Woodcutter house, Your Highness. There was an owl in the road and it frightened me, so I moved to avoid it. Then the world broke. I hit my head." His explanation sounded like a child's. He was far more eloquent when delivering someone else's well-thought-out words. Funny, he hadn't thought about his injury since finding the girl. The fey gentleman reached a hand over to examine Conrad's own noggin, and Conrad let him. The hand was warm. Suddenly the room seemed steadier. "Thank you, milord," he told the man.

"When I awoke, it was twilight. The far side of the road had been replaced by a muddy beach, beyond which lay . . . lies . . . a vast ocean. I washed myself off and made my way up the shore until I found . . ." Conrad still wasn't sure what to call her.

"You dragged her all the way here?" The fey man sounded dubious.

Conrad was forced to admit his shortcomings. "I tried, Your Highness. We didn't get far. But then a man came along driving a cartful of hay."

"Hay," the king mused. "Did this man have yellow eyes?"

The question shocked Conrad so much that he forgot his manners. "How did you know?"

"Velius!" the king addressed the fey gentleman. "That's the

same man who helped me back to the castle after my transformation. I'd bet my crown on it. We must find him!" He turned to Conrad again. "Did he tell you his name?"

"I'm sorry, Highness, he did not," said Conrad. "But his donkey's name is Bobo."

"Then we will use the beast to find the man. Thank you, friend. Please stay; my wife will see you are taken care of. Velius, quickly!" The king leapt to his feet and ran out the door.

Conrad stood quietly before the pretty young queen, unsure of what to say next. Her thin golden crown nestled deep in the golden hair that fell around the face of the girl in her lap. After a moment she held a hand out to Conrad. Since there was no one else in the room, he took it. Her eyes were as blue as the cloudless summer sky.

"Thank you," she said to him. "Thank you for saving my sister."

2

Safely Delivered

"RIGHT SIDES TOGETHER," her teacher said. "Keep the stitches small."

"Yes, mistress." Friday Woodcutter smiled graciously and did as she was bade, even though these tasks were things she had been doing from the time she'd been old enough to use the enchanted needle Fairy Godmother Joy had given her on her nameday. Friday was so ecstatic that she'd been apprenticed to the esteemed seamstress Yarlitza Mitella that she received every instruction, no matter how menial, with great joy.

She had always enjoyed her time at church with the orphans as well, but Sister Carol seemed increasingly reluctant to instruct her further in the ways of the Earth Goddess. Friday did everything the Sister asked and made no secret of her desire to one day become a dedicated acolyte, but after several seasons of resistance, Friday had stopped pushing. The children loved Friday, and Sister Carol—whom she respected mightily—had never asked her to leave, so Friday continued returning . . . and continued ignoring the feeling that she didn't fit in. She had her suspicions as to why she might not be the picture of a perfect acolyte, but she took a page from her mother's book and kept those thoughts to herself, lest the Sisters toss her out for good.

But here, lost in the slide of material in her hands and the magic needle pressed against her fingertip, the world felt right. Whatever path she was meant to follow, it would always involve this perfect expression of mending and creation: sewing. Every stitch she made was an offering of thanks to the gods.

"Right sides together!" Yarlitza Mitella ordered. Friday loved the mellifluous cadence of her teacher's voice. Mistress Mitella hailed from high in the mountains above Faerie, where the people had smooth magenta skin and silky black hair and everyone wore smart leather boots that seemed to last forever without ever appearing unfashionable.

"Yes, mistress." Friday checked for the ninth time that her material hadn't magically turned itself inside out, and then cheerfully continued with her row of tiny, almost imperceptible stitches. The push of the needle and pull of the thread was meditative; Friday could have happily gone on like this forever.

Mistress Mitella sighed loudly and threw her hands up in the air. Her teacher was the second-most animated person Friday had ever met (the first was her younger sister Saturday). "Do you know how this is supposed to work?"

Friday paused her stitching and gave Mistress Mitella her undivided attention. "I admit I do not, mistress. I am blessed to be in your tutelage, and I promise to do everything in my power to be a diligent student."

"This!" Mistress Mitella swept her arms toward Friday. "This is what I mean. It is my job to give the instruction and it is your job to complain. We must argue. Your anger then challenges you to surpass even my own skills."

Mistress Mitella wanted her to be *mad*? Even if such a thing were in Friday's nature, she was desperately afraid of losing her apprenticeship. "Between the orphans and my siblings, there is enough animosity in the world without my adding to it."

Her teacher plopped down on the cushioned seat next to Friday. The ruffles in her layered skirt echoed the fluttering of her hands. "I agree with you! And you are an excellent student!"

"But you are still unhappy."

The mistress's hands flew up in the air again. "How do I challenge you? Obstinacy, conceit — these I can instruct. I do not know how to teach to kindness and grace." She said the words as if they were the worst traits a person could have, but Friday did not take offense. She had spent enough time around Mama to know otherwise.

She could sense keenly the mistress's frustration, but took care to guard herself and not let the emotions overwhelm her or the situation, as Aunt Joy had taught her. "I am afraid," Friday admitted reluctantly.

Mistress Mitella brightened. "Yes. I can work with fear. Of what are you afraid?"

Heights, mostly, though Friday didn't see how that was pertinent to their conversation. "I am afraid of disappointing you."

Mistress Mitella squeezed Friday's pale fingers with her deep-red ones. "You won't," she said, but the words Friday heard instead were, "Make it fly." Dark storm clouds gathered in the window behind her teacher. Lightning flashed in her teacher's eyes.

Storms like this meant magic, and lots of it.

Friday bent her head over the material in her hands and challenged herself: right sides together, stitches small. "Fly," she whispered into the thread. She did not know why she had been instructed to do this; she only knew that she must. "Fly."

Pain erupted behind her eyes and in the base of her neck, as if the lightning was now flashing inside her skull. Stitch by stitch. Impossibly tiny. Impossibly quick. "Fly."

The stitches turned red as liquid fire, dark as blood spilled from a pricked finger. The fabric slipped from her hands and spread itself out before her like the pages of an open book. Friday stepped onto the floating sheet. She soared through the ceiling of their sitting room in the palace, over the carriage that waited at the gate for them, and out above the white-capped waves of the crashing sea.

This was her true fear come to life, though it diminished some with the sturdiness of the material beneath her and the breathtaking sight before her.

A wedge of swans surrounded her, leading her south for the winter. There were seven, their white wings each spreading out to almost the length of a man, their unfeathered black masks cocked jauntily like fellow bandits.

She felt the gentle brush of a wing at her side and shivered.

"Stop that," said one of the swans.

"He said not to touch her," said a second swan, with the voice of a young female.

"He didn't say that," said the one who had touched her.

"Yes, he did," said the first swan. "I was right there. He said if you didn't obey him, he was going to lock you in the stocks and let our sister beat you."

As the swans spoke, Friday's floating material began to descend, and her with it. The birds didn't seem to notice. Her fear of falling returned tenfold, gripping her heart in her chest with icy fingers.

"That wasn't a real threat. Besides, she hits like a girl."

"You think so?" said the first swan.

"Keep it up and you'll find out," said the girl swan.

The rest of their conversation was lost in a rush of wind as Friday plummeted to the ground. She opened her mouth to scream but there was no sound, no breath. Flailing, her limbs tangled in the yards and yards of material that enveloped her all the way down to . . .

. . . her bed.

A calmness settled within her breast, though her heart still ached from the phantom fear.

Not completely sure of where she was, she remained still, eyes shut, and felt the room. The sheets above and beneath her were silk and satin. The air was crisp and cool and smelled faintly of wood smoke. She could hear birds, both outside the window and within. The wild ones beyond told her it was daytime, and that the weather was fine. Her feathered friends chirped of sunshine and not rain, not storm winds and floodwaters. Inside the room, the swans from her dream still argued among themselves in the comfortable pattern of sibling rivalry.

She was not in the carriage. No longer in the company of her esteemed tutor. The bed that held her rescued body felt familiar, somewhere safe. The dream-fear in her chest melted as she woke. Happiness. There was happiness in this room, laced with concern. For her.

"You are a Grand High Bugaboo, Mikey."

"Yeah, well you're a gold-dipped bum-licker."

"Stop being ridiculous, Mikey."

"He started it!"

"Pretty sure I didn't invent being ridiculous. I would have remembered that."

Friday calmed herself and forced her mind to be silent. She would not worry the children with difficult questions that she knew would be answered in time. Orphans had enough complications in their lives without her adding to their burden. Friday sent a silent prayer to the Earth Goddess, whether or not she was listening, and called upon her strength. It was up to Friday to maintain what smiles she could in such a confusing moment.

"Listen to my darlings," Friday said with a voice far stronger than she felt. "Calling me back home with their sweet songs."

A trio of voices cried, "Friday!" and suddenly her bed was filled with children energetically clamoring for hugs.

Somewhere at the foot of the bed, a dog barked. She could see the nose and front paws of a puppy still too small to surmount this obstacle. Judging by the size of his paws, it wouldn't be an obstacle for much longer. He had a ways to grow. Just like her children.

John and Wendy and Michael weren't technically hers, but as orphans they weren't technically anyone's. Or, rather, they were everyone's. They belonged to Arilland and were therefore the responsibility of its citizens. It was a burden Friday didn't mind bearing.

"Found a friend, did you?" she said, catching them all in a bear hug and nodding to the puppy.

"He's an orphan too," said Michael.

"He got lost, same as us," said Wendy.

"It was scary," said John.

Friday rubbed the boy's back reassuringly. Not yet old enough to take on an apprenticeship, John played the role of protector to many lost children. He did not admit weakness lightly.

She hoped her darlings had not experienced anything like the memories that flashed through her mind, all of them drenched in water the color of terror. Rain upon rain, puddles and rising seas as they desperately raced north. The screams of the horses. The tilt of the carriage. Mistress Mitella's order for Friday to swim clear of the door . . . It was the last thing she remembered her teacher saying before the hungry waves consumed them.

Friday's heart sped up and her breath caught in her throat.

She wasn't sure if it was John's concern she felt or her own, but it was there all the same. In an attempt to distract the children she said, "I'm so glad you are all here. I was just dreaming about you."

"You were?" asked Wendy.

"Was I a pirate?" asked Michael. "Did I have a sword and kill trolls? Did I chop off their heads?"

Friday laughed and tousled the boy's hair. "Dearest Michael. Where do you come up with these things?"

"I have dreams too," said Michael.

"Then one day you must tell me all about them. But today I will tell you about mine. Is that all right?" The three children nodded quietly. She wished Sister Carol were here to see them like this, all clean and obedient. According to the Sisters, Friday's Darlings were usually anything but. This was not the church, though—Friday had surmised as much from her surroundings. She appeared to be back in the palace again, where her youngest sister reigned as queen.

"All three of you were there. But there were no trolls, and no swords. You were all birds. We were flying." She poked Michael in the nose. "And you were arguing."

"It would be a wonderful thing to fly," sighed Wendy. "Imagine the places we could go."

"What kind of birds?" asked John. Ever the practical one.

"Swans," said Friday.

"Swans?" said Michael, clearly disappointed. "But swans are—"

The crash of a tray and breaking of glass against stone echoed through the room.

Friday chided herself for not realizing that there was someone else in the chamber with them. A scrap of a girl with mousy hair and a scullery maid's uniform stared at Friday instead of the mess at her feet. Her large, muddy gray eyes almost swallowed up her gamine face. The wave of sadness that washed over Friday nearly drowned her again.

Friday slid out of bed without a second thought. "Let me help you," she said to the maid, and then yelled, "FREEZE!" back to her obedient cygnets. "Do any of you have shoes?"

In any palace but this, things like shoes would be required. John and Wendy shook their heads. Michael scowled.

"Best stay on the bed, then. Michael, hold . . . what's the dog's name?"

"Ben the Brave," said Wendy.

"Ben the Pest," said John.

"Ben the Troll Killer," Michael corrected.

The dog barked his own opinion.

"Ben," Friday compromised. "Keep him with you until we've managed to clean this up, all right?" Friday was mindful of her own bare feet as they touched the cool stone floor. Broken crockery was another thing with which she was intimately familiar, be it shattered by idle hands or angry ones. A family as large as the Woodcutters was not without its messes. She shook out the cloth napkin and began scooping up what she assumed was meant to be her breakfast, or lunch.

The girl knelt beside Friday, thin fingers still covering her mouth, more in shock than shame. "Don't worry." Friday put the same tone in her voice that she used with new and particularly skittish orphans. "Everything will be fine." The girl didn't seem convinced. "Are you hurt?"

"She won't say nothing," Michael called from the bed by way of explanation.

"She's mute," clarified John.

"Cook calls her Rampion," Wendy filled in. "She's the herb girl. She's been taking care of you all this time."

"Taking care of *us,*" said John.

Friday risked one of those difficult questions she'd been waiting to ask. "How long have I been here?"

"Three days," said a melodic voice from the doorway. "You've been blissfully asleep for three days. Wish I could say the same."

Friday looked up to see Velius, Duke of Cauchemar, standing beyond the threshold. King Rumbold's cousin, advisor, and closest friend was—among his many other great powers—a skilled healer. Friday was honored that this man would oversee her care . . . though her sister would have not settled for less. His beautiful fey body was the picture of health from head to toe, though Friday could feel his exhaustion from across the room. The shadow of his lithe, dark silhouette hid another boy, scruffy and slightly older than John.

Friday smiled and did her best to curtsey from her knees in the billowing nightdress. "Your Grace," she said with an affected air. The children on the bed giggled.

Velius bowed low to her and the scullery maid. "Princess Friday, how lovely to see you are doing so well that you've decided to throw your lunch across the room."

"I could not contain my joy upon waking."

"Indeed." Velius motioned to the upturned tray, and the shadow behind him ran into the room. "Conrad will help your friend clear the mess you've made."

"Rampion," Friday interjected. "Her name is Rampion." It was important to Friday that every young person have a name besides "you there" and "child."

Velius bowed again. "Forgive me, Lady Rampion." The mute girl blushed and bobbed her head politely, clasping her still-trembling fingers together tightly. Velius helped Friday back to bed while Conrad and Rampion quickly worked to clear away the spill. Even in the most elaborate finery Friday felt short, chubby, and ungraceful next to Velius; her current pitiful state did nothing to help her self-image. But she knew from the pressure of his hand that he cared for her as the sister of one of his dearest friends, and he wished her nothing but good will.

"If the lords and ladies of the bed would excuse us, I would like to see to my patient." There was much moaning and groaning on behalf of Friday's Darlings—and much whining on behalf of Ben the Conqueror—but the trio saw themselves out. Conrad closed the door gently behind them.

Friday climbed back into bed, noticing as she did so the myriad scratches that ran the length of her legs. "Is Conrad your new squire?"

"He's yours, actually." Velius released her hand and pulled a chair up to her bedside. "It was Conrad who found you washed ashore and saw you safely to the castle."

It was odd to think that she'd been washed ashore, since she'd never seen a seaside in her life. Now the mere mention of the ocean set her heart racing. Why? What had happened to her? More importantly: What had happened to the world she knew? Friday held her hand out to Velius again and he took it. Her friend. The voices in her head quieted.

"How am I?" She wasn't sure if Velius would know what she meant; she wasn't sure *she* knew what she meant.

"Remarkably well." His voice was as smooth and rich as the silken sheets. "You may not heal at the rate that Saturday does, but it seems your body has the ability to set itself to rights quickly enough in its own time."

"That time being three whole days?"

Velius patted the hand he held. "I was never worried. Nor was your family. Or the children."

"Thank you." Wise Velius knew exactly what words would most console her. Doubtless he had consoled many a distraught woman in his time . . . a length of time few could quantify. The fey blood ran strong in Velius, as evidenced by his dark hair and fair skin, giving him the innate ability to outlive many a mortal man while always maintaining the appearance of a hale and hearty youth. His father, born mortal yet addicted to magic, reputedly resided in Faerie to this very day. In his sire's absence, all called Velius "Duke," though Velius would be the first to remind them that he could not truly hold the title while his father survived.

"Forgive me, Friday, but I must ask. Do you remember what happened?"

Friday searched her mind, wishing she could recall more than the flashes of random visions that flickered before her eyes. With them, bubbles of sadness and terror burst inside her belly. She saw the swans again, and her mistress beside her, but those had been a dream. She did not want to disappoint Velius as she had disappointed her mentor. "I . . . I'm not quite sure."

Velius enveloped her hands in his larger, warm ones. His palms were surprisingly uncallused for a knight, just as hers were despite all her years of sewing. This unblemished skin was a particular fey trait they shared.

"Close your eyes," he said, and she obeyed. No harm would come to her in this world or any other with such a protector. Behind her lids the darkness turned to clouds of deepest indigo. "Breathe."

As she did, the clouds brightened and parted before her. Trees full of chirping birds surrounded her; sun warmed her skin. A soft breeze rustled the leaves above her and danced through her hair. She wore her usual costume: a plain linen shirt, bodice, and full patchwork skirt. There was a basket in her hand. Velius stood by her side, unchanged from the formal court dress he'd been wearing in her bedchamber.

"I know this place." She smiled into the sun and filled her lungs with fresh air that smelled of wildflowers and baking bread. "I often stop in this glen on the way to the church."

"I thought more familiar surroundings might set your soul at ease before we proceed. Do you mind?"

"Not at all," said Friday. "It's lovely."

"Many do not share your optimism as regards my use of magic. Especially in the wake of our former, unbeloved king."

Rumbold's father, King Hargath, had used magic to extend his own life by both literally and figuratively consuming the lives of his fey-blooded wives. Her sister Wednesday had barely escaped his clutches.

Friday raised her brows. "To decry the use of magic would slight both my own family and myself. So long as it is used for good and healing, I believe magic should never be shunned."

The duke bestowed upon her the infamous smirk that set all women blushing. "I'll be the first to admit my intentions are not always pure, milady."

Friday was not immune to his beauty. She knew he meant it politely, but she was not used to being a woman that men sought out, even in jest. Normally, girls like her were destined to become dedicates of the Earth Goddess and one day, if they were very lucky, maybe even great abbesses like her Aunt Rose Red.

Then again, dedicates, acolytes, and abbesses didn't normally fall in love with every person who came their way, either. Sister Carol might have seen this trait as a distraction, but Friday preferred to see it as a sign that she was destined for her chosen path. Humans and fey were all children of earth, and so Friday felt her seemingly endless capacity for love a boon to her Goddess. She would continue doing her best to stay true to the path of Earth; Sister Carol would come around eventually.

Friday turned away from Velius, whose inner and outer beauty almost seemed to glow in this other-place. "Even so, it is not for me to judge, Your Grace. That is between you and the gods you favor."

"You are too kind, princess." He placed a chaste kiss on the back of her hand. "This world is sorely lacking in kindness."

"Perhaps our new king and queen will set a trend." She sat on the fallen log he indicated, straightened her skirts, and settled her basket. "Can I offer you some conjured dream-pastries? I'm sure they're delicious."

Velius chuckled. "Thank you, no."

"Pity." Friday replaced the biscuit in the folds of the napkin and sucked the golden crumbs off her thumb. It was, indeed, as scrumptious as she'd imagined. "To work, then." She slid her hands back into Velius's, which were so warm with power that she almost broke into a sweat. She crossed her legs at the ankle and took a deep breath. As she exhaled, the visions came to her again, more slowly and smoothly, as if she were relating a tale remembered from Papa's knee. She forced herself to think of the recent events not as a memory, but as a story that had happened to someone else a very long time ago.

"I was in the carriage with Mistress Mitella on our way to her home in the north. We had made it as far as Hammelyn when the horses bolted." She saw their rolling eyes and blocked out the memory of their screams before they reached her ears. "There was no warning, besides the horses, of course. The driver managed to cut them loose, but the carriage never stopped moving—the earth rose up and caught the wheels and we were at its mercy. Then the water came, raining from above and rising from below. It filled up the cab as if the gods had dropped us in a lake. Mistress Mitella opened the door and ordered me to swim free." Her voice abandoned her briefly, and she paused to regain control. "That's the last I saw of her."

Friday might have been overcome with sadness had it not been for the calm strength of Velius radiating in warm waves next to her like a healing sun. Her brother Peter sometimes had this same calmness about him. "I've never been a very good swimmer."

The duke did not laugh at her. "It would not have mattered if you were. It seems the gods took it upon themselves to turn the high seat of Arilland into a seaport. I'm only sorry you were caught in the middle."

"Has there been any word from Mistress Mitella? Or the driver?" Friday stopped herself. If Velius had known, she would already have answers. "Who would have angered the gods so?"

"By all accounts, it was your sister."

"Wednesday?"

"Saturday."

Saturday? The least fey Woodcutter sibling of them all? This should probably have surprised Friday, but it didn't. Velius knew, as she did, that even without a scrap of magic Saturday had the power to anger anyone. "By whose accounts?"

"Your father, your brother, and Monday," said Velius. "Apparently, Trix spelled them all to sleep so that he could run away without your mother stopping him. Saturday did not succumb immediately, thanks to that damned sword of hers, and she managed to stay conscious long enough to throw a magic mirror after him. This particular mirror subsequently broke the world . . . and summoned pirates."

Pirates? *Of course*. It made sense when one's sister was a pirate queen. "Thursday gave that mirror to Saturday last spring, before we came to the ball. Just before we met you." There had been yards of gorgeous material in that trunk as well, and a proper seamstress's kit, thanks to the foresight of Captain Thursday's magic spyglass, or the remaining Woodcutter sisters might never have been able to attend that fortuitous occasion. Friday lamented a moment for her beautiful sewing kit, now lost to the waves of a misplaced ocean. She could kick Saturday.

"Why did Trix run away?"

"A message came for your mother that her sister, your Aunt Tesera, was dead. Her body lies in state at Rose Abbey."

"Trix's true mother is dead? Oh, the poor darling. Mama would have forbidden him to go, of course." Everything Mama said came to pass, for better or worse. That was her gift, and her burden.

"We'll never know," said Velius, "though I'll wager he didn't want to leave it to chance. Thursday took your mother and Saturday on her ship, so that she might see them safely delivered to the north. Erik accompanied them as well."

"Good." Few people could rein Saturday in as efficiently as her fencing teachers: Erik and Velius. Mama could too, of course, but not without substantial resistance and possible dire consequences. "How is Papa taking all this?"

"Your father and Peter are building a ship." He put his arm

around Friday's shoulders. "In the meantime, Rumbold has sent messengers far and wide. We will discover what happened to Mistress Mitella. And everyone else."

With that, the forest faded and Friday's bedchamber returned. The noises of the Wood were gone, and beyond the stone-rimmed casement the sunlight had dimmed to a late afternoon glow. The fallen log beneath her was now the silk and down of her bed.

Velius released her hands; Friday stretched her fingers out in the blessed cool of the room. "I shall keep you no longer, milady. I expect there are more than a few people eager to see you."

The duke nodded to her squire, who had slipped quietly back inside the chamber without anyone noticing. Conrad opened the door, stepped aside, and bowed as her family poured through with gifts and smiles and love. This time she opened her mind to their emotions, letting herself be overwhelmed by their good intentions. And whatever portion of Friday's soul that had yet to heal itself did so immediately.

3

Princess of Children

REFUGEES SWEPT into Arilland's palace only slightly less rapidly than the magical floodwaters that had evicted them. Every room was quickly filled, the larger areas transformed into mass sleeping quarters for those farmers and tradesmen who could not find lodgings in the lower city and surrounding areas.

Every morning, Friday steeled herself against the onslaught of emotions running amok through the palace. Aunt Joy had taught her meditations that allowed her to achieve calmness in crowded spaces, but silencing the ever-increasing population of Arilland was a true test of her mettle.

Sunday and Rumbold all but lived in the Great Hall. When the doors were open, they received guests and settled disputes.

When the doors were closed, they decided graver things, like where to house everyone, how to feed them, and whom to approach in the neighboring kingdoms for help. Velius took charge of the healers and turned the larger ballroom into a makeshift hospital. Princess Monday demanded the position of head nurse until Velius caved — her beautiful face at a patient's bedside worked more miracles than any panacea he could conjure.

Not one to stay idle, Friday appointed herself the Princess of Children. Every morning she, her young squire, and her Darlings would make the rounds, collecting any new children and seeing to their needs. Some parents were reluctant to leave their progeny in Friday's care — mostly the lords and ladies who felt that the unwashed masses had no business mingling with their royal betters. But after a day or two in the company of childhood boredom, these parents were all too happy to turn their young ones over to Friday.

"But what will you do with all of them?" Sunday had asked her big-hearted sister before granting her strange request.

"The laundry," Friday had answered with a smile. As she had learned from making herself indispensable to the Sisters, the best kind of fun was the kind that was also useful. This task was also best done outside, away from a palace teeming with emotions that Friday was still struggling to handle.

The weather stayed in Friday's favor — the skies seemed to have cried all their rain into the ocean and had no more to give. After collecting the children and baskets of soiled clothes, Friday and her flock marched down to the pond and set up camp.

The older boys built a lean-to to shade the babies from the sun. A few of the older girls sat with them, as well as Frank, a young man with no use of his legs but a sixth sense when it came to babies. They took turns with the changing and the feeding and the rocking and the cooing and the snuggling. There was much snuggling.

Friday broke the rest of the children into teams for sorting, washing, wringing, hanging, and mending. At first, washing was more of a punishment for the misbehaved, since, for the life of her, Friday simply couldn't dream up a way to make this fun. And then the misbehaved discovered the amusement of soap-fighting. After that, punishments turned to spot-scrubbing.

Each team had their own individual challenges. Whoever finished the task first got to sit with Friday or collect lunch from the kitchens. Whoever finished last was made to wash the babies' diapers. John and Wendy sat with Friday as many times as Michael had to fetch diapers. Only Ben the Ubiquitous accompanied Michael while attending to that particular chore.

When all the lines were hung and the bread and cheese were gone, the children were free to play their own games in the fields until dusk. In the evening, Friday returned her weary charges to their parents, happily yawning and bearing clean clothes for the palace maids to redistribute.

But the strain on the palace did not leave Friday's new Darlings untouched. As the days passed there were so many lines of clothes that no more could be hung. The children began using tree limbs, or the sunny patches of dry grass, where linens whitened best. There was less and less free time in the late afternoon. Vigorous games gave way to less energetic prospects like floating in the pond, watching the swans, or napping. All work and no play made the children irritable; Friday was eventually forced to leave some of the work undone. Worse still, the lunches began to shrink in size, though the number of children only grew.

Conrad joined Friday at the edge of the pond one afternoon, while the children played an elaborate game involving much running and screaming and barking and throwing of sticks. There was too much work to declare today a holiday, but an afternoon of idleness was sorely needed.

"You are doing the best you can," he said.

Friday smiled away a yawn she could not stifle. She was unsure how much of the exhaustion she felt was her own, and how much of it was the children's emotions compounding this feeling she was too tired to block. "And here I thought I was the only one who could sense the feelings of others." It had become a joke between them — Conrad's years of reading unspoken signs from masters in countries with an unfamiliar language seemed at many times on par with Friday's own powers of empathy.

"Be careful, mistress. Children have a sixth sense. They can tell when you're not happy."

"I promise to stitch up an extra-large smile before our journey back to the castle tonight."

"Then I will guard your sadness in the meantime," said Conrad.

Having a squire was an odd business. This boy — this young man — was her responsibility now in a way that her brothers and her charges had never been. The decisions she made would directly affect him, and no one else was responsible for the outcome save her. His complete willingness to trust her made her humble; it would have been disrespectful for her not to trust Conrad in kind, so she would and hope for the best. She thought it sweet of the young man to stay and help her instead of offering to take the first message from Rumbold and run straight out of Arilland — Friday certainly wouldn't have blamed him.

Friday let out a long breath and allowed herself to relax. "Thank you."

"As milady wishes."

Not so long ago, it would have been scandalous for a "lady" to frolic in the fields. Worse still, a woodcutter's daughter posing as a member of the royal house would have been tantamount to treason. These were different times in Arilland and — inconceivably — it had been her family who'd changed them.

Now, as long as the children were taken care of, no one cared if the princess dipped her toes in the duck pond. It's possible no one would have cared had she tossed her dress aside altogether and taken a swim. "I would rather be teaching them to read instead of training them for the workhouse."

"This is a time of adversity," said Conrad. "It will not always be like this. But it is important that they know to be useful in such times."

"It is also important that they not forget to be children."

"I was never good at that," said Conrad in earnest.

"Nor I." Friday had been put to work from the moment she'd understood the word "chore."

"Hmm. Perhaps your sister the queen chose the wrong shepherds for this flock."

Friday chuckled at that. "Perhaps."

"But as no other champions have stepped up to the task, I suppose we must bear the burden a little while longer."

Friday smiled at her squire. As if sitting beside a sunny pond in the late afternoon watching the swans and listening to the laughter of children could ever be a burden.

It was not perfection, though — there was a sorrow on the wind. The bitter, icy tendril of sadness pierced Friday's skin as easily as her needle slid through silk. She concentrated on the shrieking laughter behind her; this feeling did not come from the children playing in the field.

Friday lifted her gaze to the opposite bank of the pond. The girl Rampion stood there, tossing what looked like dried corn to the swans. The birds acted like fools for her, squabbling over the tidbits and pulling at her skirts and apron. Rampion smiled and Friday felt a laugh spring up in her throat on behalf of the mute girl. But there was still a profound wistfulness about the scene on the shore, echoes of the same sadness that had gripped Friday's chest back in the bedchamber.

Poor Rampion. It was good that the swans came to her. Like children, wild animals were always drawn to those who were pure of heart, a fact that Friday herself could readily substantiate. If the poor mousy girl had a kind heart, as Friday suspected she did, her troubles would work themselves out in the end. Only . . . this sadness felt old, cobwebbed with hopelessness and despair.

The wind kicked up Rampion's skirts; the bevy of swans — seven of them, Friday noticed — flapped their wings in the gust like a dance. The breeze caught Rampion's kerchief and blew it away. The strands of her limp hair caught the late afternoon sun and glittered like gold. For a moment, Friday saw the long limbs and innocence of a young woman. A memory struck her: Tuesday. Friday could almost feel the presence of her vibrant dancing sister, lovely in her solitude right up until the day death took her.

"Odd." Conrad's comment pulled Friday out of her reverie.

"Hmm?" Friday lifted her toes out of the water and wrapped her arms around her knees. "Odd? I think it's beautiful."

"It's odd because there is no wind," said Conrad.

Friday lifted her head. He was right. No leaf stirred, no grass blade bent, and there was barely a ripple in the pond before them. Friday held an arm out and felt no pull of the breeze on her sleeve or tickle of it across her skin, yet the scene before them played out as if trapped in a blustery dream.

Perhaps she and Conrad were too low to the ground? Friday stood, holding her body still so as to catch any stray brush of wind. Rampion caught the movement and ceased her dancing with a slight bow of the head to Friday. As she stopped, so did the wind. The swans dispersed, pecking once again at corn kernels hiding in the grass and at one another in turn. A tiny cloud covered the sun and that wistful sadness returned. Rampion was naught but a mousy herb girl once more. The dream was over.

"Magic," said Conrad, not loudly enough to carry over the water.

"Are you sure?" Thanks to the fey blood in her family, Friday had witnessed her fair share of magic spells being performed. But if Conrad hadn't brought it to her attention, she wouldn't have noticed anything out of the ordinary with the herb girl and the swans.

Her squire nodded. "It's . . . hard to explain. An old, sad magic."

His description sounded too much like the tendril of feeling that had burrowed into her. "Is it a curse?"

"Perhaps," said Conrad. "There is a dark, mud-brown magic that is not the girl's. The girl's magic is light blue."

Friday turned to him. "You see magic in colors?"

"You don't?"

Friday shook her head. "I don't know anyone who does. And I come from a rather extraordinary family."

Conrad smiled at her. "So I hear."

"Well, go on, then. What color is my magic?"

Conrad leaned back. "A deep, blood red. Also odd."

Friday raised both eyebrows in question.

Conrad cocked his head to the side. "Forgive me — this is difficult to explain. Blood-red magic to me has always been something dark and tainted."

Friday had the inclination to brood once in a great while, but she didn't feel particularly dark and tainted.

"But you are different," Conrad said quickly. "Your magic is bright and pure. It almost glows with a . . ."

"Light?" offered Friday.

"More like love," said Conrad. "As if your aura were the essence of love itself."

Friday blushed, hoping that her mysterious aura masked the red in her cheeks. "I'm flattered. And yet, you say that you have never before seen this sort of magic used for good works?"

Conrad shrugged. "I do not have academic knowledge of magic. I only know what I see. What I have seen."

"Then may your eyes only ever alight on good works," said Friday.

He bowed his head to her. "You remind me a little of my Omi."

"I do not know your Omi, but I believe you have just paid me another compliment."

"She was also a woman of much love. Fierce love. Not kindness, like yours. But we did not live in a kind place."

Before Friday could ask him to elaborate, a series of sharp barks and honks erupted into the air beside them. In the pond beyond Conrad, a swan fiercely defended his territory from Michael, who was in turn being defended by a very enthusiastic Ben.

"Is that a diaper?" Friday called to the boy. "I don't think the swan wants you mucking up his playground with that."

"But they need to be mucked out and I'm the mucker. *Again*." He pouted. "And what does he care? The swans don't live here anyway. They live in the sky tower."

"I thought swans nested on the ground, in the brush," said Friday.

"They do," said Conrad.

"Not these swans," Michael said. "These swans are fancy. They stay at the palace with the king and queen."

Since it was not safe for anyone else to inhabit the ruined tower that hid in the clouds, it made as much sense as anything for the swans to have taken refuge there. "Perhaps they got tired of you fouling their home. Who won the laundry races today?"

"Carrot Kate." Michael scrunched up his nose in mock disgust.

"Michael," Friday said warningly. "You know that's not nice. Her hair is much more like gold than carrots. Why don't you say that instead?"

"Because we have a Gold Kate now. And then there's Mean Kate, Smelly Kate, Little Kate, and Pickles."

"Pickles?" asked Conrad.

"I wouldn't let them call her Goblin," said Friday. Once more, their conversation was interrupted by hissing and honking and barking. "Wilhelm and Jacob are digging out a new latrine on the far hill. Go de-muck the nappies up there."

Michael pulled another face and Friday raised a finger. "It's not the mucking I mind so much," Michael said before she could speak a word. "It's the flirting. Flirting is worse than mucking."

"Jacob and Wilhelm are flirting with each other?" asked Conrad.

"Noooooo," said Michael. "With the Silly Twins. Elaine and Evelyn."

With every fiber of her being, Friday resisted the urge to roll her eyes. Michael's habit of labeling things would be the death of her. She looked out over the field where the children were at play. When had her army of children grown quite so legion? Perhaps there was a method to Michael's madness. Friday realized she could name them each herself, but it might take half a day.

"Take these," said Friday, and she handed the child a bunch of flowering vervain. "Give them to Elaine and Evelyn and tell them I said to take care of the nappies for you. They can muck and flirt at the same time."

A wide grin split Michael's face; he grabbed the bunch of purple wildflowers out of her hand and sped across the meadow, Ben nipping at his heels.

"What do you say?" called Friday.

"Thaaaaaank yooooou!" echoed back to her as he ran.

"There you are, sir," Friday said to the swan. "Disaster averted. You're very welcome."

The swan strutted in a circle, honked a bit, and then, curiously, seemed to bow to Friday before spreading his wings and launching high into another phantom gust of wind.

Conrad shook his head. "Magic."

Friday stood and picked what grass she could out of her fine dress—a blue velvet with silver gilt weft from Sunday's closet. It was far too fine for sitting in a meadow, but she would never refuse a gift from her sister the queen. Even so, she missed the full, patchwork skirts that she'd grown to love over the years. She'd already begun collecting items of clothing that were beyond repair in the hopes that she might fashion another one.

"The sun's gone down," she told her squire. "Let's start herding our flock."

~ellee~

Since the castle was already overflowing with refugees, John, Wendy, and Michael shared a pallet in the corner of Friday's room. She didn't mind at all, even when it sometimes took the giggling gaggle a very long time to settle down and succumb to sleep. Friday had surrendered a blanket and pillow to Conrad, who somehow made himself comfortable on the floor by the door.

She wasn't sure how Ben the Needy managed to wake her without disturbing any of the others, but there he was, pulling at her sheets, licking her hand, and whining into her palm before even a hint of sun had dispelled the dark from the sky. She rubbed her eyes and lit a candle so that she could see the puppy out to the courtyard. She probably should have woken some of the children and forced them into the role of responsibility, but she'd rather do it herself now than deal with grumpy faces all day.

Silence met Friday in the hallway — not so much as a guard or well-seasoned farmer stirred to break the stillness. Not even Conrad awakened as she tiptoed over him and slipped through the doorway like a thief.

The puppy bounded along in front of her. Where he should have turned right to make his way down to the familiar courtyard, he turned left and scampered away, his morning necessities apparently forgotten. Friday did not call after him for fear of breaking the castle's serenity, so she gave chase, shielding the candle she carried so that she would not be lost in the dark.

Down halls and around corners she went, farther and farther into the depths of the palace. Just when she thought she'd lost Ben in the shadows, there he was, nipping at her heels and sprinting away again. What was the fool pup playing at? Whatever it was, she hoped he tired of it soon, before someone caught her wandering about in her nightgown like a lost ghost.

One more hall and two more turns and suddenly she was mounting stairs, up and up and up. When she hit the third landing Friday realized with dread that she was climbing the sky tower. Even before it had been ruined she'd never had a desire to do this, but there seemed to be no turning back. Far ahead of and above her, Ben let out a sharp bark. She swore to scold the dog as she would an unruly child when she got her hands on him.

Friday concentrated on the steps and the flame. She heard the cold wind whip around the tower and through the thin windows spaced along the stairwell, but the candle in her hand never gave so much as a flicker as she climbed. The stones beneath her bare toes grew slick as she reached the misty cloud cover, and then dry again as she rose slowly above it. She swallowed hard so that her ears would pop and tried not to think about just how far below her the rest of the world was. She took deep breaths, when she remembered to breathe at all.

At the top of the stair lay an Elder Wood door, shut and latched from the inside. Softly, Ben yipped from the other side of it. Friday sighed. The room that the door had previously hidden had been completely destroyed. There was no ceiling here— just the brightest of the fading stars still twinkling in the rising dawn above her—and the walls were naught but crumbled piles. Of this room only the doorway and the floor remained intact.

The tower swayed in another gust of wind, and Friday began to pray. She knew that nothing could happen here. The evil giant king had half destroyed this place, but Wednesday had healed it. She'd come up here every day and used her magic to bind the stones together so that they would never fall. Like the tower that supported the Woodcutters' own humble cottage, this tower would be standing long after the rest of the castle had rotted into memory. Taking a deep breath of the thin air, Friday lifted one leg over the rubble closest to the Elder Wood door and entered the room.

There were naked men everywhere.

Friday realized she'd stopped breathing again.

Before her on the floor lay one, two, three . . . *seven* young men about the age of her brother Peter. The great Elder Wood door shadowed the men from the pinks and blues of the awakening sky. A few threadbare blankets were scattered among them, but the sight was mostly skin and hair. They were all quite fit, with leaner muscles than her woodcutter brother's, but well-defined all the same. The colors of their hair varied, but each was so pale it seemed as if they'd never seen the sun.

Ben sniffed and scampered around the men, but they did not wake. Friday found herself stepping into the room, one foot after another, not realizing what drew her until she was at his side.

Here slept the most beautiful of them all. His hair was long, perhaps shoulder length, dark blond with shocks of white. His features were at the same time sharp and beautiful; in sleep he looked the way she imagined one of Lord Death's angels might. She could not help glancing into the shadows to see if he had wings of feathers or fire. It was almost impossible for her to turn her gaze away.

Friday could not name the strange power that held her; she only knew — with complete certainty — that she was supposed to be here, at this time, in this place, with this man. She felt as if she knew his name, but the word would not bloom on her tongue. Was she supposed to help him somehow? Judging by the state of him, he and his comrades were considerably lacking in the three basic necessities. She wanted to give him shelter. She wanted to bring him a hot meal. She wanted to tailor his favorite shirt.

She wanted to kiss him.

Gods help her, she'd fallen in love *again*. She whispered another prayer to the goddess to guide her hopeless soul, while also secretly wishing to know the color of his eyes.

As she leaned down toward him in the dawn's early light, her wish was granted. Three drops of wax from her unwavering candle fell onto his pale, unblemished skin, and with a sharp gasp he awoke.

Blue. His eyes were deep blue and white, like the caps of the waves on Saturday's impossible sea. Blue . . . and angry. Or frightened? Confused? For once, Friday could not discern the other feelings that washed over her. She only knew they were powerful, and that she'd been caught in their net. She wasn't sure if she was supposed to hug this man, hide him, or present him to the king. All of those things were at odds with what her instincts were brazenly suggesting.

The young man did not move or speak, nor did she. She was paralyzed, frozen in his gaze.

"What is this?" another man bellowed. "Who are you?"

Friday turned her head ever so slightly. Her eyes reluctantly followed soon after, adjusting in the light to focus on the three very large, very awake, and still very naked men now standing between her and the Elder Wood door. These men were angry, there was no doubt.

"Answer me, girl," said the darkest and the strongest, but Friday could not find her voice. She backed slowly, begrudgingly, away from the young man on the floor. She forced her tongue to speak an apology. Then a high-pitched yowl broke the silence.

She had stepped on Ben's tail.

With a gasp she took another quick step back, realizing only too late that there was no more of the room left behind her.

And so, gracelessly and in her nightgown, Friday plummeted from the sky tower.

4

A Bevy of Idiots

RISTAN DIDN'T STOP to think before he dove off the tower after her. He was aware of the time, less from the light in the sky and more from the itching of quills beneath his skin. It was morning, he knew. He just hoped it was morning enough.

He could see her face as she fell ahead of him, fast, too fast, a fluttering blur of warm brown hair and white fabric and eyes, those eyes, gray as dark ice, wide with fear and piercing straight into his soul. He spotted movement in the corner of his vision: good. His brothers had been stupid enough to follow him down. Despite sheer will, and assuming this worked, he wouldn't be able to bear her weight alone.

He flattened his arms against his sides, forcing himself to

fall faster. The familiar pinch on the bridge of his nose and the pull between his shoulder blades seemed to take an eternity as the ground rushed to meet them. He curled his feet in beneath his body as his tail elongated, and resisted naturally curving his neck as it stretched, keeping his beak down.

Somehow he managed to pass her in the air; having done so, he spread his arms wide, slowing down as the brute wind pushed them upward. His massive wings shuddered as he strained his muscles to the breaking point.

Bit by bit, he felt his burden lessen by degrees as his brothers caught her gown in their beaks and pulled hard, their outstretched wings humming against the rush of the wind. Had he been able to, he would have cried in relief and joy.

Too quickly they met the overgrown rubble at the base of the tower. A sharp rock sliced along his chest, deep beneath his left wing. The girl rolled limply off of him as his brothers released her. The candlestick in her hand skittered across the ground. Tristan summoned the last of his strength to waddle over to her unconscious body. He burrowed himself into the crook of her arm, stretched his long neck out over her shoulder, and died.

"Tristan, come on. You're not dead."

Sebastien was growling at him again. It really was too bad they'd been cursed into swans. Sebastien would have made a much better bear.

He had been growling at his younger siblings for years, long before they had migrated to this pretty little palace in Arilland. It hadn't been so bad just after their escape from the islands and over the endless sea, but somewhere among the ice and snow north of the Troll Kingdom, their eldest brother had taken it upon himself to fall in love with a real swan. The rest of them had been paying the price ever since.

"No," Tristan replied. "Pretty sure . . . dead." If the fire lancing through his breast didn't usher him into the hands of Lord Death soon, the aching emptiness that lingered beneath might. He had not seen the girl since that morning, since his sister had carried his swanself away from the rock pile at the base of the sky tower. The girl lived, but would she return? He had seen the fear in her eyes, followed her down all those stories, willed her to believe in him.

Somehow, though, he knew she had believed. He didn't know how, but he *knew*.

He sucked air in through his teeth as Elisa attempted to scour his gaping wound with a damp cloth. He could say this for his little sister: all these months of toiling under the orders of the palace cook had made her stronger than ever. Tears of pain leaked from the corners of his eyes.

They had all learned the hard way — well, all but François, who was smart enough to let his idiot older brothers learn on his behalf — that transforming each night back into a larger human body meant whatever wounds they had sustained as swans would grow proportionally larger as well, and vice versa. This particular gash might still yet usher him into the hands of Lord Death, especially if his sister kept on the way she did. Idly, he wondered which of the lord's angels would come for his poor, tortured soul. He wasn't worried. In fact, his soul was calmer and more alive at the moment than it had ever been his whole life.

Were there people who actually existed in states of such bliss? How did they function?

Elisa's ministrations sent his body into paroxysms of pain; this time he did cry out. The twins grabbed him — one clamping a hand over his mouth and one holding his shoulders down as Tristan tried to squirm away from his sister.

Bernard adjusted his hand over Tristan's face to get a firmer grip. "No giving us away, brother dear."

"It's no less than you deserve," said Rene.

"What possessed you?" asked Christian.

"He's finally gone mad," Philippe said in low tones. It wasn't a question.

Tristan's almost-twin was the only one of them angrier at the world than Sebastien. Philippe was born angry at everything: his life of privilege, his inability to be the oldest or the biggest or the smartest or the strongest among his brothers, and now the curse, on top of everything else. What few words escaped Philippe's lips dripped with spite. Tristan remembered being a young man full of fire in the days before their lands had fallen into the hands of their enemy, but that was nothing like Philippe's tempered rage. And yet, Philippe had followed him off the edge of the tower without question and worked just as hard as the others to save the falling girl.

He might never understand his brother, but he loved him all the same.

Elisa stared at Tristan with scolding blue eyes and pointed to each of the speakers in turn, indicating that they were saying exactly what was on her mind, since she could not speak the words herself. She laid the cloth on him again; this time he growled like Sebastien and removed her hand. "Can't think . . . when you're . . . doing that," he said as gently as he could.

"Wimp," said Bernard.

"Girl," said Rene.

"You must let her tend to it, Tristan. It looks terrible," said Christian.

Elisa pointed at Christian.

"I'll be fine," said Tristan. "Just . . . give me . . . a moment." It hurt to breathe. Elisa summoned the breeze in to cool his skin, since he would not let her touch him, and he welcomed it. It danced through her golden hair and set the candlelight flickering. Despite all the things Tristan hated about this curse, he was glad it masked his sister's natural beauty by day, though he did miss the sound of her voice and the music of her laughter. There had been such joy in their lives once, so long ago that Tristan had almost forgotten what it felt like.

"What are we waiting for, exactly?" asked Bernard.

"Isn't it obvious?" François sat apart from them all, his nose buried in another book. "He's waiting for the girl."

"She won't be back," growled Philippe. Tristan smiled. He could tell his brother didn't believe that any more than Tristan himself did.

There was a deep, rumbling bark from the far edge of the open floor, and the brothers all turned to witness something they had not seen or heard in a very long time: Sebastien laughing. The sound was as disturbing as it was amusing. Their eldest brother scratched his short, dark beard and the sparse pelt of hair on his chest. "Tristan's in *love*."

Something else washed over Tristan then, something not pain but just as powerful. Love? Really? He'd definitely felt something since daybreak — a pull like a fist clasped round his heart — but . . . love? He didn't even know her name! Since their parents had died, none of them but Sebastien had ever been in the position to love anyone but one another.

Tristan wondered what role the girl would play in their future. She could only have found them if the Gods of Air had led her here and allowed her passage. But why?

And why did he seem to know with extreme certainty that she would be walking through that Elder Wood door at any moment?

"Dunno," Tristan managed to say. "She means . . . something."

"Trouble," said Bernard.

"Doom," said Rene.

Tristan expected no less from his elder twins.

"Perhaps it's time to break the curse," François suggested from his corner.

Tristan saw Elisa's shudder. Breaking the curse meant facing Mordant again, the man who had killed their parents and taken

Elisa for his intended bride. Their curse had been the price of her refusal. Mordant's sorceress had changed them into swans and a plain-faced serving girl. Thusly the heirs to the throne of Kassora, high seat of the Green Isles, had fled, eventually making their way west toward Faerie, into the heart of Arilland.

Though the brothers were forced into swanhood by day, it was worse for Elisa, who could not allow herself to speak a word aloud. If she did, the curse would trap her brothers' souls inside their beastly bodies forevermore. She had hopped from orphanage to orphanage until she was finally sold to the royal kitchens here at the palace. The cook seemed to genuinely care for Elisa, fostered her as well as any guardian might, and for the first time in many years the siblings held some small hope of breaking the curse. For it was not out of the ordinary for swans to inhabit the royal gardens, and no one was hunting a mousy girl named Rampion.

A gentle hand knocked on the door; had Tristan not been holding his breath in wait for it, he might have missed the faint sound. "She's here," he whispered.

The wind whipped through the broken room as Elisa startled; her spells, which had been keeping it at bay, faltered briefly. The older brothers merely stared at the door as if in fear of what lay beyond. It was François, the youngest, who finally put down his book, wrapped a blanket about his waist, and went to open it. The rest of them scrambled for skin coverings of their own as she stepped tenuously into the room.

Oh, how Tristan's soul had missed her.

What?

A nameless force clenched round his heart again. This was a ridiculous feeling — he hadn't even known her a full day! — but it was there, nonetheless.

She looked smaller than he remembered. He shook off the swan's memory; humans would not have referred to this girl as either small or slight. She was healthy, as a young woman might be who could climb terribly long flights of stairs on a regular basis. Her cheeks were flushed from the exercise. Rich mahogany curls spilled over her shoulders in a wild thicket — for a moment he saw blossoms sprinkled in that riot of hair, but then the moment was gone. She too had covered herself with more clothing this time, though merely a simple skirt and shirt, and she carried a large basket. There were slippers on her feet. Those feet did not venture far beyond the safety of the Elder Wood door.

Tristan realized how physically and mentally exhausting it must have been for her to make the journey back up here after falling so far. He wanted to go to her, to save her the trouble of having to come farther in the room to where he lay. Elisa put a hand on his chest to still him.

The girl braved one more step into the room before breaking the silence with her sweet voice. "I think you saved me," she said to him. "I think you all saved me. And I thank you for that." She set the basket down on the floor between them. "There is some food in there. A few more blankets. And a book." She did not look at François — did not look at any of them — as she slowly backed away. "I'm sorry it couldn't be more." One more step back. She was outside the door now. "I should go."

"Please." It was Sebastien who spoke the words that bled from Tristan's heart. "Stay."

The girl smiled down at her slippers; her whole body seemed to soften and relax with the expression. Tristan wished she would smile at him like that. And then, as if he'd said the words aloud, she did. Her gaze hit him like a blow to the chest and took his breath from him. Or that might have been Elisa's cloth at his wound again. He growled and slapped his sister's hand away once more.

"My name is Friday." Her voice was as soothing as a nurse at the bedside of a wounded warrior.

Elisa gave up and tossed her rag at Tristan. She stood, faced the girl, and then curtseyed low.

"Oh no, really. Please. You don't have to do that," said Friday.

"You're the princess who minds the children." Of all of them, François retained the most memories from his days as a swan. Tristan was only ever left with a stiffness in his shoulder muscles, the briny taste of fish on his tongue, and hazy, half-formed dreams.

"I am merely the daughter of a woodcutter and a devotee of the Earth Goddess," she said. "But yes, my little sister happens to be the queen here. And yes, I lead an army of laundry-cleaning children. Such a glamorous life." She pulled back the cloth that covered the basket's contents. "I wasn't sure if men who turned to swans would have the stomach for meat pies, so I selected some simpler rolls and pastries. I don't think the kitchen will miss them."

Rene and Bernard got over their shyness enough to snatch the basket out of her hand and rummage through it like a couple of starved kobolds. Elisa scrambled to retrieve the blanket they'd dropped and held it up to shield the princess from the twins' nakedness.

"Cinnamon! I smell cinnamon. Dibs on the cinnamon thing, whatever it is."

"Move your elbow, lout. Don't mind the soft rolls, the old men can eat those. Ooh, I think I see a pie! Here's your cinnamon thing. Now get your arm out of my face before I break it."

Both the "old men"—Sebastien and Christian—chuckled at the twins.

"Your kindness is most appreciated," said Sebastien. "It's not often we see such treats."

"Surely Rampion brings you bread from the kitchens," said the princess.

"We don't encourage it," said Christian. "We don't want her . . . reprimanded."

Friday took another step forward, closer to Tristan. He wasn't sure if she noticed, but he did. Her presence pulled at him, and he yearned for it. He wanted to keep her, to protect her, to save her all over again. He wanted to hold her and stop her from trembling. He never wanted her to be afraid again.

He screamed at the sky, in pain borne of frustration rather

than blood. *"WHAT IS THIS?"* Tristan yelled at the princess, at the world, at the gods, and then immediately regretted his action. His first words to her should have been ones of kindness and introduction, not anger and confusion . . . but he'd had enough of feeling this strangeness between them without being able to define it.

Slowly, Friday shuffled her feet toward his prone body. When she became uncomfortable walking, she lowered herself to her knees and scooted up beside him. "I have just as many sisters as you have brothers, if you can believe that," she said. "One of my older sisters, Wednesday, is a powerful fey. The evil king who lived here—the current king's father—tried to bind her power to him in this very room, and in doing so almost destroyed it." The more she spoke, the less she trembled. Tristan tried to concentrate on her words.

She waved a hand to the crumbling half-walls that surrounded them, but did not follow it with her eyes. "After the king died, Wednesday came back to this place and used binding magic to secure the stones and keep them from crumbling. Some who are sensitive to these things say they can still feel her magic in the mortar, fusing the tower into one solid structure."

"What does this . . . have to do with . . . ?" He didn't need to finish.

"My little sister—the queen—believes that Wednesday's magic bound together more than just the stones of this tower. Sunday thinks that Wednesday strengthened many other bonds here in the castle, both tangible and intangible. Soldiers became more loyal. Families grew closer, our own certainly. And people whose destinies were meant to intertwine have been . . . particularly drawn to each other."

"So this . . . is destiny?" As if Tristan hadn't had enough of Fate's meddling handiwork.

"Call it what you will, based on your own experiences and beliefs." The comment was worthy of a dedicate. In which of the gods' houses did she say she served? Earth? No wonder she was so ill at ease at this altitude. "Either way, I am here now, and I would like to help you. If you would let me."

"Are you a physician?" Rene asked her, despite the fact that she clearly wasn't.

To her credit the princess did not rise to his brother's goading. "I am not a healer," she said humbly. "I am a seamstress."

"Do you use skin as fabric regularly?" Bernard asked in a similarly mocking tone.

"I have experience with leather and sheepskin. And I have a magic needle." She pulled said needle from a seam inside the shoulder of her shirt. "After the king died, I sewed a goose back together with a thread made from the blood of a monster. The goose had previously been my sister Wednesday. By all accounts, both the goose and Wednesday are thriving."

"You have a strange family," said Philippe.

"So do we," admitted François. Elisa pointed at him in agreement.

But even Philippe's rancor didn't seem to bother the princess. She removed a spool of white silken thread from the pocket of her skirt. "I should warn you, though; the goose now lays golden eggs. I don't think you'll start doing the same, but I won't continue if you don't want to risk it. The choice is yours."

He didn't want to smile at her, but Tristan couldn't help himself. She smiled back at him, and in that moment she was the most beautiful creature he'd ever seen.

Destiny, maybe. But love? *Bah.* Ridiculous.

"Go on." The command came from Sebastien. "He can take it."

Friday still waited for Tristan's nod of agreement. "The goose couldn't tell me otherwise, but I imagine this is going to hurt." She reached out to touch the flesh of his marred chest with her hand and a dark blue flame of lightning shot from his skin to hers. Tristan watched as the indigo spark leapt from them to the floor, splitting and dancing between the stones.

Judging by Friday's expression, a similar event had not happened with the goose.

"Was that painful?"

He shook his head, afraid that if he opened his mouth, one emotion or another would betray him. He wasn't lying; the spark had tingled, but it hadn't hurt. No more than his current wound already did.

Her needle, on the other hand, lanced through his flesh like a firebrand. Sebastien, at the ready, shoved the corner of a blanket into Tristan's mouth to muffle his screams. He bit down hard. His muscles spasmed. His eyes welled up against his will. He could tell Friday's jaw was clenched, but she remained steady. He did his best to remain steady for her.

Stitch by stitch, she continued sewing him up with fire.

Tears began to course down her cheeks too. Did she feel sorry for him? Was she losing her determination? Her tears made him angry, which was good, because the anger kept him conscious. She knew virtually nothing about him, his past, or his family. There was no way she could know what an excruciating punishment this was. What right had she to cry?

Suddenly there was a new pain: the fingers of Tristan's right hand were being crushed by his sister. Elisa stared at the princess over Tristan's body with a look that could cut glass.

"But I don't know what else to do," Friday whispered, as if in answer to an unspoken question. "I must go slowly to make sure every stitch is right." She paused for a beat, and her beautiful features screwed up in an expression of . . . pain? Helplessness? Fear?

She shrugged, and then nodded. "Okay," she said. "It's just . . . I've never . . . I don't know . . ." Her words trailed off into nothing.

Had Tristan succumbed to delirium? With whom was she speaking?

Friday pulled her needle through his flesh one last time before cutting it loose from the thread with a small knife and replacing it in the seam of her shirt. Was she finished? Tristan's senses were so dazzled by the pain he couldn't tell. She reached out to him again, this time laying her palm flat against his wound. There was another spark of magic flame—deep red instead of blue—and the pain was suddenly gone.

Friday fell away and collapsed into Christian's arms, unconscious.

"What did she do?" Tristan sat up. "There's no pain."

"There's no wound," said Bernard.

Tristan twisted this way and that, ran his hands incredulously up and down his chest. His brother was right—there was nothing: no cut, no scar, no evidence that he had ever been injured. What *had* she done?

"She said she wasn't a healer." Tristan took the princess from his brother and cradled her in his own arms. As she shifted, her shirt pressed flat against her left side. Just beneath her left breast, a flower of blood began to soak through the linen there. Had she been wearing a bodice, they never would have seen it.

"She's not a healer," said François. "She's an Empath."

"Idiot!" Philippe yelled to the skies. He could have been referring to Friday or Tristan. Or both.

Less enigmatically, Rene smacked Tristan on the back of the head.

"You've gone and killed a princess," said Bernard.

Tristan could feel her warm body breathing in his arms, however shallow. "She's not dead," he snapped.

"Not yet," said Rene.

"She's an Empath more powerful than I've ever seen," said Sebastien. "She didn't just feel your pain; she took it from you completely."

Tristan held the princess tighter, cursing himself for the selfish thoughts he'd had while she was trying to heal him. "Will she be all right?"

"Let her go and let me see."

Tristan might not have released his hold on her for anyone

other than Christian, the most levelheaded of the brothers. Christian lifted Friday's shirt, gently and modestly, uncovering the wound and nothing more. "It's sewn," he announced after his examination, "and nicely, too. The blood there seems to be entirely superficial." He blotted it away with the corner of a blanket and lowered her shirt again. "Worry not, brother. She will heal."

"I bore the burden of the sewing, but she will bear the scar I was meant to have." Tristan tried not to be angry with her again, this time for being stronger than he.

"Who *is* she?" Tristan asked again.

"She is your destiny," Sebastien told him.

Tristan had had enough of this nonsense, magic flames and all. "But I don't want a destiny!"

"People seldom do. Just ask my sisters." The soft body in his arms shook with a chuckle, followed by a wince. "Goddess, that hurts. Remind me not to be funny again for a while."

"She's alive!" shouted Rene.

"Incredible," said Bernard.

Her eyes fluttered open and those gray depths looked right at Tristan. "What happened?"

"You took my wound," he told her. "You just *took* it. It's yours now."

She raised her right arm to her left side and winced again. "That's new."

"Luckily, you took the stitches as well," said Christian. "It already looks much better. I believe you'll be fine . . . in time."

Was his brother mad? So little about this whole situation was fine.

"I take it you don't do this sort of magic often?" Tristan asked her.

"Beyond sewing, I've performed little magic at all personally, though it does run in my family." Friday shook her head a little. "This is definitely a first."

"Well, don't go doing it again."

Those gray eyes narrowed into icy slivers. "We may share a destiny, sir, but you do not know me, my family, or the chaos that skips merrily in our wake. I will very likely do that again, or worse, and you have no control over it now, nor will you. Understand?"

It was eerie how her words mirrored the ones he'd felt only moments before. Tristan hadn't had a woman put him so firmly in his place since before their mother died. He supposed he deserved it—he just couldn't seem to control his emotions lately. "Yes, milady. Please accept my apologies, and my extreme gratitude for the healing."

"She's not a healer," the twins chorused.

Friday grinned. "They're a quick study."

"She's a seamstress," Christian finished with a smile. And then his smile fell. "A . . . seamstress," he repeated, and then shook his head. "Milady, you have found yourself among a bevy of idiots."

"Sorry?" Tristan had no idea what his brother was on about. He was too distracted by those eyes, that smile, and the happy realization that she had not yet excused herself from his arms.

Sebastien hopped up and slapped his thigh. "YES!"

Elisa quietly covered her mouth with her hands.

"It makes so much sense," said François. "How could we have overlooked that? Has it been so long?"

"The question is," said Philippe with great condescension, "can she *weave?*"

"Of course I can weave." The princess seemed annoyed at the very idea that she might lack such simple knowledge.

"Of course she can weave," Tristan repeated breathlessly, and then cradled her tightly in his arms again, hugging her close. It *was* destiny. She was going to save them. She was going to help break this blasted curse and save them all. And if she did that, she could have his heart and what little else that came with it.

Her cry from his shoulder was muffled. "What is going on?"

Christian shoved Tristan back and took her hands. "Princess Friday. How much do you know about nettles?"

5

Prickly and Proud

ETTLES?" FRIDAY ASKED. "Like stinging nettles? The weeds."

"The very same," said the elder blond man.

Friday opened her mouth to begin answering the question, and then thought better of it. She'd recovered from the shock of her miraculous empathic magic — the skin of the wound pulled beneath her breast less painfully with every move she made. It was healing quickly, enough to rival even Saturday's miraculous ability. Saturday, her younger sister with a destiny.

It was no secret that other great forces had a hand in the lives of the Woodcutter family, Fate most of all. Friday looked up into her young man's bright blue eyes again and risked losing herself there.

Oh, for heaven's sake. Enough was enough.

It was time to play the princess card.

"First things first." She shoved against her young man's now-unscarred chest and extracted herself from his arms. When she stood, the whisper of a breeze whistled in her ears. Goosebumps raised on her arms and she remembered where she was. The sky tower. Above her was nothing but stars; below her was nothing but darkness. She backed up against the Elder Wood door, away from the ragged edge that would haunt her nightmares for the rest of her life, and summoned her strength. "We still haven't been properly introduced."

After a moment of exchanged glances — Friday was all too familiar with the kind of sibling-speak that needed no words — the elder dark one cleared his throat.

"We are the former heirs to the throne of the Green Isles, in the far east, beyond the Troll Kingdom. Our parents and lands were taken from us by a usurper who wanted to force himself upon my sister. We stood against him, and for that we were punished by his sorceress. My brothers and I are cursed to take swan form by day and human form by night, when no man can look upon us." Friday raised her eyebrows at that. "At least, until now. My sister is cursed with the glamour of a plain orphan girl. She is not mute, as you believe, but if she speaks a word to anyone before our curse is broken, the spell will last forever."

Friday was at a loss for words, but still felt she needed to say something to the girl. "I'm so sorry."

Rampion shook her head in forgiveness. *It was not to be helped.*

"We call you Rampion." Friday turned to the dark brother. "What's her real name?"

"Elisa," he said. "I am Sebastien, the eldest."

"Christian," said the man who had asked her about the nettles, presumably the second-eldest.

"Rene and Bernard," said Rene and Bernard, twins to be sure, but Friday could not discern which was which. They bowed and patted their copper heads in unison.

"Tristan," said her destiny.

"Philippe," said the angry brother, the one whose melancholy hovered like a black cloud above his head. His features and coloring were similar enough to Tristan's for them to be twins too, but Friday guessed otherwise.

"And François," said the youngest, with a nod and flourish. "Elisa is one year my senior, though she's been cursed to look younger."

"You are the reader," said Friday, and François bowed his head again.

"Like you, my intent was to be dedicated to the gods," he said, "and it is still. It's a path that requires much study."

Friday did not feel it was too impertinent to ask, "Which gods?"

"The Four Winds. You might have noticed my sister is something of a windweaver herself."

"So that's why the winds don't carry us off right now. And why my candle never went out. And how you danced yesterday." Friday turned to their sister. "You're very good, Rampion. Oh . . . should I call you that?"

"It is best that no one speak her true name outside this tower," said Sebastien. "In case we are still hunted."

The girl pointed to her eldest brother, presumably showing that she agreed with his sentiment. *Rampion is a fine name. I don't mind it.*

"That may be, but I would not insult you."

And then Friday realized to whom she was responding . . . and how.

"Ah. Oh my."

Elisa's words had echoed perfectly in Friday's ears, though she had not heard them in truth. It was the same voice she'd heard earlier: *Your family has power! Heal him!* And then: *If you let him die, yours is not the only destiny that dies with him.* Those words had prompted her to reach deep within herself and somehow take Tristan's wound from him.

Though they seemed to have caught the attention of gods and fey alike, no one in her family had ever performed such powerful magic without training . . . except perhaps Wednesday. Wednesday, who had been transformed here, and who had woven her magic into the rock so that it would never crumble. Friday realized now that the stones of the sky tower contained far more power than any of them had imagined.

Elisa's eyes were like saucers. *Princess Friday, did you hear me?*

There was no reason to lie, though the brothers might pose more questions she could not answer. "It seems that I did."

Friday braced herself as the girl jumped into her arms. She was all spindly limbs and golden hair, reminding Friday of Sunday in younger days. From her spasms it felt like the girl was sobbing, but no noise came from her. Friday patted her back. "There, there. It will be all right."

Elisa pulled herself away; this time her eyes were wide with fear. *I haven't upset the curse with this, have I? Please tell me I haven't.*

Friday squeezed the girl's arms. "You can't take all the blame; we are both part of this conversation. But you haven't spoken a word out loud. I think the curse remains intact." Friday snuck a glance up at the midnight sky, still full of stars with nary a cloud in sight. Upsetting a spell of this caliber would cause a storm, no doubt, and there didn't seem to be anything brewing on the horizon.

Elisa hugged her again, more gently this time, and rested her head on Friday's shoulder. Friday could sense the brothers' combined tension and spoke to ease their minds. "Your sister is all right. She's worried that she mucked up the spell somehow. I assured her she hasn't."

"You can . . . hear her?" asked Christian.

"It would appear so," Friday replied. "I'm learning all sorts of new things about myself tonight. I only hope I still like me when it's all said and done."

The twins chortled at her self-deprecating humor. They were so much like Peter that Friday suddenly missed her brother fiercely.

It has to be me, Elisa told her. *I have to be the one to weave the shirts of nettles for each of my brothers. They must don them before Mordant finds me and . . . binds me to him forever.*

"She's telling me about your curse," Friday said to the brothers. And then to Elisa, "I will help you however I can."

I tried once. I did not do a very good job. I could not finish. It was too painful. Elisa released Friday and walked dangerously close to the outer edge of the room to retrieve something. Friday couldn't bear to look. She opened her eyes again at Elisa's delicate touch on her arm. In Elisa's apron was a crude mat of thick stalks, woven together to form a square roughly as long as Friday's forearm.

In order to make this mat, Elisa would have had to manipulate the raw nettle stalks barehanded. Friday could only imagine the pain such a creation required. "You poor thing."

"There must be another way," said Christian. "I'm not sure any of us has the strength to watch her go through that again."

"There is another way to use nettle, but it has to be broken down and the fibers removed from the inside. Like flax." Friday had learned to weave flax from the Sisters of the Earth Goddess. Sister Carol often told the story of an old mother with hands like leather who preferred nettle cloth to all else, but no one else was brave enough to manage the stubborn, prickly weed. After growing up in the Woodcutter household, Friday figured she was brave enough to manage anything. She put her hand to the wound at her side. Even destiny.

The young man whose eyes she had been avoiding hadn't moved from his spot on the floor in the center of the room. The exhaustion that the tower's magic had kept at bay for so long swept over her with a force that made her stomach churn. Her eyelids felt like anvils and she tasted bile in her throat.

"I will help you." She swallowed quickly so as not to disgrace herself further in front of her new friends. "If you can weave wind, you can weave this. I promise. But I must come back tomorrow. Forgive me, I —"

Friday lost her words and her footing at the same time, falling back against the Elder Wood door for support. Tristan lunged forward to rescue her again, but Elisa stood her ground between Friday and her brother. Friday was grateful for it. Another shock from him would certainly deplete what little energy she had, and she'd need every last bit to make it back down all those stairs.

Elisa held an arm up to her brothers, palm flat out. Once she had made eye contact with each of them, she turned and put her arm around Friday, propping her up and bearing some of her weight.

They understand that you are under my care now, said Elisa. *I will help you back to your room.*

Friday was too exhausted to express her gratitude, too exhausted to stop Tristan from approaching them further. But when he came to the door, he merely opened it for them.

"Thank you," he told her once more. She blinked at him, hoping he would interpret that as an acceptance. He stood there as Elisa helped her out onto the landing and only bowed his head politely when they passed.

"Oh, and Elisa," he added.

Elisa paused on the top step, tilting her head back to acknowledge him.

"Be sure to let us know if she starts laying golden eggs."

Friday awoke to the quiet of her bedchamber. The sunlight peeking through the cracks in the curtains was so bright, Friday was surprised it hadn't roused her sooner. Then she remembered the events of the magic-drenched night before and decided that a certain amount of exhaustion should have been expected.

She sat up slowly. Her head felt foggy, but her mind was clear. She lifted a hand to the wound on her chest; she could feel a raised line of skin and the bumps from her stitches, but there was no pain. There was no blood either. Rampion — nay, *Elisa* — had managed to drag Friday's half-conscious body out of her soiled clothes and into a nightgown.

Friday knew what a feat that was. She had performed the same task with Saturday and Peter, on the rare occasions that they visited the local pub after a long day's work and overindulged. Friday smirked at the thought of wild rumors of her inebriation spread among the parents. Her, of all people. Friday Woodcutter. The girl who did no wrong. The Princess of Children. Who would believe it?

Dear Goddess. "The children!"

The chamber door opened at her exclamation, and Conrad and Elisa came rushing through.

"Everything is fine," Conrad said calmly. "The children are hard at work and play as we speak. I started the rounds this morning, gathered them up, and set them to it. John, Wendy, Michael, and Kate are running the show. I've been checking in. It's all fine."

"Which Kate?" Friday asked.

Conrad took a moment. "I have no idea," he said finally.

"Does it matter? How are you? Rampion said . . . well, she didn't say, but she gave me the impression that you weren't feeling well."

Elisa-Rampion cocked her head and mimed a clap to applaud Conrad's deductive reasoning.

"Don't you have something to fetch?" Conrad asked her playfully. Elisa stuck out her tongue and moved to pour a cup of tea from the service laid out on the table by the fireplace. As she placed it in Friday's hands, Elisa stared at her intensely. The girl's eyes, once bright blue under the night sky, were now a dull brownish-gray. Eyes, skin, clothes . . . everything about her was that same brownish-gray, as if she'd just stepped from the canvas of a faded portrait.

More importantly, Friday could no longer hear Elisa's words in her ears. "I'm sorry," Friday whispered to the girl as she took the tea. "Thank you."

Elisa nodded slowly, and then went to find Friday some new clothes.

"I'm sorry," Friday said again to Conrad. "I —" She stopped. It was not in her heart to lie. "It was exhaustion."

It was obvious that Conrad knew there was more to her story, but he was clever enough to let it wait until she was ready. "It is not yet noon," he told her. "I was heading down to Cook to fetch lunch. The children will be happy to see you are well."

"I would have you do something for me first, if you don't mind, and then I will meet you in the kitchens." She gave Conrad her instructions, and he quickly scampered off to obey them.

"I know you're disappointed in me," Friday told Elisa after

Conrad had left. "I cannot hear your words, but I can feel what is in your heart. I have not lost all my fey faculties. Do not lose hope."

Elisa nodded again but did not meet her eyes. She helped Friday out of her nightgown and handed her a cloth with which to wash herself from the basin. Friday ran the cloth over her wound, now but a thin line of scar tissue. She wished the water were colder so that her head might feel less foggy; she sipped more tea in an effort to that end. It was a weak brew, but Friday did not care to complain. The castle's stores must surely be dwindling.

Friday let Elisa help her into some clothes. None of the Woodcutters had ever needed a maid before that spring, but there were certain roles to be played in the palace, and Friday was determined to cause as little additional trouble to her sister as possible.

When Elisa had finished tying a bow in Friday's hair, Friday took her by the hands. "I will come to the tower tonight. I promise."

Elisa planted a soft kiss on her cheek and left the room.

~~ellee~~

The children met Friday and Conrad halfway across the field. Friday took time distributing the contents of the lunch baskets, carefully doling out bits of bread and cheese. She asked each child how he or she was doing, and assured the ones who queried that she was fine, just tired, but weren't they all? When they reached the end, Friday sent Conrad back to the kitchens for a little more food, and tasked a few of the farmers' children with foraging in case Cook had nothing else to give.

She mopped her brow in the heat of the midday sun. There hadn't been enough in the baskets for a lunch of her own, but it didn't matter. A rest in the shade by the pond would suit her just fine. From there she could check on both her flocks: the children, and her now-feathered friends.

There was already a girl sitting in Friday's spot on the bank beneath the willow tree. She wore a plain skirt and blouse and a headscarf that obscured her face. Her feet were bare. Friday was about to introduce herself when she realized she didn't have to. The pair of white pigeons in the branches above them twittered a hello at her approach.

Without a word, Queen Sunday leapt up from the ground and into Friday's open arms.

In that embrace, Friday understood everything that Sunday wanted to say but could not. The weight of being a queen rested heavy on her young shoulders, and though she was brave enough to bear it, it exhausted her. Crowds of people had always exhausted Sunday, and with the country in turmoil, the audiences had been never-ending. She gathered strength from having Rumbold by her side, but Rumbold, too, was wearing thin. Such decisions they had to make — decisions about the fate of so many. There was no time for deliberation. The people of Arilland loved her and hated her, but they listened, and they carried on. Day by day, issue after issue, Sunday was feeling just as lost at sea as all those assumed perished.

Friday squeezed tightly, reminding Sunday that in this small shadow of the world, under this small tree, she was just someone's little sister. That someone would love her unconditionally, no matter what choices she made.

Friday kissed her sister on the cheek. "I almost didn't recognize you."

Sunday let out a halfhearted laugh. "I almost don't recognize me either, these days."

Friday clasped her sister's hand and they plopped back down on the grass next to Sunday's basket. Friday put on her most dazzling smile; she was sure Sunday had seen little but tears and scowls in the course of her new profession. She could already make out a permanent crease of worry between Sunday's fair brows. Sunday returned the smile, closed her eyes, and breathed in the fresh air all around her. Her scarf slipped aside and the breeze danced through her golden hair, and in that moment she was a lazy little woodcutter's daughter once again, skiving off work.

Friday turned into the breeze to see Elisa across the pond throwing crumbs to her swans.

"Cheeky," Friday mumbled under her breath. "So," she said to Sunday, "what did you bring me?"

The big blue eyes opened and the worry lines deepened. "A bribe. A meeting. A favor to ask. And company." Sunday lifted the cloth off the basket to reveal some freshly baked bread, a few thick slices of game bird, some berries, and a bottle of cider. Friday was honored that Sunday had come all this way just to seek her advice, but even Mama would have included more than this in a basket for the queen of the land.

Between the contents of the basket and Sunday's furrowed brow, Friday knew that things were far direr than they seemed. "Your company? I've missed that so much, it's worth a trade for all the others. So, tell me what's on your mind. I'm sure you don't have much time."

"I'm the queen. I have all the time I want."

"Then it won't be long until Erik or one of the other guards finds you." In her joviality, Friday remembered too late.

"Erik's vanished with Saturday to gods know where — on that sea, or beyond it. Papa and Peter are still hard at work building a ship. It isn't as much of a mission for Papa as it is a distraction."

"I'm sorry. I didn't mean to remind you."

"It's not you, Friday. The citizens of Arilland remind me every single day." Sunday offered Friday the basket. She took nothing for herself.

Friday tore off a chunk of the still-warm bread; it was sweet and divine. "What can I do for my queen?"

Sunday leaned back against the trunk of the willow tree and curled her bare feet up beneath her skirts, just as she'd done as a child. The Queen of Arilland would always be a woodcutter's daughter at heart, most at home when surrounded by trees. "Sister dearest, of all of us, you have the unique ability to make divine creations from nothing but scraps."

She was referring, of course, to the patchwork skirts

Friday created for herself from the bits of cloth left after making clothes for the poor out of tithed remnant materials. Those skirts had become near infamous in this little corner of Arilland, and by Conrad's account they had even saved her life. Friday didn't mind wearing the dresses that had been provided to her at the castle, but she had missed her skirts. Was Sunday asking her to take up her needle and make them again?

"Arilland finds itself with an overabundant population, and two needs have risen above the rest in a very short time."

"Food and clothes," Friday guessed. When a child arrived at the orphanage, these were the first needs the Sisters tended to, just as they were the first things Friday had considered upon encountering Tristan and his brothers . . . right after the color of Tristan's eyes. Butterflies cavorted in Friday's insides at the memory of his intense stare. She forced herself to concentrate on Sunday.

"So many of these families have lost everything. When I realized clothing was becoming an issue, I couldn't think of anyone else more qualified than my seamstress sister." Sunday waved at the various stages of laundry being taken care of by the children. "Your flock has already done so much for Arilland—more than they will ever know. I hesitate to ask for more."

"We are your willing and enthusiastic subjects," said Friday. "What do you need?"

"I need you to start sewing again. I will send women and men to help you and the children with what's already being done—manpower is the one item we have in spades."

"Thank you. But what about the food?" More bodies meant far more food than Friday's Darlings had to spare.

Sunday gave a very un-queenlike shrug and sighed. "Rumbold and I haven't figured that out yet. I don't suppose you have any ideas?"

Friday smiled again, eager to share happiness and hope with her sister. "Perhaps my flock can help there as well." She raised a hand and called for Niall and Rhiannon; the call was repeated across the meadow until there was an answer.

Sunday adjusted her headscarf so that her face was once again in shadow. Friday didn't know if these farmer children would have recognized her sister. She did not want to cause Sunday the undue stress of an impromptu audience with the children of Arilland . . . but she wasn't about to deny Niall and Rhiannon the knowledge that they were addressing their queen.

The children met Friday with hugs and kisses. Niall was tall for his age, with spiky blond hair and spectacles. Rhiannon was very much a child of the earth, with her cornflower-blue eyes and freckle-kissed nose.

"The woman sitting beside me is my sister," Friday whispered to the children. Niall's eyes got wide, and she gently turned his face from the meadow so none of the other children would see his reaction. "We have something very important to ask you, but I don't want to cause a scene. Please greet her as my sister and not . . . anything else. Do you understand?" Niall, still stunned, nodded silently. Rhiannon, on the other hand, smiled broadly and jumped right into Sunday's lap.

The resulting giggles made Friday's heart soar. There were few ailments for which a child's laughter was not a panacea.

It wasn't in Niall's makeup to be as unrestrained as his little sister, and Friday felt for the boy. "How may we be of assistance, my . . . er . . . miss . . ." He looked to Friday for help.

"Why don't we call her 'Aunt Sunday,' for now?" Friday suggested.

"Oh, 'Aunt Sunday'! I like that. Makes me sound all dignified." Sunday proceeded to demonstrate her capacity for said dignity by tickling Rhiannon mercilessly.

". . . Aunt Sunday," finished Niall.

Sunday instantly sobered and sat with her back ramrod-straight. In her lap, Rhiannon did the same. "Thank you, Sir Niall. Yes, let's get down to business. My problem is thus: Like a silly person, I have invited too many guests into my home. Now I need to find a way to feed them all. Aunt Friday here seems to think you two might help me with some ideas."

"How many people?" Niall asked sagely.

Sunday pulled no punches. "The entire castle."

Niall thought a moment, contemplating the true scope of the issue, and then shook his head. "Even if Mama and Papa still had their farm, we would never be able to feed so many people. I'm sorry, Aunt Sunday."

But Sunday was not put off so easily. "Pretend the castle here—the palace and all the grounds—were your farm. How would you work it? What would you bring to market to sell?"

"Berries!" Rhiannon shouted jovially.

"That's a good start," said Sunday. "Do we have many berry bushes here?"

"There are quite a few along the creek that feeds the pond," said Niall. "They go deep into the woods. We snack on them sometimes after lunch . . . but we'd need an army to pick them all."

"I just so happen to have an army," said Sunday. "What else?"

"There are apple trees back in the woods," said Niall. "Some are just crabapples, but they're all about ripe now."

"Cook could work magic with those crabapples," said Sunday. "She's a very good cook."

"There are also patches of wild onions," Niall added, growing more excited about this palace-farm project. "I've taught most of the kids here about them, but not everyone likes to eat them raw . . ."

"A handful of the boys here love them," said Friday. "You could pick them out of this crowd just by their scent."

Niall was on a roll. ". . . dandelions, violets, clover, rampion root . . ."

"Ooh, ooh!" Rhiannon wiggled in Sunday's lap. "I know! I know!"

"What is it, darling?" asked Sunday.

"Nettles!" shouted Rhiannon.

Friday froze.

Niall pulled a face. "Nonny, only Gran eats nettles."

Rhiannon stuck her tongue out at her brother. "Just because you don't like them doesn't mean other people won't."

She played with the ends of Sunday's scarf. "Gran does all sorts of things with nettles. She makes tea and beer and mashes them up and eats them and everything."

"You can make cloth from them, too," Friday said in a daze. "Like flax. But . . ." she shook off the giddy dream the coincidence had sparked. It was too good to be true, too perfect to think that the answer to the swan brothers' curse had presented itself so quickly. "But, Rhiannon, honey, we'd need lots of nettles for that. Bushels and bushels."

Rhiannon hopped up and offered Friday and Sunday her hands. "Come. You'll see."

Niall hesitated until Sunday offered her free hand to him; he accepted it with a smile. The white pigeons followed, dancing on drafts of air above their heads. They rounded the pond and let Rhiannon drag them up the hill on the other side . . . all the way to Cook's walled herb garden. The swans' honking outside the gate caught Elisa-Rampion's attention as they passed, and she followed the small party.

There was a dense thicket of golden grass behind the garden almost as high as Rhiannon's head, but the girl waded straight into it, unafraid. When they emerged on the other side, Rhiannon spread her arms and held them up to the heavens in triumph. "Behold!"

Sunday cheered.

Niall groaned.

Friday smiled.

Elisa-Rampion said nothing, only crossed her thin arms over her chest and waited.

The field before them was full of nettles, their green stalks standing prickly and proud in the afternoon sun. They ran wild all the way from the walled garden to the edge of the forest that bordered the castle lands. The white pigeons took refuge in the brush behind the children instead of seeking a perch among the stinging weeds.

Apart from being extremely fortuitous, there was something odd about this meadow . . . Friday examined the field with the eye of someone who had tended many gardens in her young life. These nettles had been cared for, watered, and weeded around. They had taken over this field by design, not by luck at all.

Clever Elisa! She'd used the plant lore she'd learned from Cook to fashion the key to unlocking her family's curse!

"Thank you, Niall. And thank you, Rhiannon, my little star." Sunday caught up the small girl in a big hug. "This could work!"

Friday turned to Elisa. "This could work."

Elisa covered her mouth, Friday knew, because she was too afraid to let the gods see her smile.

Friday was not afraid to smile. In fact, Friday smiled so widely that her whole body hummed with hope. If she succeeded in helping Elisa defeat this curse, perhaps the Sisters would find her worthy enough to enter their order despite her shortcomings!

The cheerful crew was interrupted by Conrad, who came tearing around the walled garden and through the high grass at breakneck speed. He took a deep breath. "Your—"

Sunday held up a finger, and Conrad was quick to catch her meaning.

"*Milady*. Your husband requests the honor of your immediate presence in the Great Hall." He turned to Friday. "He wishes for you to come as well."

Sunday began walking quickly back toward the palace. Friday followed, kissing the children on the cheek and sending them back to the flock. As they made their way across the hillside, she could still sense Elisa's quiet presence behind them.

"Did he say why?" Sunday asked.

"Not in so many words, but yes, I know why," Conrad answered. "He has found the yellow-eyed man."

At that, Sunday lifted her skirts and broke into a brisk jog.

Friday had heard of this yellow-eyed man in tales told by her sister and Rumbold about their meeting. After Rumbold's own enchantment was broken, he was helped home by a yellow-eyed man with a haycart. According to Conrad, that same man had come to Friday's own rescue and aided Conrad in delivering her to the front steps of the palace. Both times he had disappeared into the night, which made Friday doubt the man's sincerity, but he did have an uncommon knack for being in the right place at the right time . . . and in the Woodcutter family, such timing was rarely a coincidence.

Such a person would only be found if he wanted to be. Friday picked up her pace, wondering what fresh dire news the gods had sent this man to report.

Velius, Monday, and Rumbold were all waiting for them when they arrived. The rest of the hall was empty but for a lone, stout man in a long black coat. He had curling dark hair and a short dark beard and a very tall hat that looked as if it had been fashioned from a stovepipe. But despite his dark clothing and coloring, his yellow eyes smiled whimsically.

The man turned to the new arrivals and removed his hat, bowing with a flourish and revealing the thinning circle of hair on his pate. "I am Henry Humbug," he announced, "and I'm sorry."

"Why should you be sorry, sir?" asked Sunday. "You've saved the lives of some people who are very important to me."

"I'm afraid there's not much time."

It was then that Friday realized Mr. Humbug was not addressing the queen. She and Sunday turned to see Elisa behind them, cowering in the shadows.

"We must be quick," Mr. Humbug said to the herb girl. "Mordant is coming."

6

Silver Linings

THE IDLE NIGHTS Tristan spent as his human self were normally long, but waiting from sundown until Friday arrived at the sky tower bordered on unbearable. It had been so long since he'd had anything to look forward to beyond the sight of his sister at the end of a long day — which was a damn sight better than his brothers' bare bottoms.

He'd have to remember to thank Friday again for leaving seven sets of clothes on the tower floor to spare him that particular image again. The shirts and trousers had been thoughtfully folded in individual piles and laid out in a row by the door. There was no difference between them save one, the fifth pile from the left, on top of which rested a fading sprig of blue rampion. As his brothers stretched and dressed and fought and told the same filthy jokes they'd been telling for years, Tristan stared at the little bell-shaped flowers in his hand and waited. And waited.

When neither Elisa nor the princess appeared, Philippe was the first to voice his uneasiness. "Something is wrong."

"Nothing is wrong," said Rene.

"Elisa is probably just helping Princess Friday up the stairs with an overly large basket of food," Bernard said dreamily.

"It's going to rain," said François.

Twilight had abruptly darkened the sky, and what stars had begun to make their presence known disappeared one by one beneath the clouds. The wind picked up without Elisa there to rein it in, whipping through the ruins and making them glad to be clothed. Tristan shivered. On the breeze he caught the scents of earth, wood smoke, and unwashed humans. Many humans.

It had been a long time since it had rained, since he and his swan brothers had watched the creation of the impossible sea from their perch on high. This rain would be welcome; it did not seem the sort of storm brewed by magic. This land — and its refugees — could do with a shower. Tristan, however, spent half his day in water and could happily live without it. He hoped his sister arrived in time to spare them — and their new clothes — what threatened to be a very cold drenching.

His wish was quickly granted. The handle of the Elder Wood door turned and Elisa came through with a basket large enough to set Rene and Bernard drooling. Friday followed with three empty picture frames. Elisa disappeared back through the barely-open door and returned with a bulging sack. Who else was out there that had helped them carry all these things? After all these years, how was it that their curse was now so visible to others?

"Conrad doesn't have to stay," Friday said to Elisa, and their sister hugged the princess tightly at her words. "Yes, I can hear you again." Friday turned to the brothers, as if about to speak, and then paused.

"Something *is* wrong," repeated Philippe.

"What is it?" asked Rene.

"Who's out there?" asked Bernard.

"It's Mordant, isn't it?" said Christian.

Elisa pointed to Christian and shook her finger wildly.

The twins jumped to their feet. "Mordant is out there?" said Bernard. "Let me kill him."

"Not if I kill him first," said Rene.

Elisa shook her head.

"*Is* Mordant here?" Tristan asked her.

"Who is it outside the door?" asked Rene.

"Whoever it is, we can take him," said Bernard.

"Is Elisa safe?" asked Philippe.

The cacophony of their overlapped voices battered his own ears; Tristan couldn't imagine what Friday heard, what with Elisa's inside voice trying to shout above them, on top of the rising tension of the room, and whoever else's mind was outside that door . . .

Friday paled and stepped back toward the door. Tristan was annoyed that the bond between them did not force her magic to work both ways—he could not feel what she felt. But he could sense that she needed protection, and that he would gladly give.

Tristan closed the short distance between them and took the princess into his arms. Her body trembled beneath the emotional onslaught. He gently put a hand on either side of her head, as if he could make a helmet to shield her sensitive mind from the mess of his siblings' thoughts vying for attention.

"Stop it," he ordered his brothers and sister. He tried his best to make the words strong, but not loud enough to damage Friday further. "It's too much for her."

As soon as he spoke, her trembling stopped. "I'm fine," she said from inside the circle of his arms.

He immediately let her go.

She looked at him curiously. "How did you know how to do that?"

"Do what?" Tell his siblings to hush? Surely she had her own experience with that sort of thing.

"Make it . . . quiet." She tapped her head. "In here."

Tristan had no idea what she was talking about, but he was happy to be of service, whatever service that had been. "I'm not sure. You just looked like you were . . ." He didn't want to insult her by calling her helpless. She had that air about her, soft and kind and without malice, but he knew better—Friday Woodcutter was one of the least helpless people he'd ever met. However, she did look ". . . tired."

"Thank you." Her tone was full of such sincerity, and her eyes were filled with . . . Tristan turned away. He had never before experienced anything like this—this pull against his heart like the pull of a tide against the full moon—and it was not a conversation he was prepared to have in front of his brothers.

Everything he could think to say in response sounded arrogant or condescending, so he opted for silence, bowing slightly to her and backing away even more. He didn't want to crowd her — the bond between them seemed to tighten the closer they were together. He moved to a spot between her and the place where she'd fallen from the tower.

Elisa tiptoed toward Friday and gently touched the inside of her elbow. "Yes," the princess said to Elisa. "I will. Thank you."

Elisa's suggestion had apparently been that Friday sit, for she did so. Elisa and the rest of his brothers gathered around her like children waiting for a story. Tristan crouched, but kept his distance.

"The young man outside the door is Conrad. He's my squire . . . of sorts. I don't know much about how things like squires work."

"If you ever do want to know, I'd be happy to teach you," Christian offered.

Friday smiled at him.

Christian had a gift of setting people at ease, one of the few ways in which he surpassed their eldest brother at leadership. Tristan had never been jealous of that before now.

"Why . . . ?" François started, but then stopped, no doubt in light of Tristan's order to cease their collective inquisitive onslaught. Poor François. With his busy brain, he was possibly as much of a torture for Friday as Elisa was while speaking her silent words.

"Everything today happened so fast," said Friday. "I am not

the storyteller that my father and queen-sister are, so this is all going to come out a jumble. Please forgive me." Their nods seemed to appease her, so she went on. "A man came to us this evening. He calls himself Henry Humbug."

"Sounds like a false name," said Sebastien.

"We suspect it is," Friday agreed. "But this man's identity, while strange, is not the issue at hand. Suffice it to say that he has shown his good faith by saving the lives of me, my squire, and my king-brother on separate occasions. He seems to possess incredible knowledge that we do not. I'm not sure how this is, but we suspect it's sorcerous in nature." She said the last bit to François specifically, as if she'd read the question off the top of his mind. Perhaps she had.

"It was Mr. Humbug who made us aware of Mordant's intentions. He sails from the east even now, and should arrive three days hence."

Tristan's hands clenched at hearing this, as did the hands of each and every one of his brothers. The only news Tristan ever wanted of Mordant was the announcement of his death. For days, even months after their escape, Tristan had closed his eyes every night and seen the image of himself impaling Mordant on his father's sword. Failing that, Mordant deserved to be trampled by a kelpie or blinded by a naiad. That snake had taken what he wanted and forfeited his right to any more of Elisa's life.

They had found a sort of peace and a glimmer of hope. It should have come as no surprise that Mordant would be hot on their heels, sniffing the air, intent on tainting their happiness like the vicious dog he was. Like his brothers, Tristan couldn't be angrier that Mordant was painting himself into their picture again.

But he was also afraid. Not of what Mordant would do to him, but what he might do to Friday. She sat there beside his sister, with her silver-blue dress and silver-gray eyes, a spot of color against the stones like a flower plucked fresh from the field, beautiful in her wild innocence. He had already lost his home and his parents to that usurper. He would not lose Friday as well.

This was it, then. This was the end. The end of the curse. The end of Mordant, or the end of Tristan. One of them was not getting out of this alive.

"He won't be alone," said Sebastien. "He'll have his sorceress with him."

"Gana." Philippe spat to cleanse his mouth of the name.

Gana. She was as bad as he — she had been the instrument of Mordant's curse, but he had been the one to give the command to slaughter their friends, family, and loyal subjects. She deserved to live out the rest of her life in a torture of her own making; Mordant just needed to die.

"The woman who cursed us," Christian explained to Friday.

"Was it she who found us?" François couldn't help but ask.

"Mr. Humbug suspects that it was my discovery of you that alerted Mordant — or more likely this sorceress — to your location. It seems there are many layers of spells in and around this castle, spells whose origins died with the generations past. Some are as old as the foundation itself." Friday looked at Tristan. "And some are stronger than others."

So your sister's spell brought us together and broke through the Wind Gods' protection of our family, Tristan thought at her.

It would seem so, she thought back at him.

Tristan's eyes widened. "I . . . heard that. I heard you. In my head." The feeling was indescribable, both intimate and intrusive at once. Is this how she communicated with Elisa? Was there anything this girl couldn't do? And if Friday's sister was reportedly even more powerful, what did that make Wednesday — a god?

Realizing what he was doing, he forced his mind to be silent.

"Well, there's another new thing about me." Friday's voice was cheerful, but her demeanor said otherwise. Even the words she had thought at him had been optimistic in tone. How did she manage to put on a happy face for the world when confronted with such insanity? Magic was a romantic thing when told in stories, but when one was faced with the grim reality, magic took on another guise entirely. His own family's troubles had been enough to depress him for years; he wasn't sure Philippe would ever recover. Tristan was having a hard enough time resisting the magic that drew him to Friday, that urged him to take her in his arms again and never let her go. And yet, this girl shone in the gloom of adversity so brightly that she cast rainbows.

Practice, she thought at him in answer. He swore he could

hear laughter in her words. *My family is just as strange as yours. For different reasons, of course. Before any of this, I found magic in love and hope. And I still do.*

"This is all my fault," Friday admitted to his brothers. "My presence here, my bond to Tristan: these weakened your gods' protection and made Mordant aware of your location. I would throw myself off this tower if I thought it would make you forgive me, but I've already tried that."

Christian and the twins cracked a smile.

"My family thinks it best if you remain unseen by those who still do not know you. Mr. Humbug fears that bending the curse more than we have may hasten Mordant's arrival or endanger your lives."

"None of us wants that," agreed Sebastien.

"Your curse will be coming to an end," said Friday, "and soon enough that we don't really have time to plan. We have no choice but to act."

"Good thing we are men of action," said Rene.

"Speak for yourself," said Bernard, stretching his long body out on the stone floor beside his twin.

"But the nettles." François showed remarkable restraint by not posing a question.

"Your brilliant sister has already solved that problem."

Elisa sat up straight; Friday patted her on the back and Elisa beamed. Tristan couldn't remember ever seeing his sister quite so happy — another kind of magic, but one he knew Friday would take little credit for.

"Not only has she been tending Cook's herb garden, but

she's been nursing the wild meadow behind it. This meadow is now almost completely overrun with nettles."

"Pestilent weed," said Bernard.

"Someone should really get rid of those," said Rene.

"And so we shall," said Friday. "The whole crop is being harvested and brought into the kitchens as we speak."

"The kitchens?" asked Christian.

"The greens themselves are edible, a good thing in a palace with too many people and too little food." Friday hugged Elisa tightly. "Thanks to her foresight, your sister might have saved all who call Arilland home for the time being."

Friday held up one of the picture frames. "But now she must get to work."

Tristan amused himself at the thought of the ghost whose portrait had been cast aside for this strange venture. If there was as much magic bound to these stones as Friday would have them believe, surely some spirit from the netherworld was clicking his or her tongue right about now.

He hoped his parents' spirits were not similarly bound to the palace in Kassora. After all the chaos Mordant had created, his father and mother deserved their peace.

"Tonight I will teach you how to weave something more substantial than wind," Friday told Elisa. "We will start with simple yarn. The staff will strip down what nettles they can tonight, and we will spin them in the morning—if the curse allows it."

As always, Elisa cringed at the thought of discussing Mordant.

"I'm sorry, my dear, but I need to know more about the spell, so that I might know best how to help you break it."

"We have always preferred high, out-of-the-way places like this," said Tristan. "While we still lived in Kassora, just after the curse, we would meet Elisa in the topmost tower there. Every night before we went to sleep, we would pray to the Four Winds to deliver us. We did not expect an answer, but we prayed every night all the same. In time, a response came."

"The gods showed themselves to you?" Friday tried to imagine how she would react to receiving such a blessing.

"Yes," said François, with pure conviction.

"We're not sure," said Tristan. "There are four gods of the wind but only one person appeared to us, a blue-skinned man in white robes. He appeared on the wind, instructed us on exactly how to break the curse, and then disappeared the same way."

Tristan knew the words of the remedy as if they had been burned on his soul, but it had been so long since he'd thought about them . . . softly he began to say the words aloud, and then realized that all his brothers were doing the same.

"Gather stinging nettles if you will, though they will burn your hands and your fingers will bleed. Weave them into seven shirts with long sleeves, throw them over your brothers, and the spell will be broken. But from the moment you undertake this task until it is done, you must not speak nor laugh nor cry, though it may take years. The first word that passes your lips will strike your brothers' hearts like a knife, and you will all remain as you are, forevermore." A poetic and haunting recipe of doom.

Friday rubbed her upper arms briskly, though Elisa had

allowed no breeze to penetrate the protective barrier she'd set up to shield them from the rain. "Your sister is worried about the exact letter of the remedy," Friday addressed the brothers. "As am I."

"As are we all," said Sebastien.

Friday nodded. "Mr. Humbug assured us that we can bend the rules around the remedy, so long as we follow its exact words. Elisa has not spoken a word since the spell was cast, so we don't have to worry about that part. My concern is the making of the shirts." Friday turned back to Elisa. "Unfortunately, my dear, it looks as if all of the weaving is up to you and you alone. But it seems as though you may receive aid in all other areas."

"But she has to pick the nettles herself," said Christian, and Elisa pointed to him.

"Gather stinging nettles if you will," quoted Bernard.

"'If,'" said Rene. "Sounds optional to me."

"What about her hands hurting and fingers bleeding?" asked François.

"You don't think she's bled enough?" argued Philippe.

"She will have to weave seven shirts in three days," said Friday. "Don't worry. Her fingers will bleed." She took Elisa's hands in hers. "I will do what I can to ease the pain for you, all right?" Elisa humbly nodded her acceptance of the princess's offer. "I'm also sorry about the sleeves. I was hoping we could get away with fashioning crude tunics, but those words are precise."

"We seem to be getting away with an awful lot as it is," said Sebastien.

"True." Friday punctuated her statement with a large yawn. "Forgive me. There has been plenty to do this past day, and plenty little time in which to do it."

"You should rest," said François. "I could make a pillow for you here by the door."

Tristan would be damned if he let Friday fall asleep next to anyone but him. Friday must have heard his thoughts; she smiled at him but directed her answer politely to François.

"You're very kind. But before I rest, I must first teach Elisa the rudiments of weaving so she can practice before she gets the nettle fiber."

Elisa nodded, resigning herself to her sleepless fate with a determined grin.

"That sack is full of yarn. We can use these old picture frames as looms."

"And what would you have the rest of us do?" asked Christian.

For the first time since Tristan had met her, Friday looked taken aback. So she *could* be surprised. Either her deep concentration distracted her from every other emotion in the room, or the brothers were quickly becoming adept at restraining their feelings.

"I . . ." she started. "I'm sorry, I . . ."

"It's all right," Sebastien said with a measure of reserve that he normally used only for Elise. "We just want to be of use."

Philippe harrumphed.

"Well, *some* of us do," Sebastien finished.

"I'm quite handy at being idle," said Bernard.

Rene swatted him in the arm. "We're at your service, mi-lady. What do you need?"

"You are welcome to sort through the yarn and food we've brought," Friday answered. "I carried a few more books up as well, so you wouldn't all have to share with François."

It was so sweet, how she innocently assumed the best of them. Tristan wondered if he'd ever been so innocent in his life. Predictably, François laughed at this. Sebastien and Christian looked at each other. Rene and Bernard simultaneously found the crumbling walls fascinating. Philippe glowered. Tristan was the only one brave enough to meet the princess's eyes, and when he did so he merely shrugged, for lack of anything better to say.

"You're joking," said Friday. "Can't *any* of you read?"

Sebastien and Christian raised their hands halfheartedly. "Well enough in the language of the Isles," said Christian. "But not much of your Common tongue."

Friday put her hands on her hips. "The heir and the spare . . . to be expected, I suppose, but I have to say that I'm disappointed in the rest of you. Shameful!"

"How's that?" said Bernard. "We don't need to read to lift a sword."

"Or shoot an arrow," added Rene. "Or climb a tree. Or paint a picture. Or seduce a woman . . ." Rene elbowed his twin at this last item and they giggled like prize idiots.

Friday's eyebrows raised. "You paint, sir?"

She sounded like a princess just then, and not an amused

one. The twins ceased their playing. Rene's usual boldness fled. Instead of answering the question, he resumed his study of the crumbling stones in the wall behind him.

"As boys we wanted for nothing," Tristan explained. "We made our own adventures; we didn't need to seek solace in the tales of others."

"Oh, but reading and writing are so much more than that," Friday said, in the same tone a woman might use to describe her lover. Tristan suddenly felt jealous; as one who gave and received love so easily, Friday certainly must have a legion of suitors. Where did his affections fall among the others? Did destiny and Wednesday's binding magic work in his favor here, or against him?

He was getting ahead of himself. After so many long days and nights of waiting, everything was happening so fast. It hurt Tristan's head to think about it. It did not, however, hurt Tristan's head to think about Friday. "I would learn, if you would teach me."

Did he really just say that? Did he really mean it?

"The reading or the weaving?" Friday asked in a mocking tone.

He could have made a joke in kind, but he didn't. "Both," he said. "I'm willing to learn."

"Would you mind sewing? Or spinning?"

"I have nothing but time." Tristan lost himself a little in that gaze full of silver linings, and Friday let him. It felt like there had been a much greater conversation than the few words they'd just uttered.

Sebastien interrupted the blissful reverie. "Interestingly enough, I find myself in the same boat."

"Me too!" said Christian. "What a coincidence!"

"It's a fairly large boat," said Bernard.

"A *crowded* boat," added Rene.

"Fools, all of you." Philippe crossed his arms and leaned back against the ruined wall of the room. Spoilsport. Well, Tristan and the rest of his brothers would not shy from work, even if it was work meant for women.

Friday smiled, that dazzling smile, the one that looked as if she'd just been handed the world on a silver platter. "It's a lovely offer. A *surprising* offer, I must say. But I only brought enough materials for three people to weave."

Tristan moved to help her, striding over to the stack of picture frames. "One is for Elisa." Elisa took the frame from him gratefully, upended the sack of yarn, and made a selection. "The rest of us will take turns with the others while you instruct. How does that sound?"

For a moment, the glow of Friday's happiness wiped away the shadows of exhaustion around her eyes. Tristan wanted to bask in that glow, to pay tribute to it in gold coins and flowers, to sweep her up and carry her off to a castle full of laughter and adventures they made up all their own . . . but he did none of these things.

Not yet.

"It sounds like a dream come true," said Friday.

"Excellent. You get us started, and we'll let you get to dreaming."

7

Blood and Fire

THEY LET HER REST a while, as promised. The youngest brother fashioned her a pallet out of the empty sack, the extra yarn, and what blankets they had. Tristan planted himself at her side, as much between her and his other brothers as he was between her and the perilous drop to the ground far below. His presence was a comfort, and she let herself enjoy it. If one of the tenets of the Earth Goddess was to celebrate life, how could her acolytes eschew love?

Friday heard Sister Carol's voice echo in her head. "Love is born of the earth, and so we return our love to Her. Loving other people is a distraction."

If that were truly so, then Friday was doomed from the

start. She almost wished she had it in herself to stop trying to please Sister Carol.

The rain had come in full force as Friday began her weaving lessons, but it had not impeded their process. Elisa's protective bubble — furnished by her own natural magic and reinforced by that of the Four Winds, the patron gods of their family — became visible as the heavenly barrage hit silently and slid down the sides, as if the room they were in still had four full walls and a roof, all made of rain.

Friday stared up at the candlelit droplets, listened to the raucous sounds of refugees below enjoying their long-awaited bath, and willed herself to sleep. She would need all the energy she could muster in the next few days — there were too many things that required her attention and not enough of her to go around. Perhaps in trade for reading and weaving lessons, Tristan and his brothers would tell her how to lead an army. If she could properly give commands, perhaps she wouldn't feel compelled to take on so many tasks herself . . . just like Mama . . . though Mama could command anyone . . .

These were not thoughts that would lead to slumber. Annoyed, Friday stared up at the cascading rain-roof again and tried to clear her head. She swept all thoughts of Mama, Arilland, and everything else into a mental cupboard and shut the door. Peace, at last.

Without warning, Tristan's face popped into her mind.

Friday scowled. Thoughts of him weren't restful either. If

she couldn't drift off, she should probably stop feigning sleep and go back to supervising her novice weavers.

Softly, serenely, the twins began to sing. It was a forlorn tune in a language Friday didn't understand, but she could sense the feeling conveyed by the words, something akin to unrequited love, or longing for a faraway home. Whatever the subject matter, the lullaby was the missing ingredient to her peace. Friday was swept up in the melody and ushered off to dreamland.

She slept fitfully, half waking at a man's laugh, a word, a snore, and her dreams were strange. Saturday and Erik rode giant waves that crashed against the Woodcutter house, the top room of its tower now a beacon, calling them home ... or warning them away. She dreamt of a setting sun that threatened to set fire to the sky; to protect her family from the flames, she had to weave a carpet of thorns from the rose bushes planted around the Woodcutter house. Fires sparked and her fingers bled and the light engulfed them all ...

In that light she saw Tristan's face again, looking down upon her. Sadness, anger, confusion, and pain fell like the impotent droplets on the invisible ceiling above them. Buried deep beneath those feelings, Friday knew, lay some glimmer of hope — it was up to her to foster that spark with kindness and love. From that morass of emotions, she could not read his expression. Was he protecting her, or saying goodbye? Behind him now, the deep cerulean sky was peppered with the pink-tinged clouds of morning. And then suddenly it wasn't Tristan, in the dream way that people are not: his face and eyes had gone dark and his hair had gone silver-white. But it wasn't silver . . . or, rather, it wasn't hair. Friday felt more pain, a surge of wind, a pull at her chest, a stretching of her tailbone, a prickling of her skin. A brush of feathers kissed her cheek, and the low thrum of wings became her own heart's beat.

Friday sat up.

She wasn't dreaming.

The sky tower room was empty now, but for Friday, Elisa, and a few stray silver-white feathers scattered about the room. Friday's soul was empty too, but for a hum in her mind, the soft whisper of a frightened girl distracting herself from the tasks of the day, and the challenge of her life.

They have gone, said the voice in her head. *It was time.* Elisa's mousy scullery maid visage had also returned with the sun. Golden tresses and alabaster skin had been replaced with the scraggly hair and scrawny limbs of a young, malnourished scamp. Said scamp was currently folding her brothers' clothes so that they might be fresh upon their return.

"You should have woken me earlier," said Friday. "I could have seen them off."

My brothers have always been proud, said Elisa. *I do not believe they would like you to see the curse take power over them.* She finished folding the next shirt and plucked at her tattered apron. *I cannot do much in this state, but I will save them from what pain I can.*

Speaking of pain . . . "How are your fingers this morning?"

Elisa bent her knuckles, made a few fists, and then shrugged.

Friday took the girl's hands in her own and kissed the

fingertips . . . now free of redness. She dropped Elisa's hands, hiding what damage she had taken upon her own in the folds of her dress.

My pain. You have subsumed it.

"I promise to endure what I can, when I can. The god's remedy said you had to bleed, but it did not say for how long." Friday pretended the aching did not bother her while she helped Elisa tidy up the room. "Whenever you are not weaving, you should stretch out your arms and your fingers, just like that. Keep the muscles moving and the blood flowing. Cramps will only serve to hamper your progress."

Do you really think we can do this?

"I think anyone can do anything," said Friday. "There are miracles in all of us; we just have to find them."

When Friday opened the Elder Wood door, Conrad was standing at attention.

"Good morning, my stubborn squire. Did you sleep at all?"

"You probably know that better than I do, milady."

He was too right, the scamp. Up here, boosted by the magic Wednesday had woven into the stones, Friday could feel Conrad's exact degree of lethargy, the sore spot in his left hip, the crick in his neck from sleeping on stones, and his determination to wear a brave face and ignore all these things for the sake of doing his duty.

Just like his mistress.

Could she still . . . ?

Friday put her fingers on Conrad's neck and took the stiffness in the muscle there for her own. She was almost frightened by the ease with which she was able to make the transfer happen. The dull ache throbbed in the back of her skull as they started down the many flights of stairs; she was glad to have relieved her stalwart squire of this particular burden. The stitch in her own side had dimmed to a mere ache as well—none the worse for sleeping on stone herself.

"You did not need to do that."

It was not a scolding so much as a comment, but she sensed that she had injured Conrad's pride. And after Elisa had mentioned her brothers not wanting Friday to witness their transformation into swans! Friday should have known better.

"Please forgive me. I did not think it would work quite so well. It was not such an easy task the first time I took someone's pain. I should have asked your permission."

"As milady wishes." Conrad shifted the empty basket over his shoulder. "If I may suggest . . . ?"

"Your insight is always welcome, my friend."

"Perhaps the degree of difficulty increases with the severity of the wound."

"I suspect you are right," she said. "I also suspect the tower here has . . . well . . . stronger magic than a place like that should."

"Indeed," agreed Conrad. "To one with gifts such as myself, the stones here glow. I have only ever seen magic that strong in temples and churches: the places where your gods have touched the earth."

"My sister may be a goddess herself."

"Stranger things have happened."

Friday tousled his hair playfully. "That's what I like best about you, Conrad. Nothing ruffles you."

"It's what I like best about being a messenger. I have seen many a strange and wonderful thing on my travels."

"Are we distracting you? I would not keep you here against your will."

"Nor would I stay, milady, if it was not my will. I assure you, as soon as the atmosphere here stops being strange and wonderful, I will return to the road."

Friday considered her family and their fascinatingly complicated lives. "Then make yourself comfortable. You'll be here for a very, very long time. But worry not; you are welcome in Arilland for as long as you wish, both now and in the future."

"Thank you, milady."

"I am curious, though. When the stones in the sky tower glowed, what color did you see?"

As soon as she finished asking the question, she regretted it. Some areas of the world did not welcome magical abilities as easily as a Faerie-bordered country like Arilland, Conrad's among them. Friday stopped on the stairs and watched as Conrad's mother gave her baby to the washerwoman who hid him from the raging sultan in a basket of laundry. The vision was fuzzy, and lasted only a breath, but it was enough to tell Friday that her squire's gifts were a rare topic of conversation. She should have simply been honored that he'd spoken to her of it at all, and left it at that.

"The stones were blue. Vibrant, but dark . . . the indigo of midnight." He nodded to Elisa, a few steps ahead of them. "Her magic is blue as well, but light and shimmering as the sky on a summer day. This is the magic of the gods of air. I have seen its like before."

"And mine? Can you still see mine?"

"Yours is still red, like blood and fire. It was most vibrant at the top of the tower; it fades even as we descend. Why do you ask?"

"I saw those same colors, briefly, the night I healed Tristan. I have not seen them since, but I wanted to be sure."

"That tower room is a truly powerful thing."

"Yes. It was quite a feat that my sister was able to save it."

"It's a wonder that she saved it at all. In the country of my birth, its presence would not be a good thing."

Friday pondered this. It was true, certainly—such power really did have no right to exist outside the realm of the gods. But the way this year had been going . . .

"My mama always says that everything happens for a reason," said Friday. "I think, in some way, Wednesday knows those reasons." She thought about Thursday and her always-timely trunks full of gifts for the family. "A few of my sisters have the ability to anticipate catastrophe. When the ground beneath your feet turns to mud, you might find a stepping stone they put there years earlier, for no particular reason at the time."

"They have wisdom," said Conrad. "My Omi also possesses such wisdom." Friday knew instantly that this "Omi" was the washerwoman in Conrad's vision, and not his mother, as she'd previously suspected.

"We are lucky to have such people in our lives," said Friday. "Just as I am lucky to have met you, my young squire."

"Everything happens for a reason," he said.

"Mama would love you to pieces," said Friday. And it was true, though probably more so because Conrad was no stranger to hard work. "Would you mind starting the rounds with the children? I'll go with Elisa to the kitchens and check on how the nettle fibers are coming. We'll meet you by the willow tree."

Conrad bowed to both Friday and Elisa before leaping down the last few steps and dashing off down the corridor.

Elisa raised her eyebrows and gestured with her hands. Though Friday could no longer hear Elisa's words in her mind, she guessed what the girl might have asked.

"He's a pure ball of energy, that one," said Friday. "And he *should* bow to you. You are a princess, after all. Deposed or not."

Elisa straightened her shoulders, raised her chin, and fiddled with her stringy hair in jest.

Friday laughed. "I'm sure I could find you a tiara. Just don't blame me for the headache it gives you." Goodness, she sounded like Mama! Elisa pulled another face, and Friday dissolved into giggles again as they made their way to the kitchens. It was good that the girl was in such high spirits. These next few days were bound to test everyone's mettle.

The main kitchens were more bustling than usual. Men, women, and children alike worked hard on every surface, sorting berries, chopping herbs, and kneading loaf after loaf of bread. She could hear Mr. Jolicoeur, the butcher, calling to a group of men beyond the open back door; it seemed a lucky bunch would be dining on fresh venison tonight. A red-cheeked Cook sang as she tended a myriad of bubbling pots on the stove and hearth.

There were nettles everywhere.

Pots of all sizes and cauldrons and skillets were filled to the brim with dark green leaves. Bushel after bushel were stacked up along the walls and out the door. Scullery maids and kitchen boys with thick gloves separated the leaves from the stalks, sorting the pieces into several bags. When the bags were filled, each was carried to a different location. The bare stalks were then rebundled and hung over the fire to dry.

Cook was nothing if not organized. Friday marveled at the efficiency with which the short, plump woman ran her chaotic domain. Doubtless they were performing similar tasks in the subsidiary kitchens, even without Cook's direct supervision.

"Come in, girls," shouted Cook. "Stand close here, there's not much room to spare."

"Thank you," said Friday, obeying quickly enough to avoid being trampled by a passing bag of nettle leaves.

Elisa tugged on Cook's sleeve and pinched her nose. Friday had been so distracted by the jovial atmosphere of the busy kitchen that she hadn't even noticed the briny smell that filled the room.

"That's the nettles you're smelling, strange as yonder ocean. Don't worry, it passes. And don't go acting all high and mighty now that you've skived off being my herb girl," Cook chided Elisa. "You may be some fancy princess to the rest of them, but you'll always be Rampion to me."

Friday's heart broke a little as she realized that Cook would miss this girl as much as any woman would miss her own child. Cook had saved Elisa from the orphanage, given her a purpose, and called her Rampion. Motherless Elisa, who had no other strong female figure in her life, all but worshipped the kind woman, and rightfully so. Elisa put an arm around Cook and squeezed tightly. It was enough to make Friday weep.

"Watch out, now, girl, or you'll have me spill something." Cook dabbed at the corners of her eyes with her apron and pretended it was because of the nettles' steam.

"Are you very familiar with nettles?" Friday asked her.

"I am, milady—ate them at my mother's knee. I feel quite the fool for not thinking of it sooner."

Perhaps fate had not wanted it that way. "It is not traditional palace fare," admitted Friday.

"In our current situation, nothing is too humble," said Cook. "It would have been better to harvest them in the spring, for eating, but fall is almost as good. The heftier stalks will yield more fibers for Miss Rampion's projects. I've got them separating off the youngest leaves for blanching and eating, and the older leaves for making tea." She had one of the maids pour a cup for Friday.

"Watch this." Cook dropped a lemon slice into the cup and stirred. The rich, dark green liquid changed almost instantly to a bright, cheery pink. Friday gasped.

Cook winked. "One of Mother's tricks. Another trick is making beer—but I'll save that for later. Here's what you're after." She handed her wooden spoon to one of the maids and led Friday and Rampion to a larder just outside the heat of the kitchens.

Friday did her best not to exclaim at the empty shelves. Arilland's situation was already so dire! Inside the larder, a group of boys were hard at work. Bundles of the nettle stalks, already dried, lined up against the bare shelves. There were a few tin buckets filled with water where some of the stalks were soaking. This concentrated stench was far worse than the fishy smell of the kitchen. Elsewhere on the stone floor, the boys jumped on drenched and softened stalks with their boots, smashing them and separating the pliable outer husk from the tough fibers inside. Those fibers they then tossed in yet another bucket lined with cloth. As they dried, the last boy laid them out and carefully wrapped them around the end of a distaff.

One single distaff. For all that they had been working through the night, there was precious little fiber to show for it.

"Don't fret, my Rampion," said Cook. "You're part of our family now, and this family looks out for one another. We won't stop until you're free."

Elisa wrapped both arms around Cook this time and buried her face in the woman's broad shoulder. Friday could feel her tears. So much lost, so many years running, never staying in one place long enough to care about anyone — or have anyone care for her . . .

Cook pulled the girl out of her arms and kissed her forehead. "You must be strong now," she said. Elisa nodded, wanting desperately to say something but bound to silence. Cook put a finger over her charge's lips and then turned to Friday. "I've already sent your squire off with baskets for the children filled with whatever I could spare. And I'm to let you know your sister is meeting you out in the yard with fabric for your patchworks and a drop spindle."

Friday curtseyed. "Thank you, chef." Elisa followed her lead.

Cook handed Elisa the distaff of nettle fibers and waved them both away. "Now, now, none of that nonsense, please. I've some smelly work to get back to, thanks to a dawdling young herb girl and some clever farmers' children."

~eellee~

The rain had passed early that morning — that part had been no dream, either. The meadow before them was green and vibrant, shadowed only by the fat clouds rolling by. The children were even more full of energy than usual, if such a thing were possible, as if they'd been watered and now stretched out to the sun like sated plants. Roughly half of them still ran laundry races, while the other half were off adventuring with baskets, seeking every edible treasure they could find and presenting them to the woman who sat beneath the willow tree — a woman who was not, as Friday had guessed, Queen Sunday.

It was Monday.

The eldest Woodcutter sister sat on a large blanket, surrounded by a dozen large baskets and a sea of ivory sateen fabric. Elisa's brothers may have been cursed into swans, but Monday was the epitome of the bird in human form, tall, flawless, graceful, and white. Judging by the limpness of her overskirt, Friday suspected that Monday's underdressings had been sacrificed for the greater good. She did not grieve for the not-so-poor soul relegated to Princess Monday's castoffs.

Monday planted a kiss on the cheek of a young girl with green-tinted skin—the Kate the children called "Pickle"—who presented her with a handful of fresh berries. Her slender fingers collected the berries in a beautifully embroidered handkerchief, and she sent the child back into the fray.

"Velius has released me from my nursing duties," Monday announced. "To be honest, I'm little help to him anymore. Now that the initial rush of ocean-tossed refugees has settled, there's not much he can't heal on his own. So I'm here to be your loyal subject." She raised a basket as if toasting Friday's health. "I come bearing scads of material and sewing implements and the willingness to instruct the masses as you see fit."

Friday blushed. Ever since Sunday'd become queen, Princess Monday had returned to Arilland from her castle in the north, eager to reunite with her estranged family. Having recently become a victim of fate herself, Friday realized it was possible that Wednesday's spell had something to do with Monday's presence—but Friday knew there was more to the tale.

Though their eldest sister was still by far the most beautiful woman in Arilland, Friday felt a shadow inside her, cold and swirling like a conjured mist. Something terrible had happened to Monday, something beyond the loss of her beloved twin those many years ago. It haunted her eyes and lent a mystery to her figure that only served to make her more of a legend.

No one ever mentioned her absent husband, the dark prince who had swept her off her feet and made her the subject of romantic songs for years to come. If Monday wanted to keep her secrets, that was her business. As long as she reached out to her family, Friday would reach back.

"Elisa, you remember my sister Monday." They had been introduced last night in the presence of Mr. Humbug, but Friday felt safe in assuming that the evening had been a blur for them all. Elisa curtseyed and Monday nodded to her.

"Enchanted."

The word made Friday smile. Ever the diplomatic princess; Monday's greeting was so much more than a simple salutation.

"I must teach Elisa how to spin these fibers on the drop spindle. Once I have her started, I can help you sort fabric, cut squares, and collect a few of the children who might be interested in helping us." She was afraid of insulting her perfect sister, but Friday had to ask, "*Can* you sew?"

Monday gracefully took the question in stride. "Not as deftly as you, dearest sister, but I can hold my own among the idly embroidering ladies of the court. I do not possess a magicked needle, however. I have been known to prick my finger a time or two." She waggled those pale, slender fingers, and Friday felt her laugh at a joke that bubbled up inside that secret inner darkness.

As Monday emptied the baskets, Friday began instructing Elisa. She felt uncomfortable — who was she to be teaching anyone, when she had only just been apprenticed herself? She repeated her prayer to the gods for the safety of her mentor, and added a prayer to Yarlitza Mitella that she might forgive her brash apprentice for overstepping her bounds.

Managing the distaff and the spindle was awkward for Elisa at first, but she caught on quickly and was soon spinning like a madwoman. After about an hour she was walking around the meadow pulling the nettle fibers from the distaff and kicking the drop spindle from time to time to keep it spinning.

Elisa seemed pleased at her progress, but Friday secretly hoped the kitchen boys would be able to fill two or three more sizeable distaffs full of the stuff before sunset. They would need vast amounts of the yarn if they hoped to make seven shirts. Once there was enough to start Elisa on warp and weft, the task of spinning would pass to Friday and the brothers . . . but there could only be as many spinners as there were distaffs.

So, for the moment, frustrating as it was, Friday was allowed to sew.

Friday waved Wendy over. She told her to fetch Elaine and Evelyn and any other men, women, or children who had the patience to sit still and stitch. Friday called out to Frank and the young women watching the babies so that they could pay attention while she and Monday demonstrated the simple stitching of the fabrics.

"Right sides together," Friday heard herself repeating as she looked over her students' handiwork. "Right sides together." She missed her teacher so much her heart ached. When fear and sorrow threatened to overwhelm her again, she squashed the feelings down, repeated her prayers, steeled her will, and forced herself to carry on.

In that moment she realized the exact nature of Monday's internal shadow, though she did not yet know the reason for its existence.

For Friday, sewing the patchwork was like coming home. She lost herself in the rhythm, stitch after stitch, at the same time becoming one with her surroundings. She was the breeze that played in Monday's white-gold hair, she was the ripples around the swans in the pond, she was the grass trampled beneath the feet of laughing children. She was the willow tree, solid yet bending. She was the sun, shining warmly down upon the world and finding it good.

She looked forward to wearing her patchwork skirts again.

As twilight descended upon them all, Monday and Friday repacked the baskets. Some of the children took their squares back to the palace to work on into the evening; so passionate were their pleas that Friday didn't have the heart to deny them. Elisa carefully wrapped up her spindle and Conrad helped carry everything back to the kitchens, where they collected more fibers and food for the swan brothers.

Friday's heart was so light that she almost didn't mind the long walk to the top of the sky tower, and when she walked confidently through that Elder Wood door, every one of the brothers smiled at her.

Even Philippe.

8

Blame It on the Fairies

THERE HAD BEEN something special about this day. Tristan's senses felt heightened—he had felt more whole as his swanself than he ever had before. He could not fly high enough or fast enough or swim far enough. The fat clouds in the sky cooled the air to a perfect temperature, and he could have glided on the delicious breezes for months without effort. The colors of the world were richer: the green grass, the brown earth, the blue pond rippling with sparkles. The wind that sang through each of his feathers invigorated him, and the fish that came easily to his beak were tasty and filling.

When the sun fell low in the sky, he was almost reluctant to return to the tower, but his brothers nudged and honked him along. The transformation was virtually painless; he shed his feathers, lost his beak, and stretched his swanskin with magical ease. He did not usually remember being his swanself, but he remembered transformation, the ache of bones, the chill from down loss, and the sense that his skin would split with the effort of expansion. This day was not like all those other days, and he wondered why.

"Is this what it's like for you?" he asked François, who remembered the days but rarely spoke of them. "Is it always this . . . alive?" Tristan did not know a better word to use. Friday, so proud of her book reading, probably did.

"No." François dressed himself in the clothes that had been neatly folded for them and ran his fingers through his short mess of hair. The brothers' hair had never grown in all the years they'd been cursed, nor had any of them needed to shave. Sebastien's small beard had been the same since the day the spell took hold; the rest of them had stayed smooth-cheeked.

What would it be like to brush his hair, to bathe, to dress, to feast as a man again? Tristan missed these mundane things, or at least he thought he did. Either way, he looked forward to getting back to the painful life he had forced himself to stop wishing for many years ago. There was nothing he would miss about being a swan, especially considering he remembered very little . . . except perhaps flying. Yes, he would miss flying. Especially on days like this.

"What's it like?" Tristan asked of all those other days. "Can you explain it?"

François furrowed his brow.

Before he could respond, Christian chimed in. "Odd, isn't it, that we've never asked this question before?"

"It's never occurred to us," said Bernard.

"We all do the same thing every day," said Rene. "I guess I just assumed it was all the same."

Philippe said nothing.

"But it's not, and we know it," said Christian. "We all know that François remembers more of these days than the rest of us, but we never think to ask why, or ask him exactly what he remembers. Why now?"

"I remembered today," said Tristan. "Most of it. At least, I think so."

"So did I," said Bernard.

"So did I," echoed Rene.

Philippe said nothing.

François's smile was wan. "It was a good day. I'm glad this was a day your swanselves chose to remember. Some days are like this, but all too few. Some days are like dungeons, dark and cramped. The swanskin feels . . . strange . . . as if I've put it on wrong, or suddenly it's too small."

"Is it painful?" Tristan asked.

"Yes," François said matter-of-factly. "Usually the torture is more mental than physical. I'm fine one moment, and the next I find myself trapped in this unnatural body I cannot escape, with a mouth that will not let me cry for help. Some days my arms and legs stay with me as phantoms, unbalancing me and weighing me down. Flying is hell on those days."

For years they had wandered through this nightmare, and only François had borne the memories. Tristan felt ashamed for asking the question, and guilty that the youngest of them had shouldered this burden alone for so long. "I'm sorry."

"Don't be." François's tone shifted, and the wry grin turned to a wide smile. "Those are the days I dunk each of you under the water to make myself feel better. It's not like you remember."

Philippe stepped back as the twins jumped forth to tackle François and wrestle him to the ground.

"How dare you besmirch my honor!" cried Rene.

"My poor, pretty feathers!" cried Bernard.

Sebastien raised an eyebrow but did not break them up. It was good to hear laughter again, and there was no need to fear their discovery in this place.

"But why?" Christian repeated, almost to himself. "Why did we never think to ask François about this before now?"

"The curse is ending," said Sebastien. "Its power is waning."

Their eldest brother's anger had waned as well these past few days, turning instead to a resigned melancholia. He, too, would have remembered this day spent with his one true love, the swan Odette. She had shared her shelter on that frozen winter's day when they'd met, and she'd followed them ever since, migrating westward, unafraid of Sebastien even in his human form.

Odette — the name Sebastien swore she was called, though Tristan knew not how — preferred to spend her evenings in her nest of rushes down by the pond, but this night she had returned with them to the sky tower; Sebastien thought it best to bring her there to keep her safe from Mordant in the coming days. Her form was only slightly smaller than Sebastien's swanself, but she made herself smaller still, huddling against the crumbling wall farthest from the Elder Wood door and closest to the sky. Tristan hoped she acclimated quickly to the height and the ruckus. Sebastien kept her close, petting her gently and cooing to ease her trembling.

"I apologize to you as well, swan sister," Tristan said to the bird. "This must be so hard for you," he said to Sebastien.

"You will know my torment soon enough, little brother," Sebastien replied. "You have had only a taste of what it is to have someone so bound to you that you fear losing her more than life itself."

Tristan and Christian exchanged glances. There was another question the brothers dared not ask, about Sebastien's intentions to free himself from the curse along with the rest of them. They knew Sebastien would never jeopardize their chances of returning to the world of men, just as they knew Elisa would weave the shirts in order to break their curse, regardless of Mordant's arrival. The curse would be broken, for better or worse, and Sebastien would conquer those demons when they came . . . so the brothers said nothing. Instead, they left the eldest in peace and went to pull the twins off François.

Tristan would contemplate his own torment when Friday

walked through that door, and not before. Now was the time for the brothers to stretch their limbs and enjoy the cool twilight. They would need their strength; there was much work to be done!

As twilight faded into evening, Tristan found himself inching toward the Elder Wood door. He had reached out for the handle, compelled to open it, when Friday walked through, hugging three sticks full of what looked like tan spider webs. Her cheeks were flushed from the march up the stairs, and the wisps that had escaped her braid made a wild halo around her face. He couldn't help but mirror her generous smile.

"It was a good day," she said breathlessly.

"Ours was too." He took the sticks from her and carried them into the room.

Elisa followed with two bulging sacks, which she quickly handed to the twins, and then turned back through the door for a bucket filled with food.

"No fancy basket this time?" teased Bernard.

Friday tucked some loose strands of hair behind one ear. "I thought it might be useful as a chamber pot, if necessary."

"We've never needed one before," said Rene.

"You've never eaten much as a man before, either." Sebastien took the bucket from Friday and began laying out the food for their supper. "That's very generous of you, princess. Thank you."

"And not very princess-like," Tristan pointed out. "Be careful, Miss Woodcutter. Your true colors are showing."

Friday's grin would have had him jumping off the tower after her all over again. What was it about love that turned men into fools? Was there a way to convince the magicked stones of the tower to at least leave him half his wits?

"Arilland is a different sort of country. We blame it on the fairies."

"Rene blames things on the fairies too," said Bernard. "Especially when he overindulges on minnows."

Every one of his brothers laughed except Philippe, and the princess laughed with them. For all her earthiness, Tristan could not see Friday as a celibate, prayer-filled acolyte. Tristan felt some guilt that his dreams of the future made hers obsolete. He had lost so much in his life; he was not going to lose Friday as well.

Sebastien bowed to the princess and ordered his other siblings to attention. "François, portion out the food. Rene and Bernard, move a few stones around and see if you can't create some sort of privy. Philippe, help Christian and me sort out the contents of these bags."

He moved to pick up the bag by the door; in doing so, he passed within whispering distance of Tristan. "Tend to the girls," Sebastien hissed. "See that they have everything they need. And that they eat." As if Tristan wouldn't have done so anyway.

There was a knock at the door; three faint beats of a fist muffled by the old wood.

"That's Conrad," said Friday. "I asked him to bring up some water."

Tristan prised the door open a crack, using the Elder Wood to block his body from sight, out of habit. A thin brown arm stretched around the door with one full tin bucket, and then another.

"Thank you," Tristan said before he thought better of it.

"Keep her safe," said the boy, pulling the door after him.

Was there anyone in this castle who didn't love Friday Woodcutter? The swan brothers and Elisa depended on her. Her sister the queen gave her everything she wanted. Children—both high- and lowborn—trailed her skirts like cygnets, and strange magicians popped out of thin air to aid her on her quests. This squire would probably follow her to the end of her days, should she but ask it.

It wasn't so hard to imagine. Tristan himself had followed her right off the edge of the tower.

Without warning, the fear found him again. What if, when this was all over, Friday let him go? Tristan didn't want someone to love right now. He wanted love like his parents had . . . like Sebastien had. Tristan wanted the freedom to care about Friday and have her care about him, without the fear of losing her forever. But now that the end of the curse seemed very real, he was forced to think about what would happen after. Before he'd met Friday, he'd wanted nothing more than to return home with his siblings and reclaim his birthright. But now she was such a part of their lives that leaving Arilland would be one of the toughest things he would ever do.

As soon as Tristan considered keeping his distance from

her, for both their sakes, Friday raised her head and looked right into his eyes. His resolve shattered like the broken walls of the tower room.

Sebastien and Conrad had both warned him to take care of Friday. Who was going to let her know that he needed taking care of in return?

Friday's chest rose as she took in a breath. A quiet tear slipped down her cheek.

He didn't have to tell her. She already knew.

Only one of the remaining buckets had been designated for drinking water; the other was reserved for spinning. Friday had told them they could use their spit to keep the fibers of the net-tle thread smoothly winding together, but after hours of spin-ning, Tristan found the aftertaste nauseating.

They had all taken turns with the drop spindles, learn-ing from both Friday and one another the best techniques to keep producing the light brown nettle yarn. The princess en-couraged them to recite the Common alphabet as they kicked the spindle, in preparation for their reading lessons. François took every opportunity to lord his superior knowledge over his ignorant brothers. Rene and Bernard took every opportunity to kick their youngest brother, while keeping their spindles in check.

Since there were only three staffs full of the raw nettle

fibers — Conrad fetched three more in the middle of the night to replace the ones they finished; did the boy ever sleep? — whichever brother wasn't spinning was set to sewing patchwork. Sebastien and Christian, the only ones with practical experience on the field of battle, had some rudimentary knowledge of needle and thread. Friday had assured them that was all they needed.

Every so often, as someone picked up a new square, Friday would say, "Right sides together," and Tristan caught a faraway look in her eyes. He cursed that fey-blessed empathy for not working both ways.

And so they sat in a circle like old maids and stitched, sometimes in silence and sometimes telling stories. Rene and Bernard were the best storytellers, each trying to top the other with ridiculous — and often fabricated — tales from their childhood. Philippe remained quiet. When it was his turn to sew, he would take a pile of squares and sit against the wall beside Elisa, a companion to her intense silence.

In the darkest hours of the night, Friday asked François to read to them from the books she had brought. Sometimes the readings themselves sparked a conversation. Other times, Friday would prompt Sebastien or Tristan by asking them a question, usually about the Green Isles or their parents. Friday had shared stories about her own family as well, but only after they had assured her it would not offend them.

"Teach me how to lead an army," Friday asked the older brothers in the wee hours.

"Why would you want to know about that?" asked Tristan.

"You offered to learn how to read," she said. "I should learn something in return."

Sebastien shot Friday a skeptical look, but Christian was more open-minded. "What do you want to know? Anything specific?"

"What are the qualities of a good leader? What is it that makes one man destined to lead and other men destined to follow?" She posed the questions with a genuine curiosity that made Tristan want to kiss her needle-wielding hand.

Charmed by her eagerness to learn, Sebastien's demeanor softened. "Noble birth assigns men to their station, but there are princes who have led men to their deaths and farmers who have succeeded against all odds."

"Father would have said the most important quality was loyalty," added Tristan.

"To your men, or from them?"

"Both," Tristan explained. "Your men will not respect you if you play them false. They will desert an incompetent leader at the first sign of trouble. But if they know you will fight just as hard for them, they will happily die for you."

Friday scrunched up her nose. It was adorable. "Not *happily,* surely."

"Proudly." Sebastien scratched his dark beard. "Honorably."

"The same way you would give your life for someone you love," said Christian.

"I would," the princess whispered.

"A leader must be kind, but strong," said Sebastien.

Friday chuckled as she deftly folded another square into

her patchwork fabric and fastened it there with tiny, perfect stitches without even having to look down. "That rules me out. I can barely lift a full bucket of water."

"It doesn't have to be strength of arms," Christian clarified. "More often than not, strength of will is what sees an army to victory."

"You lead an army right now," Tristan pointed out, "for all that they are children."

"They've been called as much by some, but they are not an army," said Friday. "They are just children. I am a shepherd, and they are my flock."

"In a country being invaded by trolls, I have seen flocks like this given weapons to defend themselves," said Sebastien. "What you have is an army."

Friday shuddered. "Gods willing, my children will never be put to that test. They have been through enough already." Her eyes met Tristan's again, and once again she read his mind as clearly as if he'd spoken aloud. "As have you," she added. "I can feel that each one of you is preparing for a fight — but you shouldn't have to."

"No, we shouldn't," said Christian. "But we will."

"I know," said Friday. "And I know there is nothing I can do to stop you, but . . . I worry about Philippe."

"Why?" Sebastien, Christian, and Tristan asked all at once.

"There is a great anger brewing inside him."

"That's not new," said Sebastien.

Friday took Sebastien's hand. "I know what you feel. Through you, I have a sense of Philippe's past behavior. Believe me when I tell you that the anger Philippe is experiencing now is far beyond anything of which you ever thought him capable."

Tristan hadn't been worried about his younger brother until that moment. "I don't know if that's possible."

"I assure you it is," Friday said with perfect conviction. "That young man is very full of pain, and he is very ready to do something about it."

"Like what?" asked Christian.

Sebastien took his hand from Friday's and folded his arms over his chest. "Like kill Mordant the minute he sets foot in Arilland."

Friday gasped. "You know?"

"I know my brothers better than you think, Your Highness. Worry not. I will speak to him tomorrow."

Friday narrowed her eyes at Sebastien thoughtfully. "You might not disabuse him of this notion."

Sebastien shrugged. "Maybe I don't think killing Mordant would be such a bad thing."

"You would start a war?" she asked. "And you would put Arilland in the middle of it?"

"I might," said Sebastien.

"Then may the gods help us all," said Friday. From the girl who believed only in putting good intentions out into the world, it was as much a prayer as a statement.

Philippe had a knack for finding chaos. This was one instance in which Tristan hoped his disconsolate brother did not showcase his talents.

9

Deadly Living

HE PREVIOUS SPRING, Friday had been tasked with fashioning five gowns for her mother and sisters for a royal ball, and she'd only had three days in which to do it. At the end of those three days, one of her sisters had become a princess, and one a queen.

This time, three days passed even more quickly.

An incredible amount of work had been done; a credit to Arilland, her inhabitants, and her resident refugees. Most of the women — and some men — took to spinning, sewing, weaving, and mending. It seemed that everybody on the castle grounds now owned some patchwork article of clothing. The parents of Friday's children in particular donned the material as a mark of pride.

Most of the men — and some women — set to helping Papa and Peter with their ship; so many that it was almost completed and ready for sealing and launching. A special crew had been delegated to help Cook with the nettles and the rest of the scavenged food, though the numbers of her staff dwindled in direct proportion to the food supply. Those who left her service made their way to the grassy beaches armed with poles to fish in the surf for whatever they could catch. Velius and Monday attended to new patients suffering from heat sicknesses and sunburns, and Cook started concocting healing salves alongside her regular menu.

It had been almost a month since Saturday's impossible ocean had appeared; it was beginning to look as if it was there to stay. If that was so, Arilland was in dire straits. Rumbold and Sunday remained ensconced in meetings, sending emissaries into Faerie and beyond in search of help or trade. Queen Sunday had recruited their old family friend Johan Schmidt as seneschal, to see how far he could squeeze the gold in Arilland's coffers. He brought along his young assistant, Panser.

It was comforting to see Panser's familiar face around the castle. Friday had been in love with Panser, too, once, not so long ago . . . and yet, it felt like ages. Tristan had colored everything about her life, it seemed: not only her present and future, but her past as well.

Friday worried about them all now — the swans and their sister — as if they were her own family. Elisa was as exhausted as Arilland. She remained in the sky tower quietly bent over her weaving, day and night. True to Friday's promise, Elisa wove until her fingers cracked and bled. And true to Friday's word, the princess took Elisa's wounds as her own when she could, bearing the pain for her.

In the evenings, Elisa's hair changed to gold, and during the daylight it returned to the color of nettle fiber, but she did not budge from her spot. She wove until she passed out from exertion, and when she woke she scolded whoever was at hand for letting her sleep too long. She would have refused food or drink if her brothers and Friday had not forced it into her, keeping the looms out of reach until she wolfed something down, used the privy, and silently fought to start again.

There is not enough time to weave all seven shirts before Mordant's arrival, Elisa said as Friday took her hands and her pain once more. *Don't tell them, please. I beg you.*

"Whether you complete the task or not, will anything stop you from working yourself to the bone?" whispered Friday.

No.

Friday squeezed Elisa's newly healed fingers once more. "Then there is nothing to be said."

Elisa had four shirts completed and was hard at work on the fifth when the trumpets blared just after dawn on the third day to signal Mordant's arrival.

Mordant's ship had . . . well, not *docked,* since there was no port in Arilland to speak of, but it weighed anchor just off the shoreline. Two boats were lowered into the water from the high deck, giving Rumbold, Sunday, and their staff time to clear out the Great Hall and ready themselves to receive the visiting dignitaries.

Friday changed out of her patchwork and back into the only formal dress she had not yet given away, a Tyrian purple she'd acquired from Monday's trousseau. Though she had altered the gown down from her eldest sister's height, taken out the seams, and fit it to herself perfectly, she was instantly uncomfortable inside it. Friday might have been a princess, but only by default. She was a woodcutter's daughter and a devotee in the church of the Earth Goddess. She was more comfortable covered in flour or children.

Still, this sort of thing was expected of her now. Sunday had made it clear: if *she* was forced to wear shoes, then Friday must make herself presentable as well.

She was intercepted on her way to the Great Hall by none other than Henry Humbug. A silver chain gleamed across his rounded belly, at odds with his tattered, long coat. When he stopped, his tall hat wobbled mightily but didn't topple.

"Miss Woodcutter . . ." he began, then shook his head. "Princess Friday . . . Your Highness . . ."

Friday put a hand on his arm. She sensed a loneliness deep within his heart, and she knew that he would find the gesture reassuring. "I prefer the first address," she said. "What can I do for you, Mr. Humbug?"

"I wondered if you might consider taking an old man's advice."

Friday was often the recipient of such advice. Perhaps because, unlike the rest of her siblings, she was the one who was most likely to follow it. "It would be my honor."

Mr. Humbug's yellow eyes seemed to twinkle with

happiness at her reply. "I know what's about to happen. And I know it will not be pleasant—for any of you, but you especially."

"I expect not." Friday was worried for her new friends, and still curious as to the extent of Mr. Humbug's knowledge of the situation. She was almost positive Mr. Humbug had no fey blood in him, but there was still something other-than-human about his personage.

"Whatever happens during this reception," he said, "you must say nothing. Do nothing."

It was an odd suggestion, but Friday should not have expected otherwise from such a man. "This is a meeting of royalty, sir. It is for Arilland's queen and king to manage, not I."

Mr. Humbug nodded solemnly. "So it is. Yes, so it is. But you are royalty as well."

Friday felt a strange impulse to hug the doddering older man. "All right, then. I promise you I will say nothing."

She made it to the Great Hall with moments to spare before the new Lord of the Green Isles and his dubious companions walked down the long carpet toward the dais where Rumbold and Sunday awaited them.

Mordant was shorter than Friday had imagined.

His robes were bright red, as were those of his sorceress consort. Friday marveled at their exquisite embroidery: silver and gold thread and even precious jewels were intricately woven into symbols of royalty and power. The craftsmanship involved meant that dozens of laborers had spent hours fashioning each garment. The costume was a smart choice for this reception, communicating not only the cost of the fabric, but the number of devoted servants — or slaves — at Mordant's command.

Beyond that, the two matched only in their wide faces, mottled skin, and coarse black hair. Her eyes were almond-shaped, almost catlike, while his were beady and hid beneath bushy brows. His thin-lipped mouth formed a line under an equally thin waxed mustache.

"Slimy" was probably the best word to describe him. Short and slimy.

A cockatrice wound itself around the sorceress's neck like a deadly living scarf. Its scales shimmered in the firelight like flame itself, from the crimson feathers atop its beaked head to the copper wings folded flat against its body, to the slender drake's tail that curled down its mistress's breast like burnished gold ivy. It was leashed to her right wrist with a gold chain so fine and delicate that it did not give Friday much faith in the animal's restraint. Thankfully, it was hooded with a chained veil of similarly fine gold, and it seemed to sleep soundly on its perch.

Just as dangerous as the cockatrice — or its mistress — was their bodyguard. The man was taller than them both, broad of chest, narrow of waist, and clad from head to toe in black silk. The only bits of skin that showed were his mouth, from cheek to chin — a scarf obscured the top half of his face, with slits for his eyes. Even his gloves and boots were black. He made no sound when he walked and, like Elisa, he said nothing. His only weapon was a dagger at his waist, conveying to the company that if he wished to stop man or beast, he needed no other aid. The mystery man made himself known by briefly stepping into the room to survey the occupants, and then made himself just as quickly unknown by slinking back into the shadows.

"We welcome you to Arilland, Lord Mordant." Rumbold's Official King voice held an air of command similar to Mama's. Friday wondered if Sunday had taught him that, or if he'd picked it up from his own overbearing father.

It was too bad that Rumbold and Sunday could not instantly raise arms against this man who had done such a wrong to their new friends, but Arilland must introduce itself as a neutral party. As king, Rumbold's duty was to assess the situation before taking action. Devastating though it was, Mordant had conquered the Green Isles and was now their new ruler. As such, Rumbold was required to treat Mordant with respect.

Especially since His Sliminess had brought with him a desperately needed supply of food.

"Word of your plight has spread throughout the land and across the sea, as far as our fair Green Isles," said Mordant.

Friday smirked. The Green Isles lay beyond the Troll Kingdom, too far away for this statement to be true, and everyone in the room knew it.

"I hope you accept this bounty as a gift from my people, a gesture upon which we might begin a new friendship."

Rumbold received the gift with as much grace as he could muster. "Arilland thanks the Green Isles for its most generous forethought."

The men bowed to each other. With a wave of Mordant's hand, bushels and bags of fresh vegetables and fruits Friday had never seen before began to parade through the Great Hall. Sack after sack of sugar, rice, flour, and salt were followed by boxes of spices and barrels of wine and the preserved haunches of various animals.

Sunday called for a matching pair of guards to lead the men to the kitchens. Cook would be beside herself. "We should hold a feast in honor of your arrival."

"Think nothing of it, Your Highness. Your situation is far direr. We must see to the needs of our subjects." Mordant managed to imply not only that was Arilland broken, but also that Rumbold and Sunday did not have the means or skill to rebuild their own country without help. The "our" indicated that Mordant had no problem with the idea of conquering Arilland as well.

Friday wanted to slap the man. If only Mama were here, she could step right up to Mordant and order him to speak the truth about his intentions.

"Perhaps, in lieu of a formal celebration, Your Majesties might help us with a more delicate, political matter."

Rumbold motioned for Mordant to continue. Friday took a deep breath and braced herself.

"A young girl—a ward of my kingdom, if you will— escaped our custody, and by doing so has put herself in grave danger."

Beside her on the dais, Friday saw Monday fold her hands together in her lap. The subtleness of the gesture helped Friday remain calm.

"How terrible." Rumbold gave no evidence that he knew of whom Mordant was speaking.

"Coincidentally, my own . . . messengers . . . have sent word that she currently resides in your kingdom."

Rumbold continued to play the fool. "We have had a marked increase in population since the ocean made its appearance on our doorstep."

"Can you tell us her name?" Sunday asked. "Perhaps we can help."

"You would not know her by name," Mordant said evasively. "She would want to conceal her true identity."

"I understand completely," said Sunday. "Then what does she look like?"

Friday hid her smile behind her hands. Her little sister made a very clever queen.

Mordant took a moment to compose his reply. "We believe she has altered her appearance to the same end. Describing her to you would be similarly futile."

"Hmm. What a shame. I am afraid we can be of little use in your quest."

Friday sensed the delight in Sunday's voice. She hoped Mordant and his sorceress did not have similar powers of perception.

Mordant snapped his fingers and the mystery man once again appeared at his side. The man bowed gracefully to Rumbold and Sunday.

"If you would but allow the Infidel the freedom to search for the girl on these grounds, Your Majesties need not concern yourselves further."

Sunday and Rumbold exchanged glances. It would be impossible for them to refuse.

The urge to blurt out something — anything — to stop this madness was overwhelming, but Friday remembered her promise to Mr. Humbug. For whatever reason, for better or worse, she needed to let this act play out.

"Sir . . . Infidel." Rumbold addressed the mystery man. "Have we met?"

The Infidel took to one knee and bowed low before Rumbold, turning his silk-clad body into little more than a smudge against the carpet.

"The Infidel does not speak," said Mordant, "the better for him to concentrate on his duties. But if I might answer on his behalf, I do not think it likely that your esteemed path has crossed his humble one."

"Thank you, Lord Mordant." After another long pause, in which none of his advisors was able to offer up any objection, Rumbold said, "You may proceed with your search."

Friday wanted to cry. Poor Elisa. What good was the power to feel, when everyone around you was frightened or in pain? Why couldn't Friday have been given some useful power, like invisibility?

The Infidel bowed lower — as if such a thing were possible — and then fluidly snapped back up to a standing position. He leaned in toward the sorceress, careless of the deadly beast around her neck. She whispered something into his scarf-covered ear and he vanished like smoke down the hallway.

Conrad quietly slipped out of the Great Hall after him.

Friday said nothing about that either.

Searching the whole of the palace and castle grounds was an impossible task for any one man. Friday should not be worried—but she was. There was something *wrong* with this Infidel, though she could not put her finger on it. She could not get a clear sense or feeling from any of these visitors from the Green Isles, as if they were wooden figures with neither hearts nor souls. There was something wrong with all of them, and the sooner they left, the sooner Arilland could go back to healing itself. Until that time, Mordant, his sorceress, and his Infidel would fester like blight.

"Lord Mordant, if you and the Lady . . . ?" Sunday let the address float in the air until Mordant deigned to fill the silence.

"Gana." The "g" was hard and guttural. The lady in question tilted her head toward the dais.

". . . Lady Gana would like to stay, we can have rooms prepared for you." Sunday left the impetus on Mordant to rudely announce how long he intended to darken their doorstep.

Sunday was *good* at this game.

"Thank you, Highness. You are most gracious. We will trespass upon your kindness one evening and no more."

"You have such trust in your . . . man's . . . abilities?" Sunday would not bring herself to call anyone "Infidel."

Mordant's answering grin made Friday's skin crawl. "He is very good at what he does."

Friday wasn't sure how much longer she could keep her

wretched tongue from disobeying her. "I need to leave," she whispered to Monday.

Monday kept her eyes on the red-robed figures as Sunday summoned guards and maids to see the guests to their rooms. "You cannot go to them," Monday replied without so much as moving her wan smile. "You will draw unwanted attention."

Friday fought back tears, hating the wellspring of emotions that spilled over so often that she was constantly left weeping in its wake. "I must do something."

"Go to Cook," said Monday. "She will be overwhelmed."

Friday realized Cook would have her hands too full with Mordant's bounty to concentrate any more of her efforts on confounded nettles. She reached forward and squeezed Monday's hand. "I will. Thank you."

Monday squeezed back. "And stay away from the pond. If luck is with us, they will find nothing and leave by daybreak."

~~elle~~

Luck was not with them.

The already-short autumn day passed all too quickly. By late afternoon they assembled in the Great Hall once more, and the Infidel stepped from the shadows with Elisa in tow.

Friday could not hear Elisa's thoughts, but she felt the girl's exhaustion and fear. Instinctively she leapt forward, but Velius held her back. Elisa was tossed to her knees on the carpet before them, hands bound.

"Your Majesties." Mordant stepped forth and bowed before

Rumbold and Sunday. The sun setting through the windows behind the dais lit the gems in his magnificent robes and made him sparkle with power. "I request that this girl be executed immediately."

Sunday and Monday gasped. Friday would have too, but all the air had left her body. Arrested? Of course. Restrained, perhaps. Thrown into the deepest, darkest dungeon even, but . . . execution?

"I am not in the habit of executing my subjects," Rumbold said carefully, "nor the subjects of any other country without a fair trial."

Sunday did not have Rumbold's restraint. "What is her crime?"

"She was once a princess of the Green Isles, under the reign of the previous monarchy. After my armies defeated those of her family, I took the throne, ceased the fighting, and spared her life out of mercy. I put to her the task of caring for the other orphaned children of the palace . . . poor souls."

Sunday's eyes didn't actually roll, but Friday felt it just the same. "What happened to the children?"

Finally, the sorceress spoke. The gilt-red cowl framed her black hair and eyes, giving her equally red lips a magical, hypnotic quality. "She killed them, Your Elegance." The Lady Gana's voice was deep and heavily accented. "She sacrificed them to her gods in exchange for magic."

"Did you do this?" Rumbold asked Elisa.

Elisa shook her head.

"Of course she would deny any charges put against her," said Mordant. "She is not a fool."

"Nor am I," Rumbold said seriously. "Were these children under your care?"

Elisa nodded.

"And they are now dead?"

Sadly, Elisa nodded again.

"Do you know what happened to them?"

Elisa stared at Rumbold for a very long time. She gave a half-shrug, and then slowly nodded her head once more. She pointed at Mordant and his consort, and then turned up her palms in a pleading gesture.

"She will not even speak in her own defense!" Mordant cried.

"She is mute," said Sunday.

"She is not," said the sorceress.

Reluctantly, Elisa nodded again.

"The girl is silent by choice," said Gana. "And wisely so, for she cannot incriminate herself this way."

Rumbold sat back in his chair. "It seems we are at an impasse, as neither party can present proof of these claims."

"Oh, there is proof," said Mordant. "We just had to wait for it."

And with that, the sun set.

Before their eyes, Elisa's form shifted from that of a dull, gray, mousy little scullery maid to that of a spindly-limbed young woman with long golden hair and wide, cornflower-blue eyes.

"You deny now that your appearance has been altered by magic?" Mordant accused Elisa. She spread her arms wide in answer, as if to say, *As you see.* "And those children died because of you."

Once more, Elisa nodded. Her eyes met Friday's in desperation and grief.

Tears streamed down Friday's cheeks. She could feel Elisa's frustration, but without the added magic of the sky tower, she could not read the girl's mind to hear her side of the story and come to her rescue.

Tristan was going to kill her.

Ultimately, Elisa's fate was left to Rumbold. "I am still not convinced that this is enough evidence by which to hold an execution."

"Fine," said Mordant. "Release her into my custody, as a subject of my kingdom, and we will depart with the tide."

Sunday, Monday, Friday, and Velius all sat forward at this request, but Rumbold held up a hand to stop them. "I would like the evening to mull over this decision. Rooms have already been prepared for you. If further proof presents itself overnight — or if the girl decides to speak and defend herself — I will consider it in my final ruling."

"And if there is no change?" asked Mordant.

"Then she will be yours come morning."

A morning that would mean Elisa's death sentence. Friday could not read the pair's emotions, but it was clear they had no desire to postpone Elisa's execution until they got back to their ship.

"As Your Majesty wishes," Mordant said through his teeth.

Friday's grip on the seat of her chair was so tight that she began to lose sensation in her fingers. Rumbold had given Elisa all he could: one more night to finish the nettle shirts and break the spell.

Once Friday returned with Elisa to the sky tower, she would find out what exactly had happened back on the Green Isles . . .

"In the meantime, I request that she be thrown in your deepest, darkest dungeon," Mordant added. "You do have one of those, don't you?"

Rumbold and Sunday exchanged glances. Well used or not, every proper castle had a dungeon somewhere. "I'm sorry, my dear."

Gracefully, Elisa got to her feet, curtseyed deeply, and awaited her fate.

Rumbold nodded and motioned for his guards. "Take her away."

As the two guards lifted her, Elisa slumped over, unconscious. Friday was unsure what had finally overcome the girl, but was somewhat grateful that Elisa would not feel pain for a little while. From the corner of her eye, she saw Velius stretch his fingers. Mordant gave the duke a nasty look. Velius gave him nothing in return.

Friday waited for her brother and sister to dismiss the wretched assembly, making plans to join Elisa in the dungeon all the while. So far from the sky tower, Friday would no longer be able to communicate with the girl at all . . . not that it mattered, really. Friday and Conrad would collect the supplies from the tower and bring them down to the dungeon. They would continue their task and Friday would help Elisa in whatever way she could.

By morning, one way or another, this curse would be broken.

10

Swansbody

TRISTAN COULDN'T BELIEVE his ears. "But . . . you just sat there and did nothing?" She would have felt the cruelty in his words. His anger didn't let him care.

"It was not my place," said the princess. "When it comes to the politics, I am merely a piece on this game board. I must act — or not act — accordingly. There would have been no wisdom in showing my hand. Or my heart."

"But how *could* you? Perhaps you have no heart." No one believed these words, but Tristan said them anyway. He needed to lash out, and thanks to this wretched curse, his hands were tied. He could do nothing but sit back and wait for Friday to report the news to them. That she had sat there and said nothing

. . . done nothing . . . He should probably be praising her composure under such duress, but deep down he just wanted to smash things.

Friday turned and walked away, crossing the room to collect Elisa's materials so that she and her squire could deliver them to the *dungeon*. Tristan seethed. He wanted to march down those steps and give Mordant a piece of his mind — right before he put a dagger in his brain.

"Stop it right now." Sebastien grabbed Tristan by the arms and shook him out of his spiral of hatred. "You're being rude and inappropriate, and you're scaring Odette."

Tristan glanced over to where his brother's swan-lover smoothed her feathers fitfully in a crude nest of rushes. "What do you care?" he spat. "You don't even want to break the curse."

Friday might not have punched him for his nastiness, but Sebastien had no such qualms. To his elder brother's credit, the pain did help Tristan focus. Somewhat.

"Better?" asked Sebastien.

Eyes watering, Tristan nodded and rubbed his jaw. If he spoke, he might have fought back, and he did not want the anger to overcome him again. Satisfied, Sebastien retreated to Odette's pathetic makeshift nest.

Tristan caught a glimpse of Philippe, hovering in the shadows against the crumbling wall. His perpetually furious almost-twin smiled sardonically.

The Elder Wood door opened slightly and three more staves of nettle fiber slipped politely through.

The true twins ignored their brothers and addressed Friday

over the sack of food she'd tossed them upon her arrival. "You want us to keep spinning?" asked Bernard.

"Please, if you don't mind. Conrad can return later to collect what you've done. This shirt is almost finished, and I'm hoping Elisa can finish another while she's . . ." The words didn't need saying. Even if Elisa was allowed to weave in her cell, the shirt she might complete this night would still leave them one tunic short.

Sebastien's dark form curled around his nervous swan-love; he smoothed her feathers and spoke in soft words. A shortage of tunics might leave him free to remain a swan, Tristan realized. Free of the responsibilities of the heir to the throne of the Green Isles. Free as a bird.

But the brothers needed a leader. Sebastien was the most mature, the most logical, and the most ruthless. He had been their father's prize pupil; he alone understood best their parents' intentions and plans for the future of the country. As a man, Sebastien would have done whatever it took for his family to regain their birthplace.

As a man, Tristan would also do whatever it took. "I'm coming with you." He picked up the completed shirts and stuffed them in another empty sack. He grabbed Elisa's crudely woven nettle mat with bare hands and threw it in for good measure, hoping the stinging pain it left behind would keep him clearheaded.

Friday would decline his offer, sweetly, and with the reason that they had been instructed to not test the boundaries of the curse any further than they already had. Yet hadn't the damage been done? Mordant had found them and Elisa now faced execution. Ending up stuck as a swan for the rest of his life seemed trivial in comparison.

Sebastien would spend this last night pining over his love. Philippe would brood. François would read. Christian and the twins would spin the last of their hope and joy into that nettle fiber, futile as their actions might be. But Tristan could not sit idly by. "Nothing you can say will dissuade me."

"I imagine not." Friday reached down into the bag she held and removed several dark items of clothing and a pair of black boots. She shoved it all into his hands. "Just put these on first."

There she went, surprising him again. "What's this?"

"That assassin of Mordant's — the one he calls 'the Infidel' — wears all black, including a mask that covers his face. You're about his build, if perhaps a little scrawnier, but not enough for anyone who might be awake at this hour to notice."

Tristan stared at the black bundle. "I . . . I mean, I . . ."

"I'm not sure if he's under Mordant's command or the sorceress's thrall," Friday continued. "Like Elisa, he doesn't speak, but that could be choice as easily as geis. Either way, it only adds to his air of deadly intrigue." She shuddered. "The next time I see him will be all too soon."

Tristan lifted the top item with fingers that still ached from their brush with the raw nettle mat. It appeared to be a scarf with two holes cut in it. He scowled down at Friday. "Scrawnier?"

Friday stuck her tongue out at him before turning to face the door. "Hurry, or I'm leaving without you."

Stairs. So many stairs. Tristan couldn't remember the last time he'd encountered stairs. If this eternal descent didn't make him miss his wings enough, the inevitable climb back up certainly would. Every step he took in those heavy black boots was jarring. Perhaps he could time the return journey for sunrise. If they reached the bottom by sunrise.

And if Elisa lived that long.

Friday's squire had remained just outside the Elder Wood door; when Tristan walked out, Conrad had done little more than nod politely. Tristan didn't know anything about the dark-skinned boy besides his unwavering loyalty to Friday, but Conrad's show of respect had just earned Tristan's own. He did not insult the princess by asking how much of her squire's watchdog presence was also for his brothers' protection.

He adjusted the scarf on his face again so that he could see better through the holes. The fabric kept riding up the incline of his nose and bunching between his eyes. Did the Infidel have this problem? Surely not; such aggravation would have led to many botched assassinations.

Tristan was less bothered by the mask than he was the gloves. For all its refusal to stay where it was put, the mask felt a bit like the one he wore every day as a swan. The gloves, however, drew his attention to his hands. With his hands encased in leather, he couldn't stop thinking how strange they were, or how large, or how hot.

Friday caught his arm when he stumbled. "Pay attention to your feet," she said. "They're the most important right now." She removed the gloves from his hands and stuck them inside a pocket of her voluminous patchwork skirt. "You can put these back on when we reach the bottom."

He trailed one of his emancipated hands along the outer wall in an effort to keep his balance. The stones were cold and damp and often obscured by random wisps of fog. "You've done this every day," he said somewhat breathlessly.

"It was necessary," she said, as if anyone else would have done the same. Friday was truly as rare and precious a person as she seemed.

"Has it gotten any easier for you? The height, I mean." Gods knew the rest of their situation had not.

"It has, a little," she replied. "I am less afraid, knowing that if I fell, you would save me."

He lost himself in her eyes again. Gods, those eyes were incredible. He recalled being angry at her not long ago, but for the life of him he couldn't remember why.

Tristan slipped again on the next step down, catching himself this time. He growled slightly and tried to resume his concentration.

After an eternity, they finally reached bottom. The hall beyond the archway to the tower was covered in thick carpet dimly lit by a row of sconces, a few of which had gone out. He was as happy about the carpet as he was for level ground; he wondered if anyone would notice if he removed these blasted boots as well.

Friday took one of the torches from the wall and gently blew it back to life. "Don't get too comfortable. We still have to get to the dungeon." She reached in her pocket, returned the gloves to him, and waited for him to put them on before march-ing determinedly down the hall.

Tristan tried to think about his feet instead of his hands. *One foot in front of the other. Stay behind Friday. Stick to the shadows. Don't make eye contact with anyone* — Friday had said that the In-fidel's eyes were black and red, certainly not the bright ocean blue of his own. Above all, he must not speak.

Apart from the servants, they only encountered one person roaming the late-evening halls as they crossed from the wing of the sky tower to the dungeon. That person was the most beauti-ful woman Tristan had ever seen.

She glided like a ghost from the hearth-fire stories his broth-ers used to tell. Her long white-blond hair and whiter flowing gown almost glowed around her as she moved in the dim torch-light. She was a wild doe in the forest, graceful and fleet, with eyes of deep and soulful wisdom. As she neared, Tristan noticed a silver circlet upon her brow.

The woman stopped before them, leaning down to place a kiss on Friday's cheek. "Sister dearest."

Ah. The legendary Princess Monday. Friday had spoken of her eldest sister's beauty to the brothers, but since Friday seemed to think everyone she met was beautiful in some way, Tristan had never imagined . . . this.

As Monday straightened, she scrutinized Tristan's dark fig-ure. She turned to Friday and arched one angel-feathered brow high. Friday smiled — was she blushing? — and placed a finger over her lips. Monday smiled back, then tilted her head in a small bow to Tristan.

She knew who he was, then. From that sibling bond that needed no words, Monday knew, and she would keep her peace. Tristan bowed low in return.

From farther down the hallway they heard the shuffle of feet, and Friday drew in a breath. The shadow of what looked like a short man in a tall hat rounded the corner. "Please . . . ?"

Monday reached out a pale, slim hand, and caressed her sister's cheek before moving to intercept the stranger.

Friday took Tristan's hand and they fled deeper into the darkness.

Tristan tried to remember every twist and turn they took from the tower, but by the time he reached the dungeon, he was lost. As they descended, Tristan worried for his sister's health in this dank, damp hole. It was obvious the dungeon of Arilland was rarely used, which spoke highly of its rulers, but as a result the place was in an unfortunate state of disrepair. The wooden boards of the narrow stair creaked beneath Tristan's weight, and small creatures — or what he hoped were small creatures — skittered out of sight.

At long last they reached Elisa. She was slumped on the bare ground behind her prison bars, hands still tied before her. If Mordant had hurt her, he would use these last hours as a man to rain vengeance down upon him. Tristan ran to his sister — and was stopped by a shadow. A very strong shadow with a very sharp knife. The blade bit into Tristan's neck, forcing him upright.

Tristan faced his attacker and met the eyes of the man in black. Mordant's Infidel.

The lighter skin that peeked from beneath the black mask marked him as being not of Cymbalese origin. Mordant traded regularly with the Troll King; it would have been nothing for him to acquire a Cymbalese slave for his mistress. And this man was clearly under Gana's thrall, as was evident from the red ring around his muddy green irises. Gana would have taken his will so that he would do Mordant's bidding without question. Tristan was not sure what crime deserved such a punishment. Then again, no one deserved to be plagued by Mordant and his witch.

This man could slit Tristan's throat without so much as a thought. But if the enemy of his enemy was his friend, then by all rights the Infidel should be his ally. His irises were not fully red; perhaps there was some small spark of the man's soul that could hear him. The blade dug deeper into his throat.

"Please," said Tristan.

The pressure of the blade did not decrease, but the man stayed his gloved hand.

"I love her."

The Infidel's eyes slid over Tristan's shoulder to where Friday stood right behind him, and then back to where Elisa lay silent in her cell.

"I love them both," Tristan clarified.

"Do you remember love?" Friday asked. It was a strange question, but one that caused the blade of the Infidel's dagger to lift away from Tristan's neck.

"We don't want to release her," said Tristan. "We just want to help her."

At Tristan's words, the dagger pressed into his neck once more.

"Friday," he whispered, "speak again."

"We won't release her," Friday repeated calmly. "In fact, we'd prefer it if you locked us both in there with her."

Tristan's instincts had been correct: the dagger fell away. He wasn't sure if it was because the Infidel's captor was a woman, or because of that magical, lilting quality Friday's voice possessed — not that it mattered. They had found the key to their survival, and the key to Elisa's cage. The Infidel unlocked the iron door and let them in.

Friday fell to her knees beside Elisa's unconscious form. She looked unharmed, for the most part, though the skin of her wrists was raw. Friday put her hands on the rope that bound her and looked up at the Infidel.

"Please."

The word was magic. The Infidel's dagger flashed through the air and Elisa's bonds fell away. Then the cell door slammed shut behind them, and the Infidel disappeared back into the darkness of the dungeon.

"Nice fellow," said Tristan.

"He's as much a prisoner as your sister," Friday chided him. "Here, help me wake her."

Tristan sat Elisa up while Friday dampened a bit of her skirt and dabbed at Elisa's bloody wrists.

Elisa was warm in his arms, and sound asleep — a blessing, and one he felt some guilt at disturbing. "Come on, baby sister. We're so close. Don't give up on us now."

Reluctantly, Elisa's lids finally lifted. When she realized where she was, her eyes opened fully, as if she were screaming at them.

Tristan and Friday both wrapped their arms protectively around her trembling body. "It's all right," Tristan whispered. "We're here to help finish this thing."

"Give yourself a moment," said Friday. "I brought some water and some bread. When you are ready, we'll begin again, yes?"

Tentatively, Elisa nodded. She cradled her head on Tristan's shoulder while Friday sorted the contents of the sacks they'd brought down from the sky tower. Elisa's trembling stopped after she finished off two sweet rolls and a substantial amount of water. She sat up on her own now and, for all that she'd been through, she looked more alert than she had in days. Perhaps that tiny blessing of rest had done her good, after all.

Tristan offered his sister a third roll, but she declined. She grabbed his hand, though, scrutinizing him in the dim light before smirking at his outfit.

Tristan tugged the scarf-mask off his head. "It was her idea."

"It worked, didn't it?" said Friday. "Besides, you look rather dashing in that getup."

Elisa smiled and pointed to Friday, showing that she agreed with the princess.

Tristan rolled his eyes and threw the mask into a dark corner. "Women."

Elisa's smile grew wider and Tristan's heart grew lighter.

Friday tossed Elisa the first loom. "Ready? Let's do this."

They worked deep into the night and beyond. Reinvigorated, Elisa's fingers flew through the weaving. At some point, Conrad entered the dungeon, and Friday persuaded the Infidel to let him slip the new spools of spun fiber through.

"Is this enough?" Conrad asked Friday.

"It will have to be," she said. "We don't have much time left."

"Can I get you anything else?"

"Refill the lantern and light another torch before you go?" Friday requested. "It's terribly dark in here."

"Tell my brothers we are well," said Tristan. "Remind them to stay strong."

Conrad nodded, did as he was bade, and fled back up the steps.

It was hypnotic, watching Friday and Elisa work. Tristan filled the quiet chamber with song, thinking that the cadence might lift their spirits — something he never would have done in the presence of his brothers. He did not have Sebastien's baritone or François's perfect pitch, but Friday smiled at the silly tavern songs and Elisa smiled at the nursery songs and Tristan felt like the finest virtuoso in all the world.

Friday stitched up the fifth shirt while Elisa dashed off the sixth, and they were well on to the seventh when Tristan felt the quickening in his blood. He did not need a window to know that daybreak approached.

Elisa looked up from her loom. She could feel it too.

Tristan fought the prickling of his skin and crossed the cell in two long strides to pull Friday up into his arms.

"What are you—?"

"I want to thank you," said Tristan. "In case I don't have the chance later."

"Dawn?" she asked. There was sadness in the word, and fear.

He ignored the question. "Thank you, Friday Woodcutter, magical princess, for saving me and fighting for my family."

"But Tristan—"

He stopped her there. He wanted the last word he remembered to be his name on her lips, so he pulled her to him and kissed her deeply.

They might not have been in the sky tower, but Tristan needed no meddling fairy magic to feel the bond between them now. Friday tasted of warmth and sugar and spice. She felt like cool breezes and home. He held her tightly—so tightly—dreading the day to come and knowing he could not stop it. But this moment . . . this moment would stay with him forever, and no spell or sorceress would ever take that away.

Friday welcomed Tristan's embrace, kissing him back with equal fervor. Her arms came up around either side of his neck and she wound her fingers into his hair. He forced himself to remember that touch as the quills shot up through his skin, as his beak hardened and left her lips, as he fell to the ground in an ungraceful puddle of black material.

Tristan threw back his long neck and honked a curse to the gods.

11

Vengeful Angels

FRIDAY HAD NEVER FELT so fulfilled as when Tristan kissed her.

She had never felt so empty as when he disappeared beneath her fingertips.

There was a prickling under his skin and merely a brush of feathers before the pressure of his embrace vanished. She opened her eyes to the harsh reality of the dim, dank dungeon and freed the swan from his black-cloth prison. Elisa sat before her, back in the scrawny body of mousy Rampion, her head in her hands as she silently wept. Laid out on the ground before her was the last shirt, the seventh, incomplete. They had managed one sleeve, but not the other.

Tears fell from Friday's own eyes to join Elisa's on the

muddy ground. Friday cradled the swan in her lap, smoothing its feathers with one hand and holding Elisa with the other. The Infidel reappeared out of the darkness, as if summoned from thin air, and opened the cell door. Friday stuffed the shirts into the sack while he bound Elisa's wrists again and marched her out of the dungeon. Friday followed close behind, clutching the swan to her breast.

When they reached the outer doors, Friday released Tristan to join his brothers in the tower. The struggling bird erupted from her arms and lifted himself into the sky without so much as a backward glance.

There was only a small crowd gathered on the shore off which Mordant's ship had weighed anchor, and Friday thanked the gods for their favors. She dreaded what was to come; if tragedy were to strike, she was glad there would be few to witness it. Gentle waves crashed over the murmur of the crowd, and a flock of noisy gulls landed on the grassy shore to meet the dawn with them. There was a sharp bark, and the gulls burst into the air again.

Friday scanned the shoreline and found Ben the Boisterous's companion. "Michael! What are you doing here?"

"Ben needed to go outside."

Friday stared unyieldingly at the boy until he amended the white lie.

"I had to see. I wanted to know."

Beyond Michael, the Infidel had escorted Elisa to a pair of beached skiffs surrounded by Mordant's guards. Friday didn't have time to be much more than brutally honest with her charge. "Michael, things might not go well here this morning. I would rather you not have to carry disturbing memories with you."

"You can't protect us from everything, Friday."

"I cannot. But one day, when you have children of your own, you will know why I can't ever stop trying." Friday put a hand on his cheek. "Stay safe, little darling. Be strong."

"I will." It wasn't much of a promise, but Friday didn't have time for more. She crossed the field to the gathering of her family.

"I cannot allow Mordant to do this on Arilland soil," said Rumbold.

"I will not allow anyone to do this at all," cried Sunday.

"That's our girl," said Papa and Peter.

"We are taking her to the ship," said the red-uniformed commander. "No king has dominion over the sea."

The king and the Woodcutters argued, but Mordant's soldiers stood their ground. The Infidel crossed his arms and remained an imposing shadow. Elisa, shoulders slumped, looked beaten.

One skiff was filled with kindling and one was empty, save for a set of oars. Friday's heart skipped a beat. The soldiers might have been taking her to Mordant's ship, but they had no intention of delivering her. They were going to put Elisa into the skiff filled with wood, tow her out into the water, and then burn her!

As the rest of the crowd realized the same thing, sadness threatened to overwhelm Friday. She wrinkled her nose to stave off the emotion. She only had one chance to get this right, and she must not waste it.

"NO!" She waved her arms like a madwoman. "YOU CAN'T DO THIS!" She flung herself at Elisa, embracing the unprepared girl with such vigor that she almost toppled them both. Friday let the momentum swing the sack in her hands forward; it disappeared amongst the wood in the boat. Friday needed to keep up her histrionics in order to cover what she'd just done, so she channeled the one person she knew who could stun everyone to silence: her mother.

"YOU CAN'T DO THIS!" She pointed to the guards, and then to Sunday and Rumbold. "YOU CAN'T *LET* THEM DO THIS!"

Oh, if only her words held the same weight as Mama's, this nonsense would never need to happen!

Rumbold, bless him, allowed her to beat on his chest a moment before trapping her hands in his. "I must, sister. I gave my word to Mordant as King, and I cannot go back on that."

"BUT THEY'RE GOING TO KILL HER!" Friday's dramatic show of emotion was so at odds with her normal behavior that the rest of the crowd looked at her curiously. "YOU HAVE TO DO SOMETHING!"

Sunday screwed up her mouth and furrowed her brow. Friday was familiar with that particular expression: Queen Sunday knew exactly what her sister was up to, and she was trying her hardest not to laugh.

Rumbold, whom Friday could tell had some idea of what was going on but remained unsure of the goal, continued to play along. "I know, Friday, but my hands are tied. Blame me if you must, if it makes it easier for you."

He tried to embrace her but she pulled away, wrenching herself from his grasp with fire in her eyes. "You are a fool," she said to him, and then collapsed in a patchwork heap of sobbing at his feet. Her tears were genuine — she called upon all that fear and sadness she had pushed away earlier and let them take over. She soon felt Sunday's hand on her back as her queen-sister cradled her in a show of comfort.

"Are you all right?" It was a valid question.

"I'm in love with a swan whose sister will die if I mess this up," Friday whispered in reply. "I'm a mess. And don't you dare laugh."

"You're making it incredibly difficult," Sunday said into Friday's sobs. "I believe you've addled my poor husband. I just hope this works."

Friday hiccupped. "Me too."

Sunday pulled Friday back to her feet. Monday swooped in and took over soothing the slightly-less-dramatic-but-still-overly-emotional sister. Friday leaned into her eldest sister's skirts. She breathed in Monday's honey jasmine scent, called upon Monday's peaceful restraint, and calmed herself. She needed her wits about her now.

"Enough of this," said Mordant's commander.

"It is well past dawn, sir," said another soldier.

Mordant's commander clicked his heels at Rumbold. "Then we will be on our way."

Rumbold could do nothing but nod. The Infidel lifted Elisa

into the kindling skiff and tied the long end of her bonds to the rowlock. He took hold of the tow-rope and boarded the empty skiff. The soldiers shoved both boats out into the waves before jumping in with the Infidel and rowing out to sea.

Friday did not know how close they would get to Mordant's ship before they set Elisa's boat aflame. Friday squinted into the rising sun — she could see two red-clad figures on the deck of the large ship, waiting. What she didn't see were archers with flaming arrows, or any other evidence of fire. Then how were they going to do it?

Mordant's sorceress stepped forward against the rail of the ship and raised her arms to the sky. She threw her head back and yelled to the gods in a language that sounded like the sea itself. The wind picked up, ripping the red scarf from her head; her long black hair swirled around her like dark fire. Her cockatrice, awake now, flew in a circle above her. As the pet's scales and her fingertips caught the light of the sun, both the fiery bird *and* Gana's hands burst into flame.

The crowd on the shore gasped. Friday gasped with them. Ben barked his disapproval.

Slowly, Gana lowered one burning hand and pointed to the skiff before her. Elisa stood tall, feet planted in the center of the boat, facing the sorceress. There was a flicker and a puff of smoke as the prow of the skiff caught fire.

Friday died a little when she saw the boat burning. She willed Elisa to scoop up some seawater and extinguish the fire, but the girl made no move to do so. The flames grew higher. Gana's triumphant cackle echoed across the water.

Friday stepped away from Monday and ran to the water's edge, heedless of her skirt. Ben was loud and quick on her heels. She pushed through the crowd that had already braved the water; she would have leapt into the waves, but her inexperience with oceans held her back. They were not out that far. Perhaps if she started walking . . .

From the corner of her eye, Friday noticed that another figure had waded into the shallows. In the dawn light, Mr. Humbug's hat cast a long shadow and his yellow eyes almost glowed. He turned to Friday and raised both his eyebrows and one index finger.

Wait.

Friday drew in one slow, deep breath and let it out just as slowly. Another screeching flock of seagulls drowned out Gana's laughter, until Ben's bark scattered them again. Barking, and then more barking . . . and then more *not* barking. Honking.

The swans had come.

Friday watched them soar over the hill in a majestic "V," large and white and determined as vengeful angels. The sunlight gleamed off their bright wings, blinding everyone below in their glory. Friday cheered them on as they passed above her. The crowd on the shore cheered with her.

The swans broke formation as they approached the skiffs; five headed for Elisa and two veered right, straight for the red-clad figures on the large ship. They batted Gana's cockatrice out of the air with their enormous wings; the sorceress's laughter turned to a scream. She tried to catch the smoldering body of her unconscious pet before it slipped overboard. Mordant crouched, as if to use the rail as a shield. At the cry of his mistress, the Infidel dropped Elisa's tow-rope, and the second skiff rowed quickly to the large boat. The soldiers on the deck rallied, but did not know where to attack. The birds continued to swoop and fly and dive again and again.

While her enemies were distracted, Elisa snatched up the bag Friday had dropped in the boat. Hands still bound, she awkwardly dumped the contents onto the smoldering sticks at her feet. One by one, she tossed the shirts into the air. One by one, the swans surrounding her dove into them and fell into the ocean until there were only two left.

Though the birds had not yet transformed back into men, Friday knew which brother-swans had attacked the ship: Tristan and Sebastien. Tristan would have led the charge and Sebastien, the brother who did not want to return to the world of men, would have been right at his side. Friday did not know which of them would be forced to wear the shirt with one sleeve, or what the consequences of that might be—she only hoped they had done enough to break the spell.

Satisfied that the other five were safe, the Tristan and Sebastien swans left Mordant and his sorceress and spun back toward their sister's burning skiff. Elisa valiantly tossed the last two shirts high into the air over her head.

Before the swans could reach them, the shirts burst into flame.

The birds attempted to dive inside the shirts anyway, but

the material fell to ashes around them. Elisa covered her mouth with her hands; Friday could feel Elisa's scream in her throat and so Friday yelled it for her.

Gana, who had regained her footing, clapped her flaming hands together in triumph.

Elisa bent down to the bag again, but Friday knew that no more shirts would magically appear inside. They had only managed seven — and barely that. They had failed. She had failed. And Michael, her family, the *kingdom* was present to watch her defeat.

Elisa straightened again with one more thing in her hand: the crude stinging-nettle mat she'd first made. With nothing left to lose, she threw that up into the air as well.

The brothers fought — not to catch the mat, but to force the other to do so. Sebastien-swan and Tristan-swan honked and swooped. They beat at each other with their wings and feet, nipping with their beaks when they could. Feathers flew into the air around them and fluttered down to the sea. They fought as human brothers would, ultimately tangling their limbs together and plummeting into the waves. One swan shifted, pushing the other into the mat that floated there upon the tide — and then the two of them sank out of sight.

Friday held her breath, straining to see above the waves. Had it worked?

"I am Elisa, Princess of Kassora and the Green Isles!" The mousy girl's unused voice croaked at the large ship. "I accuse the sorceress Gana of witchcraft and the murder of innocent children, and I seek asylum in Arilland!"

Elisa grew taller as she spoke, her thin limbs filling out beneath her tattered dress into the form of a healthy young woman. Her hair became longer and lighter, shining like hammered gold in the waxing sunlight. In the water around her, lumps of feathers and fiber changed to thrashing human limbs. A strong wind from the east swirled around Elisa's skiff and extinguished the flames.

The curse was broken.

With a wave of Rumbold's hand, his guards rushed forth into the sea, followed by most of the crowd. Mordant's ship, now with the Infidel safely aboard, lifted anchor, raised sails, and fled into the open waters. The masses cheered again, hurling increasingly inventive threats and insults at the retreating vessel.

Amidst the excitement that threatened to overwhelm her at any moment, Friday saw Mr. Humbug walking toward her through the surf. He took her by the hand. "It's over," he said. "You did well, princess."

"Thank you," said Friday. She let him lead her out of the water and back to where her family stood on the shore. But it was not finished. She would not be satisfied until she had seen Tristan emerge from the waves.

"We did it!" Sunday said as she put her arms around Friday.

"Did we?" asked Friday, but no one answered. She refused to feel anything until she saw the siblings back on dry ground. All of them.

"Mordant escaped." It was obvious that Velius blamed himself for not having enough power to make the man pay for his crimes.

"For now," said Rumbold. "Only for now. He has made enemies this day."

The crowd on the shore rushed forward to help the men walking out of the waves. Friday saw François, Christian, Philippe, and the twins. The five of them wore only the nettle shirts that now covered them to their knees, but they seemed whole and hale.

There was not yet any sign of Tristan or Sebastien.

Rumbold's guards swam to Elisa's skiff and sawed her bonds free. She was carried to shore and met with blankets and kindness and the embrace of the doting crowd and her tall, strong brothers.

All but two of them.

Rumbold and Sunday moved to greet the siblings with the rest of the crowd. Friday stayed, frozen in place, staring at the flaming boat on the horizon and the empty waves surrounding it. Monday stayed with her. The sun had risen enough now that the clouds were no longer pink with dawn.

"He didn't make it," Friday whispered into the wind. "I couldn't save him." She could still feel the joy of the crowd, the relief of the swan-brothers, and the concern from her family, but in the middle of all that was a numbness, a hole that would never again be filled. The stories said that those who lost their soul mates were destined to wander the earth as soul wraiths, forever lost and alone. If that were true, Sister Carol would have no reason to deny her the life of a dedicate. Not that it would be much of a life at all, without Tristan.

"You saved *them*." Monday indicated the five brothers and their sister.

Philippe joined them. The magic nettle shirt had grown along with him, covering him to his knees like an oversized shirt of chain mail. "It's what he would have wanted."

"Yes." Her tears fell freely now. Friday said the word because she knew it was true. Saving his brothers and sister *was* what Tristan would have wanted. Sebastien as well. But at what cost? They should at least have been resigned to life as a swan instead of no life at all. She turned to the brother who looked so much like Tristan that it was almost painful. She could sense something still eating away inside of him. Something dark. "What would *you* have wanted?"

Philippe's unyielding stare never left Mordant's ship. "To kill Mordant, no matter the price."

Friday's hurt drowned in the intensity of Philippe's hatred. It was as if the curse keeping him a swan had also kept this unabashed loathing bottled, and now both it and its master were free.

"I will not rest until I feel his blood on my hands. I will sever his head from his body and hang it from the ramparts of Kassora by his entrails. His bitch will die far more slowly and painfully. Her body will be cut into a thousand tiny pieces and scattered on the wind."

Friday wasn't sure which made her more ill: the gruesome mental images, Philippe's unrestrained desire for them to come to fruition, or that she felt herself swept up in the anger with him, mourning the loss of her beloved and desperate to strike back at *something* in return. She swallowed the bile that rose in her throat and attempted to calm both herself and Philippe. "Mordant will be defeated. Your brothers will see to that. And Arilland would love nothing more than to come to your aid." Technically that last part wasn't in her power to promise, but she did it anyway. "Right now, you should be concentrating on your family." As she should concentrate on hers, but just now her heart wasn't in it.

He turned to her, his eyes burning with a blue fire hotter than what Gana had been able to summon. "I assure you, princess, for the past few years I have concentrated on nothing but my family."

There was nothing to say but "I'm sorry."

He smiled then, and that smile scared her more than falling from the sky tower. "There is nothing to forgive, Friday. Through your efforts, our curse has been broken. But this is far from over." He turned back to the sea. "Worry not; I will end it."

Don't worry? There were few things in Friday's life that had ever worried her more.

Ben barked again at a lone gull spinning over the burning skiff and heading to shore. Friday wiped away the tears blurring her vision. It was not a gull. It was a swan. Only one.

Friday and Elisa both ran sluggishly through the water to where the swan landed on the shore.

"Is it . . . ?" Elisa began, with a voice still strange to both of them.

"One of ours?" finished Friday. "It must be."

"But which one?"

Friday was afraid to guess and ashamed to admit she couldn't tell. And then Ben began to bark again. The swan joined in the cacophony with excited honks. Beside them, a body covered in feathers washed up on the shore. Friday and Elisa fell to their knees to pull him out.

It was Tristan.

Heart racing, Friday tried to move the overly large feathers obscuring his face so that he could breathe . . . but for every feather she tried to shift, three more swept back in.

"Why won't these blasted feathers move?" she yelled in frustration.

"Oh, Friday," gasped Elisa.

Friday pulled Tristan's body into a sitting position and the feathers fell away . . . but they didn't go far. She slid her hands up Tristan's bare arms and around his back to where the giant white wings attached in a downy patch between his shoulders.

"What have I done?" whispered Friday.

"You saved us," Elisa whispered back, as Tristan coughed up mouthful after mouthful of water. When he'd caught his breath, Friday peppered his face with kisses and hugged him as if she'd never let him go. Friday felt Elisa's joy at the sight. The girl had five other brothers to fuss over — she could do without this one for a moment more.

Someone else, however, could not.

A shadow fell over Tristan and Friday. Above them, a large man cleared his throat. Friday looked up to see Papa and Peter blocking out the bright sky with their huge bodies.

"I'm happy to see you're well and all, son," said Papa, "but I am forced to ask: What are your intentions toward my daughter?"

Tristan smiled. Peter swallowed a laugh. Friday blushed, suddenly realizing how this must look to her father.

Apart from the giant feathered wings, Tristan was naked as the day they'd met.

12

Infernal Wings

RISTAN BENT HIS KNEES and hunched forward, curling into a ball in an attempt to cover
himself. He had not been embarrassed in Friday's presence before, but he was starting to be. This was not the way he wanted
to greet the world as a man after so many years.

A third shadow joined Friday's father and brother above
him. "Greetings, Tristan. I am Rumbold, Friday's less-hulking
brother."

Rumbold . . . the king? *Fantastic.* "Forgive me for not rising
to greet you, Your Majesty."

"Don't mention it. In fact, that's why I'm here. I believe I
have just the thing for that."

Tristan hoped the man didn't offer his shirt; he was fairly

sure there was no way to get any sort of tunic around the monstrous wings now sprouting from his back. It was one thing to have an impressive wingspan when one was a sizeable swan, but this? Would he have to go bare chested the rest of his life?

Thankfully, King Rumbold did not remove his shirt, only the knee-length velvet cape around his shoulders. One of the king's men—not a guard, Tristan could tell from his clothing, possibly some higher-ranking official—wrapped the cape around Tristan's hips and affixed it on the side with a pin.

"Thank you." Tristan was incredibly grateful to the slender, black-haired man. Friday was the sort who would have seen to the task herself and, in doing so, completely mortified him. The man extended his arm and helped Tristan to his feet with surprising strength.

"I'm Velius," he said. Tristan nodded and began to release Velius's arm, but the man held tight. "Give it a moment. I expect your balance isn't quite what it used to be."

He was right, of course. The moment Tristan stood up fully, he almost toppled backwards from the weight of the wings. Good Lords of the Wind, were they waterlogged? They weren't going to be this heavy all the time, were they? He tried to shift them forward and alter his center of gravity; he succeeded only in swatting both the king and Friday's father in the face.

Fantastic.

There was an ever-growing crowd gathered around him on the shore. Behind the contingent of Woodcutters and their royal majesties now stood his brothers, and behind them, half of Aril-land. No one spoke above the cry of the gulls and the bark of that dog. That pesky, wonderful dog.

Tristan looked at Friday, Friday's father, Rumbold. He wasn't sure what to say. He was beginning to feel like an attraction at the local market fair.

Velius placed an incredibly warm hand on Tristan's shoulder, and the pain between his shoulder blades eased a bit. Rumbold was a smart ruler indeed to have a healer in his retinue. "We should get you inside," he said. "I'd like to see for myself that you and your brothers are all right. We'll see if we can't scrounge up some suitable clothes for you. And then—"

"We should have a ball!" This suggestion came from the delicate young woman who had slipped in between Friday's two brothers. Judging by her optimism, her pixielike face, and the curve of her lips, this could only be Friday's little sister the queen.

Queen Sunday nodded slowly, as if taking her own idea into consideration. "Yes. We should definitely have a ball. Tonight is too soon . . . we'll say tomorrow. Arilland needs something to celebrate, and there's nothing this country loves more than a ball. Also, you need a distraction, or you'll never get off this beach." Sunday winked at Tristan before turning to announce her intentions to the expectant crowd.

"My wife comes from clever stock." Rumbold's expression quickly shifted from joviality to sincerity, the mark of a true leader. A move that would have made Tristan's father proud.

"You must take it slowly," said the king. "I am all too familiar with what you're going through right now. Not that long ago, I was in your place."

"You had wings the size of a small ship?"

Rumbold didn't miss a beat. "No. But every now and again I have an incredible craving for flies."

Tristan laughed at the comment, and was pleased to see smiles wash over the people around him. His new wings may have been unbearable and socially unacceptable, but his heart held hope.

"Come," said Rumbold. "Velius and I will escort you and your family to the guards' training ground. The palace is chock-full of faces — you'll not find any solace there. The practice yard has facilities large enough to see to your needs, and we can more easily assure your privacy."

"I'll come with you." Friday's words almost startled Tristan. Until then, it had not occurred to him that they might be separated at all — but Monday stepped forward to intervene.

"Sunday will need your help with the ball preparations," said Friday's beautiful sister. "As will I."

"And you need to sleep," Christian chimed in. "We all do."

Elisa yawned at his comment; Tristan's poor sister looked as if she might fall over at any moment. Friday noticed this too and nodded reluctantly.

"I'll go with him," said Friday's squire. Conrad's company was a poor substitute for his mistress, but his offer seemed to appease her.

So, mere moments after the curse had broken, they were

being separated for the first of what would undoubtedly be many times. He was unhappy about the prospect—possibly even a little frightened—and empathic Friday knew it. Tristan dared not embrace her again in front of her family, but he held his balance well enough to let go of Velius's arm and take Friday's hands. He kissed the back of one, and then the other.

"Soon" was all he said. She would know what he meant.

The smile she gave him was so dazzling, he vowed to keep it with him for all of his days.

At the mention of festivities, the enthusiastic crowd began to dissipate, and the king's guards led Tristan and his weary family up the long hill to the training grounds and the Guards' Hall. Peter accompanied them, as did Friday's father. Conrad walked beside them, proudly holding Sebastien's large swansbody in his spindly arms. The king excused himself to rejoin his wife in the palace, but he left Velius and a stout man in a tall hat behind in his stead.

Tristan could have done without the extra company, but if it meant that he would not be separated from his brothers and sister, then he would tolerate them. Later, when he was more himself and fully clothed, he would have to thank Rumbold. In the meantime, he concentrated on remaining upright. If he crouched forward and used his arms to bear the burden of the wings, it seemed he could balance tolerably well. The extra weight was not insignificant—it seemed as if every stone in the path to the training grounds sought out the tender pads of his seldom-used feet.

The guards led everyone straight into the bathhouse. Vapors

rose from several tubs that were already being filled. One was surrounded by screens and two maids to ensure that Elisa had her privacy—but not so much privacy that she could fall asleep and drown. After all they'd been through these past few days, this was a danger for every one of them.

Tristan the swan had spent almost every day in and around water, but Tristan the man couldn't remember the last time he'd had a bath. Even now, he wasn't quite sure how he was going to manage this with the wings. The other brothers didn't hesitate—they tossed off their nettle shirts and jumped in the hot water. Contented sighs filled the air.

Velius gently nudged Tristan's elbow, careful not to brush his wings. "Down the steps there is a small pool where you might be more comfortable." Tristan followed the man down to a common resting area where, indeed, a pool was being filled with fresh water. This water didn't emit steam like the tubs in which his grimy brothers now soaked. He dipped a toe in, resigning himself to yet another cold bath.

"Wait," said Velius. The lithe man knelt beside the pool and placed one hand flat against the surface of the water. *"Pyrrho."*

The water didn't so much as ripple, but within moments, steam began to rise. Tristan raised his eyebrows at the man.

Velius shrugged.

Tristan removed the king's cloak and waded in. The water so eased his skin and his weary muscles that he gave up the idea of keeping his wings dry and simply submerged himself altogether. A guard handed him a brush and a cake of soap, and

Tristan set about the job of scouring several years of cursed magic and filth off his skin.

Leisurely, each of his siblings bathed, dressed, and wandered down to the sitting area by Tristan's pool. Elisa was first; after the maids took her measurements for a proper gown, the guards provided her with a squire's undershirt and breeches to wear. She padded in on bare feet, curled up on some large pillows by the fire, and was instantly fast asleep. Sebastien-swan waddled up beside her and joined her in slumber.

Each of his brothers arrived, dressed in unadorned guards' uniforms and sipping from large steaming mugs of something that couldn't be alcohol, or they'd have been just as asleep as their sister. Philippe carried nothing.

François set a mug down beside Tristan's pool. Tristan glided over to try it; it was indescribably thick and sweet and bitter at the same time. "It's a stimulant."

"Granted, it would have to fuel the sun to keep me from slumber for much longer," said Christian.

"You'll have your rest," said Velius. "We just wanted to chat with you briefly first, about Mordant."

"And the curse," said Peter.

"And my daughter," said his father.

Tristan did not rise to Woodcutter's semi-playful goading. At the moment, Tristan was still too concerned about the well-being of his own family to complicate it with anyone else's. While the bath had relaxed and risen the spirits of everyone else, it seemed to have done nothing for Philippe's demeanor.

The others sat, but Tristan's almost-twin remained in the doorway, arms crossed, brooding impatiently.

Only one thing could have been eating at Philippe: their unfinished business with Mordant. Philippe stared at Tristan until Tristan slowly closed his eyes in concession as if to say, *Yes, brother. Nothing has been forgotten. We will deal with this. Just, please, give me a moment.*

Philippe nodded tersely and sat, arms still crossed, in the chair closest to the door.

Tristan surrendered to the lovely embrace of the water once more, and then forced himself to stop putting off the inevitable. "All right," he said. "Let's get this over with. But can I at least have some pants?"

Velius waved his arm for the squire. "Grinny's working on a sort of shirt for you. He's no Friday Woodcutter, but he can make a man's armor fit as well as a second skin. In the meantime . . ."

Conrad stepped forward. Folded in his outstretched arms were the black trousers Tristan had worn while pretending to be the Infidel. He dried off, donned the trousers, and found a stool in the room on which he could perch comfortably. With these wings, there would be no more stuffy, high-backed chairs in his future. He spread his arms out to the men before him. "Who's first? Ask me anything."

"Can you fly?" the twins asked simultaneously.

"Really? You've been with me the whole time, numbskulls. I haven't exactly had the opportunity to find out. I promise, you'll know as soon as I do."

"Can you move them at all?" Velius's question was more realistic. Tristan raised his arms out to the sides, and the wings spread along with them. He lowered his arms, and the wings lowered as well. Then he tried to move each limb independently. It took a great deal more concentration — a bit like having four arms now, instead of two.

"Would you mind if I took a look?" asked Velius.

"Not at all," said Tristan, and the dark-haired healer moved to examine his back.

"Fascinating," said the man in the tall hat. "I'm Henry Humbug, sir, and I know some minor magic . . . though nothing compared to His Grace here."

Velius was a duke? Proper titles and addresses were things Tristan hadn't worried about in a very long time. "Friday spoke of you, Mr. Humbug. My family owes you a great deal."

Humbug shrugged off the compliment. "Minor magic. Nothing more. But tell me, sir, are you in pain?"

Tristan moved the infernal wings again. They were still heavy, and his back and shoulder muscles would continue to ache for as long as it took him to get used to this new form, but there was no true pain. "No."

"Good, good. And you've been under this spell for how long — seven years? Ten?"

"I'd guess roughly between those, yes," said Tristan.

"But none of you have aged in all that time."

"Apparently not."

"Good, good," Humbug clucked. "And where did your brother meet his swan-mate?"

Tristan was caught off-guard. "Maybe a year or two after we left the islands. We encountered Odette somewhere in the frozen wilds north of the Troll Kingdom."

"Fascinating," Humbug said again. "There is a tale from that region about a cursed swan princess who was betrayed by love and forced into a swansbody forever."

The circumstances were too strange to be coincidence. "And you think Odette was that princess?"

"I'm not sure we'll ever know," said Humbug. "But I have my suspicions."

"Birds of a feather," François said into a yawn.

Tristan shuddered as Velius ran his fingers down the length of his wings, tracing the muscles that now grew seamlessly into his back. After a few more moments of contemplation, Velius stood. "Unfortunately, I don't believe removal is possible, magical or otherwise."

"I'm not sure if I'm happy or sad about that news. Mostly I'm just glad we're alive. If not all human."

They all looked to where Sebastien-swan lay curled up against Elisa; their brother had made his choice. "Not much to be done about that either, I'm afraid," said Velius. "A curse is a curse."

"Which makes Christian now the heir to the Green Isles," said François.

"Bastard," Christian said to the swan.

"What action will you take?" asked Velius.

"Find Mordant and kill him. With all due haste." Philippe was back on his feet, staring them all down.

Christian held up both hands. "It would be rash to decide anything now."

"There's nothing to decide," Philippe said plainly. "Mordant is evil. He and his minions slaughtered many of our people, killed our parents, and cursed us. It is time for him to die, so we can rightfully regain what is ours."

Philippe had a point, but that was not for Tristan to say.

Their plan of action was Christian's call now. "Leading an army to reclaim a country involves more than the murder of one man."

"Does it? I disagree."

"I'm sorry you feel that way." Christian turned back to Velius. "Your Grace, I'd like to speak with you, the king, and anyone else who might have ideas on how to proceed."

"A wise decision," said Mr. Woodcutter.

"A ridiculous decision," spat Philippe.

"Yet it is the decision I have made," Christian said more firmly. "And you must abide by it."

"No," said Philippe, and with that, he walked out the door. Velius stood. "I'll go after him."

"Give him some time to cool down," said Christian. "Philippe was born angry, and Mordant's curse only served to hone that anger. It will pass."

Tristan hoped Christian was right. There would be no turning back at twilight this time.

A wizened old codger limped his way down the stairs. He had bushy brows, a squinty eye, and a white cloth in his hand. Tristan assumed this was Grinny, the armorer. Grinny had brought a shirt, but not a functional one. It had a high collar and was a size or two too large, which made the sleeves billow out tremendously. It had been completely split down the middle in the back.

"Put this on. There's a good lad. Don't mind the back. That's what I'm here to figure out."

Several dozen pins sprouted from what Tristan hoped was a false knee; Grinny circled Tristan, folding fabric and making "hmm" noises. Tristan lifted his arms and wings as best he could. After a few more grunts and much prodding, Grinny bade him remove the shirt and vanished up the stairs again.

Tristan turned back to the company. His brothers had abandoned him and escaped into sleep, and there were still the Woodcutters left to deal with. *Fantastic.*

Tristan perched on his stool once more and tried his best to ease the tension between himself and these men. "Are you really the family of the infamous Jack Woodcutter?"

Of all the things he might have said, few could have been more perfect than this. Friday's father seemed to relax at once. "You've heard of my son?"

"His stories are told even as far away as the Green Isles," Tristan affirmed. "Legend has it that he visited once, though I would have been too young to remember it. Christian might, though, or . . ." He'd almost said Sebastien. Now he wasn't sure what to say.

Jack Woodcutter the Elder raised a hand; it was large, and attached to an arm the size of a small tree. The man could have ripped Tristan's new wings off without a thought, had he been so obliged. "There is time enough for that," he said. "First, we must speak of my daughter."

Tristan nodded. "I love her, sir."

"Everyone loves her, son. You've got to do better than that."

Tristan took a deep breath. "I believe she is part of my destiny, far beyond the breaking of this curse. I mean to do whatever it takes to see to her happiness."

Friday's father considered this for some time . . . enough time to make Tristan uncomfortable.

"I can ask no more of a man," he said finally. "But I warn you. Friday is special"— Peter laughed at this —"yes, as a father of seven gifted daughters, I can honestly say that each one of them is special. Friday is practical and resourceful, much like her mother, but she is also loving and generous to a fault. She has a heart as big as the moon. And should even the tiniest part of that heart break, I will take my ax and chop you into many unfindable pieces."

Peter crossed his equally massive arms over his chest and nodded slowly, grinning widely as he did so.

Tristan swallowed. "Yes, sir," he squeaked.

"Excellent. Just so long as we understand each other." Jack Woodcutter smiled, the picture of ease. "Now, about that legend. Tell me a story."

13

Hopes Come to Life

RIDAY STOOD on the balcony, away from the din of the ballroom, and looked out over the Queen's Garden. With the exception of a few late-blooming roses, most of the flowers had gone to seed. The leaves had begun to turn and fall; there was a chill in the air. Friday rubbed her arms beneath the gossamer sleeves of her gown in an effort to keep warm. There had been little to the back of this dress to begin with, and Friday dared not waste precious fabric fashioning a shawl.

She'd had no desire to wear one of Monday's elegant white princess gowns, but the eldest had insisted. And so the afternoon had been spent taking out seams and hemming, while doing the opposite for her own court dress so that Elisa had something proper to wear. The deposed princess was taller than Friday and a good deal more slender; cinching in the waist had made the skirts of Friday's old gown billow out prettily. On the other hand, no matter what Friday did to Monday's dress, she never stopped feeling like a giant cloud about to rain on someone's wedding. What would Tristan think of this ridiculous display? Mistress Mitella would have been disappointed at her lack of confidence. The children had braided ribbons and wildflowers into her hair and proclaimed her beautiful, and that was all that mattered.

She shook her head, trying to rid herself of her fears, trying to rid her mind of the hatred she'd seen in Philippe's eyes and the darkness she'd felt in her soul. As for Tristan . . . well, he had bigger things to worry about than how silly she looked in her dress.

"You're missing a lovely party." Mr. Humbug's tall hat was perfectly framed by the glass doors that led to the brilliant ball-room. He toasted her with his glass of green punch, yet another nettle concoction of Cook's.

Friday searched Mr. Humbug's strange yellow eyes. "Did you know how the curse was going to end?"

"I had my hopes. There were several outcomes I did not anticipate. But then, there always are."

"You knew so much about this . . . and you seem to know so much about my family. Are you a god?"

"You flatter me, child. No, I am not a god."

"But you are not human."

"Only slightly less than you, I suppose. Consider your

family, my dear. In comparison, I believe a great deal of us would be found wanting."

Friday deserved that. Her bloodline ran with so much fey magic, she wasn't sure she'd consider herself entirely human, either. "True enough, though I don't feel as stupendous as the rest of my family, most days. Even with a magic needle." She patted the seam where the gossamer sleeve met her bodice; still a woodcutter's daughter in this extraordinary ball gown, Friday was never without her nameday gift.

"I hope your gifts continue to surprise you and bring you joy. Which reminds me." He lifted his hat and scratched the thinning hair beneath, proving to Friday that it was not permanently affixed there after all. "I believe it is time for your surprise." He bowed to her before opening the door to the ballroom. "After you, milady."

The children had been waiting for her; they parted as she stepped into the overly warm room. Wendy took one of her hands and — because for the life of her she couldn't bring the child's surname to her addled mind — Carrot Kate took the other. The girls wore patchwork ribbons in their hair that matched their patchwork pinafores. In fact, all the children wore something patchwork about their person. In her stark white gown, Friday was a lone ghost in a field of wildflowers.

Trumpets sounded, and the Grand Marshal stepped forward onto the landing. "It is my great honor to announce the arrival of Princess Elisa of Kassora and her brothers, the crown princes of the Green Isles!"

Friday grinned at the announcement, though she wondered

what Sebastien was doing right now. Hopefully, he was at peace in the embrace of his swan love and unconcerned with the fete celebrating his family.

Elisa was the first to descend—the crowd below welcomed her arrival with a distinctly unroyal chorus of whistles, calls, and whooping. Friday's gown looked lovely on the princess. Its golden color flattered the long golden waves of her loose hair, and the new green trim—a nod to the colors of Elisa's homeland—brought out the vivid blue of her eyes. Above her, Sunday's fairy lights twinkled in the ceiling like a river of diamonds. Watching Elisa walk down those stairs was like seeing her hopes come to life. Friday could hardly imagine anything more delightful.

And then the brothers came down the stairs.

The twins were the first to descend, framing their sister's beauty. They wore uniforms of the Royal Guard of Arilland, only the sashes and epaulets had been changed from burgundy and gold to forest green and silver. With their deep auburn hair washed, trimmed, and brushed, Friday hardly recognized them. François and Christian followed. As heir apparent, Christian wore one of Rumbold's seals of office to note his station. He waved in response to the generous cheering by the women in the crowd below.

There was no sign of Philippe.

One more figure appeared at the top of the stair, but this time the crowd fell silent. Unlike his decorated brothers, Tristan wore only a pair of black trousers and a full white shirt with billowing sleeves. The shirt had a high collar, and his waist was secured by a wide belt with a series of straps and buckles that fastened at his side. The shirt fell away at the back, like Friday's own gown, but where Friday merely had skin, Tristan had wings.

Tristan looked down at the crowd, and Friday sensed his discomfort. While she knew the silence was borne of awe and reverence, she could tell that Tristan was afraid he was not welcome. She saw him pause, take a step back.

Friday leapt forward before he could flee. She let go of the girls' hands and caught up the voluminous material of her skirts so that she wouldn't trip as she bounded up the steps. She felt the pins in her hair slip and knew she must be trailing a stream of flowers and ribbons in her wake. She didn't care.

Tristan met her halfway. Friday released her gown, letting the material fall back down to her toes and anchor her on the steps while she caught her breath. Tristan took her hands in his. "It's good to see you too, princess." He kissed the back of one, and then the other, just as he had when they'd parted on the shore.

This time, the roar of the crowd was deafening.

"I was beginning to think you wouldn't come," said Friday.

He smiled wanly. She loved his smile. "I was beginning to think I wouldn't, either."

She'd have been sad if he had left her to celebrate their success all by herself. "What made you change your mind?"

"Your brother swore to me that I am not the strangest thing this country has seen."

Friday wondered which of the Woodcutter tales Peter had

chosen to tell Tristan. "He is right. But you must know there is nothing strange about the sight of you. You are magnificent. Like an angel."

He kissed her hand again. "Sweet princess, you are much closer to a true angel than I'll ever be."

"You flatter me."

"You saved my life, Friday, long before the curse was lifted. I owe you far more than flattery, and I mean to repay that debt."

"Do you?" she teased. "How?"

"With all I have," he whispered solemnly. "For the rest of my life."

Friday's heart grew its own wings and fluttered in her breast. She felt her cheeks redden at his kind words. "What would my father say?"

"Quite a bit, actually," said Tristan. "I was the recipient of both a stern lecture and a rather odd story about your mother and a white goose. I think it was a humorous tale, but I admit, I was afraid to laugh. I'm pretty sure your father could break me in two with one hand. Have you seen the size of his arms? He and your brother just finished building a ship. Single-handedly, I've no doubt."

"Have you seen the size of your wings? I've heard tales of swans who could break a man's bones with much less." Friday put a hand on Tristan's chest; she could feel the heat of him through the fine silk shirt and yearned for that warmth.

"Excuse me," said Peter.

"Peter!" Friday exclaimed. "You've finished the ship! That's wonderful!"

"Thank you, sister dear," said Peter. "But if it's all the same to you, half of those people down there are holding their breath to see if this oversized crow is going to fly away with you, and the rest of us would like to start dancing. So when you've quite finished exchanging sonnets, would you both mind floating down here among the rest of us?"

Peter hopped down the stairs, swept Elisa up into his arms, and signaled for the music to start. With a cursory glance to the king and queen for approval, the merry band complied.

"Where is Philippe?" Friday asked quickly before they reached the main floor.

"He got upset and walked out," said Tristan. "Don't worry. I'll find him."

Friday *was* worried, but there was no time to explain. As expected, once she and Tristan finished descending the staircase, there was no more opportunity for a private chat. The children fawned over Tristan with an unabashed adoration the adults could not show, asking politely if they could touch his wings, along with a myriad of other questions.

"Do your wings hurt?" asked Pickle Kate.

"My shoulders and back ache a bit; they're heavier than they look. But where you're touching them, it kind of tickles."

"Can you fly?" asked another John.

"I don't know," said Tristan. "I'm a little afraid to try."

"Because it might work?" asked another boy. "Or because it might not?"

"Both," said Tristan.

"Are you going to take Friday back to your kingdom with you?" This was from Michael. The boy faced Tristan in a defensive, cross-armed stance.

Tristan's mottled blue eyes met Friday's. "We haven't discussed that yet."

"But you are leaving, right? To take your castle back from that evil man and his witch?" Had the boy been talking to Philippe?

"I'm not much of a prince without a kingdom, am I? Your Friday deserves more than some plain old man with messy hair and wings."

Most of the children nodded approvingly, but Michael did not let up on his scrutiny. Tristan got down on one knee so that he and the boy were eye to eye. "I promise you that I will not do anything without asking Friday's permission first. All right?"

Michael let his arms fall. "All right."

If there was more to their conversation Friday did not hear it, as Christian caught her up in the next dance. All the brothers took their turn with her—Friday was ready to beg off dancing altogether when she was pulled in once more by the strong arms of her father. He swept her off her feet in a giant bear hug and then twirled her around the floor like he had when she was a girl.

"It's good to see you, Papa."

"Likewise, sweetheart. How's your white-winged scoundrel?"

Friday laughed. "Tristan is a good man, Papa."

"And as soon as he proves that to me, I'll consider his worthiness with regard to my daughter," Papa said. "Your heart has had dubious taste in the weaker sex before." He raised his eyebrows at a corner of the room, where a tall, gangly lad sat by himself sipping gingerly at a glass of green punch.

"Oh, poor Panser. I had quite the childhood crush on him, didn't I?"

"Poor boy, indeed! He'll probably never be the same again."

Friday turned to follow Panser's gaze across the dance floor—he was staring at a brown-skinned young girl who was standing by herself with her own glass of punch, swaying gently to the music. "I think he'll be just fine," said Friday.

"And you, my sweet one? How will you be?"

"I will be as I always am, Papa. Happy and free and surrounded by people I love until the day I die."

"That's my girl."

Without warning, the trumpets sounded again. The Grand Marshal stepped forward once more and cleared his throat. "Prince Sebastien Swan and the Princess Odessa."

Friday's mouth dropped open, as did everyone else's in the room. Sure enough, the dark-haired prince appeared at the top of the stairs. The slight woman on his arm had golden skin, black eyes, and long hair as white as Tristan's feathers. Much as Friday had, Sebastien's siblings bounded up the stairs to tackle their eldest sibling with hugs. Tristan beat them all, spreading his wings and lifting himself above everyone to make it to the top first.

Well, then. That answered *that* question.

"Surprise," whispered Henry Humbug.

Friday turned to the man in the stovepipe hat. "You did this?" she asked.

Mr. Humbug rubbed his round belly. "The only ones who can break a curse are the gods, or the sorcerer who placed it," he said. "But another magician can . . . bend the rules."

Friday had heard of this bending of magic before: Rumbold's godmother had attempted something similar when Aunt Joy had cursed the then-prince into spending a year as a frog. "So they're not human again," she said sadly.

"Oh, they are," corrected Mr. Humbug, "but only every full moon. It was the best I could manage."

Friday gave the stout man her own bear hug. "You are wonderful, Mr. Humbug. So very, very wonderful!"

The man's cheeks flushed above his mustache. "Thank you, milady."

"Might I request the pleasure of your company in this next dance?"

Mr. Humbug chuckled. "It would be an honor, my dear. An honor, indeed."

Friday laughed as she spun around on the dance floor once again, happy and free and surrounded by people she loved. If there was to be another night in her life as glorious as this one, she felt hard pressed to imagine it, so she made sure to fill every second with joy.

Some time long into the dancing, Tristan finally managed to take her aside. "We didn't have a chance to finish our chat," he said.

"We didn't," said Friday. "What do you suggest?"

"Things seem to be winding down. Why don't you meet me at the base of the sky tower in, say, an hour or so? Unless you're tired, of course."

Friday never wanted to sleep again. "I'll be there."

As soon as she said the words, the crowd pulled them apart once more, but Friday didn't mind. She would be meeting the man she loved in an hour or so, and they would have the rest of this glorious night to plan their future.

When the time came, Friday used Monday's yawn to excuse herself. She bade everyone good night and gave hugs to all that she passed on her way back to the tower. The torches in the wall sconces were dim, but her heart was light, and she danced down the corridor until she arrived at the base of the steps to the tower where she and Tristan had met.

Friday leaned back against the cold stone walls and remembered that night she'd fallen from the tower, and those days afterward. She stood until her legs got tired, then slid to the floor, lost in her happy memories.

When she woke—had she fallen asleep?—she wondered if she'd heard Tristan wrong. Had he wanted to meet at the *top* of the tower? He would have had to pass her here in the hallway—unless he'd flown. Second-guessing herself, she began to climb the steps of the sky tower, stopping only when she came to the first window. Judging from the fluffy white clouds on the horizon, it was well past dawn.

Tristan had not come for her.

14

Nefarious Purposes

RISTAN AWOKE and regretted it instantly.

His vision was blurry and it felt as if a kelpie had danced on his noggin. His body ached from tip to toe and his face was pressed into . . . the floor? There wasn't enough nettle punch in the world to make him fall asleep on the floor fully clothed, not that he'd had time to drink any.

What had happened?

He remembered his conversation with Friday on the stairs at the ball. After he'd very reluctantly left her side, there hadn't been so much as a pause in his conversations with his sister, his brothers, and the residents and refugees of Arilland. He'd only run into Friday once after their parting; he remembered that too. She had promised to meet him at the base of the sky tower. She was probably there now, waiting for him.

But he was here . . . wherever here was.

Wincing, Tristan opened his eyes. He couldn't straighten his wings without standing. As he didn't seem to be able to summon the energy for that, he waited for his sight to adjust in the darkness. A cool breeze brushed the cheek that wasn't kissing the ground. There was a tang in the air. The floor beneath him creaked. He was on a ship. And there was only one ship he was aware of that had recently been in the vicinity of Arilland.

Mordant's.

A shaft of light sliced through the cracks in the porthole and illuminated his surroundings. He was in a prison cell, a large cage, in the hold of a ship. Several other bodies lay unconscious on the floor beside him. The brightness of the light told him it was morning.

His addled brain brought back his conversation with Friday. She was supposed to meet him. He hoped to the gods that hers was not one of the bodies here with him. Tristan got to his hands and knees to check on his cellmates. He discovered one brother after another and finally Elisa, curled up in the corner around a large swan. Sebastien. All his family was here, then, except Friday. And Philippe.

Had Tristan felt better, he would have laughed at the irony. Philippe had never returned after walking out of the bathhouse. He might still be cooling off somewhere or — more likely — he had stolen a horse and was attempting to hunt down Mordant and kill him all by himself. If Philippe had only been patient and stayed with his family, he'd be exactly where he wanted to be. Funny how Fate worked out.

The rest of Tristan's human brothers groaned and shook off the sleep spell. If Mordant wanted to kill them, he would have done so already. Imprisoning them like this meant that Mordant had more nefarious purposes in mind. For Elisa, death would be more pleasant than another moment in Mordant's company.

Tristan shivered. Rumbold's armorer had made this shirt suitable for a warm ballroom, but not much else. Tristan stretched his wings out as far as he could and worked on wrapping them around himself like a cloak. The effort alone made him sweat, and for that he was thankful.

How had Mordant captured them? The ship had fled after the breaking of the curse, but then it must have doubled back around under some sort of magical cloak. Gana could have easily managed that sort of thing, once her power had recharged.

Philippe might not yet know of their kidnapping, but Friday would raise the alarm and send Rumbold's forces after them in all haste. She would know he had not left her willingly. She would do whatever it took to be with him again.

Wouldn't she?

Tristan tried to imagine the scene from Friday's point of view. Many would believe that the siblings, now returned (mostly) to their former selves, would waste no time in going back to the Green Isles to reclaim their birthright. Only Velius had Christian's word that they wanted to proceed with caution, and Friday had Tristan's promise. He had promised her — in front of her flock—that he would not do anything with regard to their future without asking her permission first. And then he had disappeared.

Somehow, he needed to send her a message.

"Where are we?" asked one of the twins.

"On a ship," said Christian. "Mordant's, no doubt."

The twins had a few other, more colorful names by which they referred to their captor.

"I wholeheartedly agree," Christian said to the twins. "Has he taken all of us?"

Elisa sat up and wiped the sleep spell from her eyes. "I am here."

Tristan loved the sound of her voice.

"Sebastien is here with me"—the swan honked at the sound of his name—"but not Odette."

"Then she isn't far behind," François pointed out. "Or she's hiding on the ship somewhere."

"I propose we do nothing until Mordant reveals his intentions," said Christian. "We'll be able to make a better plan when we have more information."

While they waited, the twins decided that their cage was sturdy enough to resist being smashed to pieces, and that they were hungry enough to eat a whale. François found a lock but he was useless without a pick, so he busied himself by stretching his slight body as far as he could through the bars and trying to pull the contents of the hold—mostly crates and barrels— closer to their cell.

Elisa worked to keep Sebastien calm. Swans were not meant

to be caged, and Sebastien made sure everyone was aware of that fact. Elisa smoothed his feathers and spoke to him in a low cooing voice that eventually served to soothe the bird—and the rest of her brothers as well.

No one was prepared for François's scream. He writhed against the bars of the cage, left arm pinned awkwardly against what looked like . . . nothing. And then nothing's face appeared, a shadow from the shadows with its black mask and red eyes.

The Infidel.

"Elisa, tell him to stop," said Tristan. A woman's voice had worked before; perhaps it would again.

"Please stop," Elisa said softly. "You're hurting my brother."

The Infidel remained still as a black stone. So much for that theory.

"That will do, my pet." At the sorceress's words, François's body dropped to the ground. The twins flung themselves against the bars, swiping at the Infidel, but the man slunk back into the shadows. The sorceress's cackle filled the air, as did the cloying smell of her perfume. "I trust you've all realized the futility of escape. The lock is charmed, and there is nothing but sea for miles."

"What do you want from us?" Christian asked.

Gana reached a thin arm through the bars and traced the line of Elisa's jaw with a crimson-nailed finger. "Such hopeless-ness. Such fear. Mmmm." She kissed the finger. "You will be de-licious."

"I'm going to lose my punch," said Bernard.

"Can't you just put us back to sleep?" asked Rene.

"Why would I do that? We're almost home."

Home. The Green Isles. If it hadn't been Gana speaking, the words would have been music to Tristan's ears. But after so long an absence, what would they find?

Gana smiled and turned back toward the stair. "I'm sure there's something in this hold to keep you occupied." She vanished into the light and let the heavy wooden hatch slam shut behind her.

"Almost home?" asked Bernard.

"Magic," answered François. "It's the only explanation."

"I wish she had magicked a different cologne," said Rene.

"She smells like dead people," said Bernard. "Has she always smelled like that?"

Elisa nodded. "Be glad you were swans those last days in the palace."

"But what does she want with us?" Christian asked again.

"I think I know." Elisa eased the swan off her lap and moved to the center of the cage. She lifted a hand, and the porthole opened a crack; not enough to afford an escape, but enough to send a breeze through the hold to rid it of Gana's ghastly stench. Bernard was right — it did leave that lingering odor of rotting carcass. Finished with her bit of magic, Elisa folded her hands before her. "She's going to kill us."

"If Mordant wanted us dead —" started Bernard.

"— he would have killed us already," finished Rene.

"Not Mordant," said Elisa. "*Her.* She needs magic. Killing people is how she increases her power."

"Of course," breathed François. "That's why she smells like a graveyard."

"The lost children in the palace," remembered Tristan. Elisa's punishment for not accepting Mordant's proposal of marriage had been to see to the well-being of a group of orphaned children whose parents had died in the uprising—nothing so large as Friday's army, of course, but enough that it was noticed when the children began disappearing, one by one. Tristan and his brothers did not know what had happened to the children, so they had not been able to tell King Rumbold the truth when their sister's life was at stake.

But Elisa could tell them now. "Yes, the children were murdered, and yes, I knew they had been murdered, but it was not I who took their lives. One by one, Gana stole them away from me, making it look like I had lost track of them. When people began asking questions and the magistrate discovered the bodies in that shallow grave . . ." The rest of the story was lost in Elisa's sadness and guilt of the past.

"They blamed you," said Tristan, "but they shouldn't have."

"Shouldn't they?" she asked. "I might not have been able to speak, but was there really nothing I could have done to save at least one of them?"

Christian stepped forward, took her into his arms, and let her cry. She gasped, hiccuped, and expelled such great, heaving sobs that Tristan was afraid she might pass out from the effort. But none of them tried to stop her—there was near a decade's worth of tears in that release. Elisa cried for the children, their parents, the loss of their old home, the loss of their new home, the loss of control of their destiny, and who knew what else.

Finally she regained control of herself, taming the weeping into sniffles. "She drinks the blood," Elisa said. "Or bathes in it; I'm not sure which. But it's definitely something to do with blood."

"That's why she needs us alive," said François.

"We are walking, talking blood bags," said Rene.

"Pleasant thought," said Bernard.

"And our family possesses the power of the Four Winds in our veins, though Elisa may be the only one able to harness it," Christian added. "I suspect that makes our blood particularly . . ."

". . . attractive," finished François.

". . . delicious," added Rene.

"Tristan," said François.

"What?" asked Tristan.

"We need to cause a distraction and find some way to set you free so you can fly back to the mainland."

"First of all, I'm not even sure I can fly. Glide, sure, but fly? And over such a long distance? I'd most likely end up in Troll Country."

"I'd rather take my chances with Gana," said Bernard.

"Sebastien can fly," said Rene.

"But would Sebastien know where he was going?" asked Christian. "And how would he pass along a message once he arrived?"

"He'll be human again at the full moon," offered François.

"We'll be dead by the next full moon," said Elisa.

"Let's keep thinking," said Christian. "François is on the right track. Let's not lose faith."

None of them contradicted their elder brother, but neither did they rally. Trouble was, they didn't have much faith to begin with. Their dreams had gone from the beaches of Arilland to the palace ballroom and no further. Faith was a thing sewn into the patchwork skirts of a girl on another shore.

Tristan tired of standing and curled back down onto the hard floor. Bernard and Rene took over François's task of trying to pull the boxes to the cage to see what was in them. Finally, their fingers found purchase enough to inch one forward. After a lengthy period of prying and kicking and pounding and cursing, they managed to smash into the side of the box. The two men removed handful after handful of packing material in search of the contents . . . until they realized the packing material *was* the contents.

An enormous pile of spun yarn stared at them all from the edge of the cell.

Elisa gagged.

But Tristan smiled. Gana's little prank would be her downfall.

"See if you can pry the lid off," Tristan told the twins, "and don't break the frame. I want to do a weaving."

"Are you mad?" asked Philippe.

"In the finest sense of the word," Tristan said proudly.

The twins managed to remove the box's cover and slide it through the bars of the cell. They broke out the inner plank so that only the frame remained. Tristan wiggled the boards—nothing as sturdy as a picture frame, but they would do. He tied one loop of yarn around the bottom corner of the loom and began creating a warp.

"I can't watch." Elisa huddled back into her corner of the cage beside Sebastien. If she wasn't already shaking, Tristan could tell she was about to start.

"You don't have to, dearest," he said. "Rest yourself. Pay your featherbrained brother no mind."

The comment was meant in jest, but as soon as he said it, he realized that a feather would be the perfect tool with which to thread the weft strands through. He tried pulling out one of his own, but he couldn't force himself to do it, nor did he have the proper angle.

"Help me," he asked of his brothers. Christian stepped forward.

"Turn around." Christian stuck his hand into the patch of feathers Tristan had indicated. Tristan turned his body away and braced himself for the pain. It was not insignificant.

Tristan collapsed on the floor, biting back a scream that would have brought Gana back to the hold—or worse, the Infidel. When he recomposed himself, he stood and faced his brother. Christian held out one bright feather roughly the length of his forearm. It would do.

"I tried to make it quick."

"And for that I thank you," said Tristan. "Let's hope it's not necessary again."

Tristan leaned back against the bars, selected a separate yarn for his weft, and began to weave. It would be difficult, but he wanted to incorporate some sort of message into the cloth if he could. A more talented man would have sewn the words she had taught him into the border or hidden some longer, more complex message, but his skills were crude at best.

After a while, Elisa overcame her disgust and eased over to help guide Tristan's hand. Between the two of them they managed to incorporate something that looked more like a swan and less like a giant white blob—at least, Tristan thought so. They added green spots to represent the Green Isles, and a red ship of sorts. Elisa had her doubts. But if even a scrap of fabric got to Friday at all, she would know who had sent it, no matter what the pattern or the quality of the work.

"You should probably work faster," suggested Bernard.

"He's working as fast as he can," said Rene.

"I just wish I knew how much time I had," said Tristan.

"She'll stay on the deck to maintain the spell on the boat," said Elisa. "Though judging by the smell, she's close to the end of her strength."

"Have you thought about how you're going to send this?" asked Christian.

Tristan nodded as he wove the quill through the warp. "My shirt," he told his brothers. "We can use the buckles to strap it to Sebastien."

Rene considered their cage. "He probably *could* fit through the bars."

"He's not going to like it," said Bernard.

"Do you think he'll be able to fly all that way?" asked François. "Or know where he's headed?"

"We don't have a choice," Tristan said. "It's the only plan I've got."

"I can help him," said Elisa. "I can summon the wind beneath him so that his wings don't tire as fast, and I can set him on a current that will take him as far west as he cares to go. We'll have to trust him to find the palace on his own."

Christian unbuttoned Tristan's collar and set to unfastening the buckles of his shirt. Tristan never stopped weaving. Elisa had done this for all their sakes, for three straight days.

"If I didn't appreciate you enough before, sister dear, then I certainly do now," he said as he pulled another strand through the warp.

Elisa kissed him on the cheek. "This will work. I know it will."

"Oh yes? How's that?"

"Destiny," she said confidently. Tristan didn't argue, mostly because he was too cold to do so. Elisa saw him shivering and called a breeze from warmer climes in through the porthole to thaw his frozen fingers.

When the crew began to cry the sight of land, Tristan stopped weaving. Bernard and Rene sawed at the warp threads with broken boards from the crate until the weaving fell away from its frame. Christian wound it up in Tristan's shirt and buckled the bundle tightly across Sebastien's back. The swan did not struggle, which gave them hope that, somewhere inside that body, their eldest brother had heard the plan and intended to fulfill it.

As expected, the swan did not enjoy being squeezed through the bars, but the twins made it happen, apologizing the whole time. Then Elisa set to blowing the porthole open as wide as she could. She managed a few more inches before it wedged against another crate and budged no farther.

Suddenly there was a great honk, and a substantial white body came hurtling through the porthole, knocking the crate aside and throwing the window wide open.

"Odette!" cried Elisa.

"I bloody love that woman," said Bernard.

"Quickly!" cried Christian.

Elisa stirred the air in the room, setting the two swans aloft. In a whisper, they had cleared the porthole. Tristan watched them speed into the horizon with the fate of Kassora strapped to their backs. Silently he wished them well, and prayed that Fate wished the same thing.

15

Wild Swan Chase

FRIDAY DIDN'T EXACTLY run from the base of the tower to her room, but her brisk walk left her almost breathless by the time she arrived. She removed Monday's fancy ball gown with some difficulty and shoved it into the back of the wardrobe. She put on a clean linen shirt and a patchwork skirt and ran her hands through her hair, haphazardly scattering the ribbons and fading flowers onto the floor.

She paused by the window to frown into the sunrise. Arilland still looked the same as it had before the heirs of Kassora had arrived; there was no reason to expect it to appear any different now that Tristan had stood her up. Surely he'd had his reasons for not being there, first and foremost his family. Friday, too, might have abandoned her liaison with a new crush for the sake of her family, if it came to that. He would find her this morning; he would come to her and apologize and she would forgive him, just as she forgave everyone.

This was the greatest disadvantage of seeing the best in people: for the most part, they inevitably disappointed you. But sometimes, rare times, faith in a person was all it took for him to achieve greatness. Those times were why Friday never stopped believing. Determined as ever, she straightened her shoulders and went to collect the children.

As she opened the door to leave, Conrad came rushing through, almost toppling her over in his haste. "I'm sorry, mi-lady, I can't find him anywhere."

She could feel Conrad's exhaustion, a sapping of strength that meant he had run from one end of the castle to the other, possibly more than once. This wasn't exactly what she'd expected.

"Gone? Surely he hasn't just *vanished*. Have you asked the rest of his family?" He was a smart boy; of course he had. "What did they say?"

"That's what I'm trying to tell you. None of them — not Elisa nor her brothers — are anywhere on the castle grounds. I've searched everywhere."

Stunned, Friday plopped down into the chair closest to her. "Maybe they went after Philippe. Tristan told me that he'd walked out on them earlier. He was incredibly mad, and hell-bent on exacting his revenge on Mordant immediately. I could feel the hatred pouring out of him when we were on the shore, after the curse was broken."

"They all went after him?" asked Conrad. "Even Elisa and the swans?"

Her squire was right. Friday closed her eyes to think, and then snapped them open again. "You don't suppose they've gone home already, do you?"

Conrad shook his head. "With no preparation? With no word to anyone? Especially you . . ." Friday put up a hand, and whatever else Conrad meant to say faded into nothing.

"I fell asleep," he said instead.

"As did I," said Friday. "It was a long night."

"Friday, I'm a trained messenger. I don't just fall asleep. Especially when I'm tasked with keeping an eye on a particular subject."

That much was true; even Mordant's Infidel had not managed to disappear from beneath Conrad's watchful gaze, and Friday had asked her squire to watch over Tristan when she could not. Friday wondered how a young man acquired such training. And where. And why. "I warned you that extraordinary events surrounded my family."

"You did," admitted Conrad.

"Do you not think it reasonable that we both succumbed to exhaustion after the events of the past few days?"

"Yes, but Friday——"

John, Wendy, and Michael burst into the room. Wendy threw herself into Friday's arms in greeting; Friday hugged the enthusiastic girl back tightly, wishing that some of Wendy's innocent hopefulness would rub off on her. Friday winced at Ben the Extremely Loud's enthusiastic barking.

"Good morning, Friday."

"Good morning, John."

"Did you sleep all right? You don't look well."

Friday attempted to distract both herself and the children by standing Wendy up and straightening her dress for her. "I imagine it will take me a bit before I've caught up after . . . the excitement of the past few days. Would you all help me collect the flock and get work started this morning? I would be ever so grateful."

Michael wasted no time. "Where's Tristan?"

Friday answered honestly. "I don't know."

"He's gone," Conrad said.

"No, he's not," said Michael.

Friday's heart skipped a beat. "You've seen him?"

"No, but he's not gone. He can't be. You would know if he was."

Friday cocked her head. "Why do you say that?"

Michael shrugged. "Because he promised."

Friday froze. Tristan had indeed made that exact promise to the boy, right in front of her. He wasn't the type of man to go back on his word. And if that were true, if he and his brothers hadn't left to chase Philippe or return to the Green Isles of their own accord . . .

. . . then something was very, very wrong. She turned to Conrad. "You and I falling asleep. You think it was magic, don't you?"

"I do."

"So do I." Friday stood and made her way to the door of her chamber. "I'm sorry, my darlings. I have to go."

"Can I come?" asked Michael.

John held his brother back. "We'll see that all the children wake up and get started on their chores. Go."

Friday didn't need much prompting. She turned on her heel and sped down the carpet to the Great Hall with Conrad close behind.

Sunday and Rumbold were very awake and very occupied upon her arrival, settling a particularly vociferous dispute between a merchant and a landowner. The Grand Marshal ushered her into the salon and promised to get word of her arrival to their majesties with all due haste. Friday sent Conrad to fetch Monday, Peter, and Papa while she waited. And then she paced. And paced. And paced some more. After a while, she began to tidy up the room, fluffing pillows and shaking out the curtains to keep herself occupied. She was moments away from rearranging the furniture when the door opened and the Woodcutters came pouring in.

"What is it, Friday?" Rumbold asked, eager to get to the point.

Sunday held up a hand. "Before that, let me first thank you for rescuing us from that never-ending battle. If those two men waste any more of this country's time, I'm ordering them both to . . . to . . ."

"Clean the dungeon," Conrad offered as he entered the salon, followed by the rest of the Woodcutters.

"Perfect." Sunday snapped her fingers. "Exactly that."

"Where's your boy?" Peter asked Friday. At Papa's stare he continued more politely, "I assumed you'd be spending the day with him."

"Tristan is gone. They all are." Friday's comment was met with the same stunned silence she'd felt all morning. "There's something wrong. There must be."

Rumbold and Sunday exchanged looks.

"He didn't strike me as the sort of person to vanish off into the night," said Sunday.

Rumbold folded his arms. "Think about it, though. What would you do if you suddenly had the chance to save your kingdom from a madman and his gang? Would you wait patiently to consult with your new friends? No offense," he said to Friday, who felt her face flush.

"I did hear that his younger brother ran off last night in quite a huff," said Sunday.

"It's true," said Velius. "I never saw him again after he left the training grounds. Perhaps they've just gone after him."

"We considered these as well," said Friday. "But—"

"He promised," finished Conrad. "He promised the children that he wouldn't do anything without asking Friday's permission first. Especially something as rash as leaving without supplies."

Monday clucked her tongue and took Friday's hand. "Friday, dearest. It wouldn't be the first time a man gave a woman an empty promise."

Friday wrenched her hand away. Her family meant well, but she needed to make them understand. "He wouldn't have left me. We have a bond." The pressure of that bond still weighed heavy in her chest. "We're meant to be together. Papa, you wouldn't have left Mama without telling her why, would you?" She turned to Rumbold. "Nor would you have ever left Sunday."

Rumbold looked deeply into his wife's sky-blue eyes. "I might if it meant saving my people," he said. "If it meant coming back a hero and proving myself to the one I love."

Sunday read all she needed to in that comment before turning to Friday. "It's true."

Friday couldn't believe what she was hearing. The *Woodcutter* family refused to believe in something? Could this be some part of Gana's foul magic as well? Each of them faced her, as if they might attack at any moment. The only one standing by her side was Conrad. Thank the gods for Conrad.

Friday took a step back. "He did not leave me," Friday said adamantly. "Something happened to him. Something happened to them all, and I'll bet my needle it's Mordant's doing."

"Even if it was, what could we do?" Rumbold asked.

Papa considered the situation. "Peter and I have finished the ship."

Friday felt a glimmer of hope flutter in her belly, but she refused to fuel it falsely.

"We need that ship to find relief for Arilland. Our country is on the verge of collapsing under the weight of all these people." Rumbold sighed and turned to Friday. "Do you have any proof—hard proof—that the heirs of Kassora left under some sort of duress?"

Other than Tristan mysteriously vanishing and going back

on his word, or a curious instance of oversleeping? No. "Do you have proof that they did not?" Friday countered.

Sunday threw up her hands. "It's like arguing with Mama."

Friday raised her chin. "I'll take that as a compliment." Papa actually chuckled at the exchange.

Rumbold bowed his head in defeat. "I'll send out the ship at first light. If you like, you may travel with them."

"And me," Conrad said quickly.

"And you," added Rumbold. "But the ship's main purpose will be to find ports from which we can acquire food and other supplies. I can't go sending this country's best hope of survival on some wild swan chase."

Then what was the point of going? But Friday had to try. She had to do *something*.

"I wish you wouldn't," said Monday.

"I have to," Friday said to her. And then to Rumbold, "Thank you. We'll be ready at first light."

~elle~

The rest of the day was torture. Friday would have used the opportunity to catch up on all the sleep she'd lost, but she feared the horrible visions of certain death that wouldn't stop running through her mind. She concentrated on the children, seeing to the babies and the laundry and the games and the collection of what little food was left to scavenge on the castle grounds. She did not let herself stop to rest where she usually did; the pond by the willow tree was now as empty as her heart. Nor could she bring herself to visit the guards' training grounds, or Cook's herb garden. When Friday needed to pause, she sat herself on a blanket out in the middle of the field where the children played, beneath the merciless eye of the sun. She figured it was best to prepare herself — there would be no shade on the ship.

There would be little packing for this sea voyage; she didn't own many articles of clothing these days. Perhaps Sunday would allow her some coin to trade for what she'd need when they found port. How long did it take a ship to cross to the sea beyond the Troll Kingdom? Weeks? Months? She'd bring a trunk of raw materials and spend her time wisely, sewing and mending and making herself useful to the crew.

"I want to go."

Ben the Intrusive's bark snapped Friday out of her reverie. "What?"

"If Conrad gets to go, I'm going too." Michael stood with his hands on his hips and his tiny chest thrust out defiantly. Ben barked again. "And Ben too."

"Oh, my darling," Friday sighed. "Who said anyone was going anywhere?"

Michael was not having any of her subterfuge. "All the children know. It's why they haven't been bothering you today; Elaine and Evelyn told everyone to let you alone and come to them instead if they had a problem. You're leaving on your Papa's ship tomorrow to find Tristan."

Friday considered recommending Michael to Rumbold as a spy. As it seemed he already had all the facts, there was no use glossing over the truth for him. "I've been invited to join the crew, yes, but the mission is to find food and supplies for our people. There is a very slim chance we'll even hear about Tristan." But she wanted to be there when they did. If they did.

"Your chances are better if you bring me along."

Friday tousled Michael's hair and pulled him into a hug that sent Ben hopping around them in wild fits. "I wish I could bring all of you," she said into his neck. When she released him, she looked him straight in the eye. "I need you here, to make sure things run smoothly. I don't know how bad this situation's going to get, and I need you to keep everyone in good spirits." Look at her, delegating tasks like a true leader! Tristan would be proud of her.

"Why me?"

"Don't you know? The children look up to you, Michael. Because you are brave." Friday looked down at Ben. "You even have a squire. You're practically a knight already."

Michael's face burst into a brilliant smile at this, and he galloped away on his invisible horse, brandishing his invisible sword to beat invisible foes. Friday's foes were far less invisible. She hoped she wasn't sending herself on a fool's errand.

The sun lingered in the sky, postponing the inevitable, but eventually it set itself to rest, as all things must. Friday should have been excited about a sea voyage, an adventure, a trip into the unknown, but that was Thursday's territory. Or Saturday's. Friday was content with . . . well . . . being content. She enjoyed her quiet little life. She was a seamstress, not a seaman. She pulled everything out of the wardrobe except the white ball gown and laid it out on the bed.

She ate the light meal Conrad had delivered to her room, and changed into her nightdress far earlier than usual so that she could spend all her remaining time with her Darlings. She played games with John, Wendy, and Michael, wrestled with Ben, and told them a few of her favorite Papa stories. Conrad even contributed a few stories of his own, dark tales of endless sands and priceless treasures and young men who defeated demons with nothing more than their wits.

They were all reluctant to sleep—especially Friday— but she settled her Darlings in, kissed them good night, and blew out the candle anyway. She lay in her own bed, staring into the shadowy darkness, wishing for sleep to wash her away. She imagined the Angel of Dreams descending from the moon astride a white horse, headed for her window.

Friday sat up. Something was indeed headed for the window, but it wasn't an angel.

"WATCH OUT!" she managed to cry before two white bundles of feathers crashed through the casement, tumbled across her sheets, and came to a sprawling rest at the children's feet.

Swans.

"Is it Tristan?" Michael tried to approach the unconscious birds, but John held him back. "Is he a swan again?"

"I don't think so," said Friday. "If I had to guess, I'd say this is Sebastien and Odette."

Wendy crouched carefully beside the swans and put a gentle hand on their bellies. "They are alive," she said, "but they look really tired."

Friday could verify that. She had never before been able to

sense the feelings of animals, but it seemed the same thing could not be said of humans trapped in animal bodies. The couple's exhaustion was so complete that it made Friday's limbs heavy. "They've come a very long way," she said.

"I can see why." Conrad leaned forward to unfasten the buckles that wrapped around the first swan. Friday felt a tickle in her chest, the sense that Sebastien had been held against his will and somehow escaped, but details beyond that were hazy. Conrad unsheathed the dagger he kept in his belt and sawed at the rest of the bindings — white as Sebastien's feathers — until they fell away.

Friday moved to lift up the bindings and examine them. As soon as her fingers touched the fabric she knew what this was: the modified shirt Tristan had worn to the ball. Despair gripped her as a small bundle fell from the tattered shirt.

"Why would Sebastien-swan bring us a carpet?" asked Michael.

"It's a mat." John swatted his little brother. "It's not big enough to be a carpet."

Wendy unrolled the mat and handed it to Friday. "It's woven," the girl said, "like the magic shirts."

From what Michael had told the children after returning from the shore that day, they now assumed all woven fabric contained magical properties. Friday hoped they were right about this one. A weaving could only mean a message from Elisa. When Friday took hold of the small mat, both her arm and the weaving glowed in the dark with a powerful blue light.

"It *is* magic," breathed Michael.

Friday smiled into the light and a single tear slipped down her cheek. It wasn't from Elisa. This mat was from Tristan, woven by his own hand.

"What does it say?" asked Conrad.

Until the messenger posed the question, Friday hadn't considered that the weaving said anything at all. But there was the message, right before her eyes.

"It says, 'Red blob, white blob, green blobs,'" said Michael confidently.

"It says we have to get this to the king and queen immediately," said Friday. She lit the candlestick once more and handed the weaving to Conrad. "Let's go."

"Right now?" asked John.

"In our nightclothes?" asked Wendy.

"Do you want to meet the king or not?" Michael called from the doorway. Ben was already halfway down the hall. With a hoot and a holler, Michael tore after him into the shadows. The pair made enough racket to wake half the castle, but Friday didn't care. The five of them raced, nightclothes and all, down the corridors to the royal bedchambers. Ben barked their arrival to the twin guards who stood outside Rumbold and Sunday's door.

"Their Majesties are asleep," the first guard told Friday.

"Well, then, wake them up!" said Friday.

Behind the guards, the oversized door shifted open a crack. "Mission accomplished." Sunday yawned. "Friday, dearest, what is it?"

Friday took the weaving from Conrad and thrust it in her

sister's face. "Proof!" Sunday took the mat from Friday and squinted at it. The second guard took the candlestick from Friday's trembling hand and held it steady for his queen. "Tristan didn't leave here willingly. He's been captured by Mordant and taken back to the Green Isles."

"White blob, red blob, green blobs," Conrad translated for Michael.

"Where did you get this?" Sunday asked.

"Sebastien and Odette. Tristan used his shirt to strap the message to Sebastien and buckle it tight. They've flown an awful long way, but I can't say how far. We need to hurry and launch Papa's ship immediately!"

Sunday sighed and rubbed her eyes. "Friday . . ."

"Tristan wove that message for me," Friday said quietly. "With his own hands."

Sunday shook her head, but Friday could see a smirk hiding there. "Only you, my sister with a heart as big as the moon, could teach a prince to weave well enough to send you love letters. Rumbold!" she called back into the room. "You need to write me love letters!"

"Yes, dear," mumbled the sleepy voice inside the chamber.

"Tell Mr. Jolicoeur to summon the crew and ready the ship," Sunday said to one of the guards, and he took off running. "Collect your things," she said to Friday. "I'll wake the king and get his assent. May I bring this?" She indicated the weaving, and Friday nodded reluctantly. Whatever it took to convince Rumbold to let her go and take an army with her, she would do it.

Unfortunately, King Rumbold didn't have an army to spare. "I'm sorry," he told Friday on their way down to the grassy shore. "We're spread thin enough as it is. I can give you Velius and a small strike force, but that's all."

"Against Mordant's sorceress *and* his Infidel?" Friday prayed to the gods it would be enough. As it was, Rumbold was giving her full control of Papa's ship when he desperately needed it for trade. Friday dared not ask for more.

Rumbold, Sunday, Monday, and Velius all accompanied her to the ship. John and Michael carried her carpetbags and Wendy held Friday's cloak. Conrad managed his own things. Friday held only Tristan's weaving, tight in her frightened grip. Together they climbed the slight berm that had undoubtedly saved the palace from flooding.

At the top of the hill, Friday froze. Beneath her stood Papa, Peter, and half of Arilland. On the water behind them floated her father and brother's beautiful ship. It was a glorious sight to behold.

Even in the predawn darkness, the people of Arilland were awash in colors. Almost everyone present — and their children, who were up far earlier than they should be — wore patchwork. To Friday, the fabric would always be a symbol of love and generosity, and she was touched by their kindness. Mr. Jolicoeur waited for her in the boat meant to take her to the ship, but the children stopped her before she reached him.

"Just a moment, Princess." Mr. Humbug's tall hat waded through the colorful crowd. When the people before him parted, Friday noticed a patchwork handkerchief peeking from the front pocket of his coat. "Arilland has a few gifts for your journey."

Friday wanted to jump in the water and swim for the ship immediately, but there was the small matter of her not being able to swim.

The young twins Elaine and Evelyn stepped forward, each holding one end of something. When they stopped before her, they unrolled the item and presented it fully: a flag. More precisely, a patchwork flag, in the middle of which swam a majestic white swan.

"Your ship needs to fly this," said Elaine.

"They are your colors," said Evelyn.

And so they were: all the colors of the rainbow. Friday hugged the girls and a cheer went up from the crowd.

"I have this for you as well," said Mr. Humbug. He placed in Friday's open hand a sphere that looked a bit like a brass bed knob. "When you are aboard the ship, cup the sphere between your hands and whisper where you want to go. This should speed your journey." Friday hugged Mr. Humbug as well at this, and placed a sound kiss upon his cheek.

"Well, well." He blushed. "Don't get too excited. It's just a bit of conjuring. Nothing more."

"You have been a great help to me, sir, and my family. To all the people I love. And I thank you for that."

"Well, well," Mr. Humbug sputtered again. "Good, good."

Friday raised her free hand to the crowd. "I love you all! I can't thank you enough for seeing me off. I will remember this forever!"

A freckled, ginger man — he could only be Carrot Kate's father — wrung his hat in his hands. "I'm not sure you understand, Princess."

The man's patchwork tunic was utterly charming. "Understand what?"

"We're not here to see you off," said the twins' mother. "We're here to fight for you."

Friday covered her gaping mouth with a hand. Michael tugged at her skirts, and she turned to look down at him. "You needed an army, dintcha? Well, we got you one." The boy raised his arms, and the children in the crowd joined his battle cry with raucous screams. So many children on the shore . . .

No. It couldn't be. Friday's shock deepened and she scanned the crowd again, this time examining each face. These weren't just concerned citizens of Arilland, they were the parents of her children. All of them. High- and lowborn alike.

"I — I can't . . ." stammered Friday. "I can't . . ." These people had children! Besides, she didn't know the first thing about leading an army. No, that wasn't quite right — she did know. Tristan had taught her. She could almost hear his voice in her head: *The most important quality is loyalty. If they know you will fight just as hard for them, they will happily die for you.* The weaving he'd sent her felt warm beneath her fingers.

"I took the liberty of selecting the halest and heartiest of the bunch for your crew," Velius told her. "The ship will sail at capacity."

"It's already decided, Captain Friday," said Mr. Humbug. "Your Patchwork Army awaits your command."

"I can't let you do this," Friday finally managed to spit out, but rafts and canoes full of people were already spilling off the shore and heading to the ship. High above them, two large white swans drifted on the breeze.

"It's out of our hands, milady," said Kate's father as he helped her into Mr. Jolicoeur's craft. "We can't disappoint our children, no more than you can."

Friday urged Mr. Jolicoeur to row as fast as he could; she wanted to thank each and every person as they boarded the ship. There were tears in her eyes as she shook hands and received hugs and listened to parent after parent gush their praises of her. With every person she touched, she could feel her resolve strengthening. Every person, that is, but one.

She reached out to a tall, cloaked man as he boarded, but he did not take her hand. Confused, Friday looked up into the man's shadowed face and saw ocean-blue eyes glaring back at her.

"It seems we have the same destination," said Philippe. "Just don't get in my way."

16

Demolished

BY THE TIME Gana returned to the hold to check on her prisoners, Tristan had restrung another loom and was weaving once more. It was Christian's idea to continue the project instead of attempting to clean up everything they had so obviously destroyed. There was no need to mask the act of weaving, he pointed out, just that they had sent the first as a message.

Rene and Bernard took the game to heart and began decorating the cage with whatever they could pull out of the carton. Elisa joined in, laughing and criticizing their choice of colors and patterns. François selected the sturdiest yarn and fashioned a sling for his wounded arm. He and Christian sat in the dead center of the cell, suggesting ideas for how they might overpower Mordant and his forces. Christian listed their assets: not much beyond Elisa's power over wind and Tristan's wings. François invented ridiculous and impossible methods of attack. Normally, Tristan would have reined him in, but they truly had no idea what they were in for. None of them had set foot on the Green Isles for almost a decade.

Unfortunately, Sebastien's absence was the one thing they could not cover up. They would simply have to deal with whatever punishment Gana doled out when she realized he was missing.

The sorceress's smell preceded her. When the air turned cloying, the siblings immediately huddled together in the center of the cell. They would not let another of them be caught unaware by that shadow-hugging assassin.

The sorceress's first reaction was laughter. "I underestimated you."

"Never underestimate our ability to take a joke," said Bernard.

The sorceress considered the scene as she stroked the gleaming scales of the once-more dormant cockatrice around her neck. Tristan waited for the humor in her eyes to turn to stone. He did not have to wait long. The bars of the cell began to smoke, and all the decorative yarn was reduced to cinders. Even the loom and its contents turned to ashes in Tristan's hands.

"Where is the bird?" She did not ask politely.

"He's a *bird*," Rene said boldly.

"He doesn't do well in cages," said Bernard. "So we encouraged him to go."

"It wasn't an easy decision," Christian said solemnly. "Our family draws its power from being together."

Tristan turned to his older brother in surprise. This wasn't something he'd considered before, but it was certainly plausible. He only hoped it wasn't true. Gana seemed pleased at the concern on his face; if Christian had been saving that little gem for just this sort of reaction, he'd done extremely well. Tristan hid the remnants of the expression behind his wings and concentrated on soaking up the heat from the cage bars.

"Bind them." Gana said the command to thin air, and from that invisibility strode the Infidel. He waited for the sorceress to wave a hand over the lock to disenchant it, then turned the key and opened the door. The brothers sucked in a collective breath as the Infidel's hand gripped the still-glowing metal bars. Even with his gloves, the heat should have been unbearable. Tristan could detect the stench of burnt leather on top of soot and corpse rot, but the Infidel did not so much as flinch.

As the masked man approached, Tristan could make out the exact quantity of red in his eyes, so much more now than the mere outline that was present only a few days ago. The iris was almost completely obscured by the color, as if all the blood had burst inside his eye sockets. Blood that glowed.

From a sack, the Infidel pulled not rope but chains: shackles with great manacles and a separate key for each. He lifted them as if they weighed no more than one of Tristan's feathers, and never selected the wrong key as he locked them tight.

Satisfied, Gana marched them up the stairs to where Mordant's soldiers stood waiting. For a moment Tristan's wings got wedged in the opening; the Infidel pushed them into his back and shoved Tristan up, scraping his wings painfully. He cried out and fell to his knees on the deck. It was a moment before his eyes adjusted to the bright light of day.

Mordant stood before them as if he were posing for a portrait. He still wore the red robes of office that had been his uniform while he was advisor to Tristan's father, the uniform he'd been wearing when he stood over the fallen king's body in triumph. He'd used that same bright red to decorate his soldiers and his mistress.

Mordant grinned, a gesture that pulled lines in his pockmarked cheeks. Everything about Mordant was slimy: the mustaches sprouting from his mottled skin, his limp black hair; even his eyebrows looked damp with malevolence.

"I informed Gana that I did not want to kill you before this moment," Mordant said without preamble. "I wanted to see your faces when you laid eyes on your homeland once again."

This time, Tristan did scream. He dove for Mordant with every intention of strangling him to death with the chain between his manacles. The Infidel leapt on him from behind, pinning his wings, and Mordant's soldiers tripped up his feet, slamming him into the deck. Unsatisfied, Tristan thrashed and pounded at the wood until he felt Gana's spell of stillness wash over him. From then on, he could do nothing *but* look.

The pain was greater than if Mordant had pulled out each of Tristan's feathers, one by one.

There was no longer anything green about the islands that lay before them, hugging the churning blue sea. The land was dead. Demolished. It looked as if a dragon had ravaged the once beautiful city, but there were no dragons in the world anymore. The instrument of this devastation was Mordant. Edifices that had stood tall, honoring Kassora's achievements beneath the eyes of benevolent gods, were now nothing but sad ruins, one pile of rubble indiscernible from another. From beach to horizon, the land was naught but one solid mass of brownish-yellow dust.

This was someone else's kingdom in someone else's world, a nightmare where demons and dragons still roamed free. There was no solace for a man in this place. Even if they somehow did triumph over Mordant, Tristan could never bring Friday here.

"What happened?" whispered Elisa.

"I happened," said Mordant. "I proved to the subjects of this land that I was not a power to be trifled with, and they trembled before me."

Tristan squinted into the wreckage, half expecting to see lines of shackled citizens, but there was no one. No children played in the streets—if there were still streets beneath the never-ending piles of debris. No buyers or sellers called to one another in the market that once stood on the nonexistent pier. Not so much as a gull dared breathe a sound over Mordant's sad playground, so awesome and terrible was his power.

"Where is everyone?" It was Bernard who whispered this time. Nor would Tristan have dared raise his voice—it felt like yelling in a church. Or a graveyard.

"The agreeable were allowed to live," Mordant said gra-

ciously. The red guards among them nodded proudly. "The disagreeable were . . ."

". . . put to better use," Gana finished.

Judging by the complete absence of anyone, it seemed the
people of the Green Isles had found Mordant as agreeable as
everyone else did. Tristan only hoped the empty harbor meant
that most of the population had escaped before Gana "put them
to use." He cut a glance to the Infidel, who stood quietly behind
Mordant. He wondered how much innocent blood the slave had
shed on behalf of his dark mistress . . . and if the man trapped
inside that body had been forced to witness it.

Tristan and his siblings were lowered onto the docks by
their shackles. Tristan's toe caught a rotted board and he toppled over, forcing Mordant's guards to help him to his feet. He
might have spread his wings to keep his balance, but they hadn't
plucked him yet; he didn't want to draw attention to himself
and give them any ideas. For now, he was content to play the
useless, grotesque half-man.

The twins took Tristan's lead. They tripped on every other
step in the dock and knocked their guards about, all the while
apologizing profusely. His brothers were not insubstantial in
human form; the twins were the broadest and the tallest of
them, a full head and shoulders above Mordant. The ginger
mops glanced at each other and smirked over the red guard
before tumbling again. They only stopped when Gana threatened to turn them into swans once more—or some other,
less desirable creature. She stroked the animal around her neck

again, forcing Tristan to wonder if the cockatrice had once been human as well.

Slowly, painfully, Mordant and his sorceress led them up the hill. Tristan's tender feet tried to avoid cracks where the grass had grown up through the unattended path, sometimes creating razor-sharp edges in the pavement. On either side of the main road they traveled, there were no buildings left to speak of. Tristan tried to remember each one as he passed so that he might honor their fallen memories, berating himself when he could not recall a certain corner or lane. The least the fallen heirs could do to honor their parents was pass on the stories of the great kingdom that had flourished under two great rulers. Tristan felt keenly the responsibility for every person and shop lost due to his faulty memory.

Behind him, Elisa sniffled. Her tears fell quietly in the dust at her own bare feet.

"May the gods lift them to their breasts," Tristan whispered to her.

"And find them worthy enough to be rid of their burdens," Elisa finished the litany.

At the crest of the hill lay the largest ruin: the Temple of the Four Winds. All the brothers to a man fell to their knees. Tristan lowered his wings into the dust of what was once the four great statues and sought forgiveness from his patron gods. Elisa clasped her hands together, her knuckles white, her face red. She might have created a waterspout or a tornado with her fury, but something was suppressing her elemental magic.

Gana pulled Elisa up by her dirty hair and dragged her forward. The guards were less kind to Tristan and his brothers. The sharp pommels of their daggers left welts.

They passed through the steppe behind the temple, and Tristan's sore feet enjoyed the blissful reprieve through the meadow. Farther they went, down into what was once the lower city, just outside the castle walls. Here one temple did remain, its red-and-gold-adorned tower standing brazenly against the cloudy sky. The Fire Temple.

Priests and priestesses of Fire were zealous and unpredictable. Dedicates of Fire by and large were beautiful, worshipped the God of Passion, and catered to the baser needs of the public. The Fire Temple of Kassora had been tantamount to a pleasure garden, its more powerful celebrants little more than troublemakers. It was no surprise that Mordant had collected his sorceress from among the more promising dedicates of that house.

As they neared, Tristan realized that the Fire Temple had not completely escaped the wrath of whatever (or whoever) had demolished the city. Here and there, a lintel was cracked. An ornament had shattered. Sections of stained glass were missing, leaving gaps in the crimson flowers and beasts that frolicked there.

Inside, there were bones. Everywhere. Human bones.

Bones formed patterns on the floor and hung from the chandeliers. Long bones lined the grand archway. Small bones made up elaborate designs in the moldings and cornices. The altar at the far end had been completely encased in skulls, their screaming grins staring blankly at what had become of the rest of their bodies, their brethren.

"I believe we have found the disagreeable," said Christian.

Tristan shivered. It was a unique, artistic sort of gruesome, and it all smelled like stale death. Like Gana. Tristan imagined he could hear the voices of imprisoned souls calling from deep beneath the stone floor. Death reigned in the parapets as well, painted as they were with the images of the god himself. In the classic depictions, both sacred and profane, Lord Death was only ever accompanied by his Angels of Fire, those designated to deliver unjust souls to their ultimate retribution. Here, though, the Angels catered to their human penitents, bestowing upon them lavish gifts and worldly delights.

Had he not been in shackles and surrounded by the bones of Kassora's most loyal subjects, Tristan might have laughed at the unmitigated hubris.

Gana strode forward and stepped onto the dais, standing before the altar. She spread her arms wide, her voluminous sleeves opening out like the wings of the angels she worshipped. The cockatrice at her neck stirred, hissed, and licked the air with its forked tongue. What vermillion light shone through the incomplete windows did not flatter her, and her position atop the dais made Mordant appear even more diminutive — and no less slimy.

"Alight!"

At Gana's command, hundreds of candles throughout the temple burst into flame. Tristan had not noticed their presence for the bones, but the soft glow brought the skeletons in the architecture to a kind of life. Shadows danced in eye sockets and wax began to drip like sweat. The scent of smoke and tallow mingled with the stench of old death.

"Bring them to me!" Gana's cry caught in the domed ceiling and amplified into godlike tones. Dutifully, the red soldiers pushed Tristan and his siblings forward. "I would have you witness the power that brought this city to its knees."

Tristan could imagine Gana having the power to speed a ship across the seven seas, but he could not see her — or anyone beyond a god, for that matter — creating the wreckage that was their former kingdom.

Mordant's mistress crooked a finger at the guards. "Bring me the eldest."

"Sorry, but the eldest has flown the coop," said Bernard.

"Would you like to leave a message?" asked Rene.

Both the twins were slapped by the guards for their insolence, but they bobbed back up, red cheeked and smiling.

"She'll settle for the eldest brother present," sneered Mordant. With a wave of his hand, the guard beside Christian pushed him forward.

As one, the siblings sprang into action.

Rene and Bernard quickly overpowered their respective guards and ran to surround Christian, but François had already beaten them there. He leapt upon the back of Christian's guard and, heedless of his weak arm, wrapped the chain of his shackles around the man's throat. Elisa bit the guard who held her. When he yelped, she dropped to the ground, rolling her body so that he tripped over her petite form. When he fell, she grabbed his dagger and held it to his throat.

Before Tristan could launch himself into the air, the Infidel had pinned his wings behind his back. Tristan's body snapped down with a thud that rattled his bones.

"Drop your weapons," growled Mordant, "or he'll rip his wings off."

Elisa's dagger clattered to the ground. François released the guard. He did not leave Christian's side, however. The brothers surrounded Christian, each of them facing out, hands raised in attack positions, despite the shackles.

Suddenly, Tristan's shackles began to warm. Elisa was the first to scream as her flesh sizzled beneath the hot iron.

"Stop this!" cried Christian. He pushed his way out of the circle of his younger brothers and strode forward of his own accord. He bowed before Gana. "I will come to you willingly. Just please, stop hurting my family."

Mordant's smirk mirrored the one on Gana's face. "But of course. The hurting always stops in the end."

In the end. Meaning the hurting would stop when they were all dead.

"Why do you need our blood?" yelled Tristan. "What difference does it make?"

"The stronger the blood, the stronger the power," said Gana. "You are children of the Four Winds. When I consume you, I will consume your power as well. In doing so, I can increase my own power greatly for a short time, or choose to stretch it out, savoring each of you to prolong my pleasure."

"'Consume' us?" asked Bernard.

"Does that mean what I think it means?" asked Rene.

"If it means am I going to drink your blood, then yes," said Gana. "The temple will partake of you as well." She indicated the bones in the floor beneath their feet, and Tristan realized that the maze was a series of grooves meant to channel the blood and direct it into a certain pattern . . . perhaps a sacred rune of the Fire Gods. There was nowhere to run and no way to separate his bare feet from the floor. In minutes, his toes would be awash in his brother's blood and the room would be flooded with vile power.

"It's just as well the eldest got away; he would have been little more than a snack." Gana reached forward and raked her red nails across Christian's cheek. "I will reap a far greater reward from you, my precious."

"And what do you get out of this?" Tristan addressed Mordant. "Aren't you afraid she'll 'consume' you too when she's finished with us?"

"I made her," said Mordant. "I saved her from the wastrel refuse and molded her into the figure you see before you. Her loyalty belongs to only me."

Again, Tristan bit back a laugh. Bernard and Rene weren't so successful.

"You fool, she'll have you for breakfast," said Rene.

"Who's the ruler of the Green Isles *now?*" asked Bernard.

Tristan felt his shackles burn again, and the twins fell to their knees in pain.

François seemed to have been waiting for this opportunity. Up he sprang, hurtling his body toward Gana. The burning chains between his shackles pushed into her dress and the fabric began to smoke. The guards on the dais were so concerned for their mistress that they missed Christian's duck and lunge, deflecting Mordant's unsheathed dagger. Christian moved to add his strength to François's, but it was too late.

Mordant's blade had already pierced François's heart.

17

The Wrong God

PAPA HAD NAMED his ship *Seven's Seas,* and Friday stood proudly upon her deck. The patchwork flag snapped in the wind in all its glory. Mr. Jolicoeur had begun referring to Friday as "Captain" immediately, and though she tried to dissuade them, everyone else on the ship followed suit without question.

Everyone but Philippe.

In this, Friday agreed with the swan brother. She couldn't think of anyone in her family less suited to be captain of anything. Her skills would be put to better use mending sails. What would Thursday say? With any luck, her seafaring, pirate-queen sister would never find out.

Friday cupped the brass bed knob in the pocket of her skirt. It remained cool to the touch, though she had not let go of it since they had set sail. Mr. Jolicoeur suggested they not use her gift until they were well clear of the shore and out into open waters.

"Does the height bother you?"

Philippe's question drew her attention to the sheer expanse of the water below her—the water she had almost died in at the ocean's creation. He wore a thin shirt of mail and a sword at his hip, purloined, no doubt, from the training grounds.

"No," she answered honestly. "I am not afraid."

"Good," he said. "Because if you fall this time, I'm not coming after you."

"I wouldn't ask you to," Friday shot back at him. "Right now, I have Tristan's love and the faith of every person aboard this ship. I feel like I could conquer the world."

"Luckily, we only need to conquer one island nation."

Friday took a deep breath. "I think I can do that."

"I'm not asking you to."

"Of course not," said Friday. "You don't ask for help. You punch first and ask questions later." She took hold of the railing and turned her face into the wind. "I have a sister like you."

The boat rocked over a particularly large wave, forcing Philippe to grab the railing as well to maintain his balance. "I like her already."

Friday smirked. "She's the same one who created this ocean."

"Hmm. Then I take it back."

"But you would do the same, wouldn't you? You would break the world and let chaos reign, just as long as it meant you could kill Mordant."

"Yes." There was no hesitation in his answer. Friday shivered from the passionate intensity that one word held.

"It's amazing," she said. "You look so much like him, but you feel so . . . different."

"Different how?" he asked. "In a way, you were as much a part of my destiny as his. What is it that binds you to him and not . . . the rest of us?"

But Friday did not hear Philippe say "the rest of us." She heard him say "me." *What is it that binds you to him and not me?* Friday looked at him, and for the first time, she was able to sense beyond the anger with which he shielded himself from the world. Deep inside that steely young man was an incredibly frightened little boy. One very tired, very lonely little boy.

Friday slid her hand down the railing toward his. She wanted to reassure him that all was not lost. She wanted to promise him that he would find something, someone — that his heart would heal in time, if he only had the patience to let it. The second her hand touched his, indigo-blue sparks jumped between their skin.

Philippe immediately pulled his hand away and fled to the other side of the ship.

Friday stayed where she was, dumbfounded, one half of her hand a mass of pins and needles. She had embraced all the rest of Tristan's brothers at one point or another, had danced with them at the ball . . . but she had never touched Philippe before this moment. She had been Elisa and the brothers' destiny, yes, and Tristan had been her destiny, hadn't he?

Hadn't he?

"Milady. *Friday.*" Conrad's voice pulled her out of her shock. "There's someone in the hold asking for you. I believe she's a Sister of Earth."

"Thank you, Conrad." Friday released the railing and followed her squire down into the ship's hold, an area made surprisingly airy and spacious due to their considerable lack of cannons. At the far end, leading a circle of men and women in a prayer to the gods, was Sister Carol. Friday waited politely for the closing chorus before embracing her first mentor.

"It is so good to see you!" Friday said with relief. "Here I thought I had greeted everyone. I had no idea you'd come aboard."

Sister Carol gave a wry grin. "You had no idea I survived, you mean. We tough old birds don't give up that easily. Oh my." She put a hand on Friday's arm. "That was careless of me, my dear. I've heard about your recent adventures with the swans, of course. Please forgive me."

Friday forced herself to smile. "It is you who should forgive me, Sister. I'm afraid our plans to make me a dedicate to the Earth Goddess have been thwarted." Earth acolytes were destined to live only for the Goddess. Once Friday had fallen in love with Tristan, she knew this path would become closed to her. Not that she minded; the alternate path set out before her seemed lined with roses. Assuming, of course, that *Seven's Seas* arrived in time for her to rescue her beloved. "Though if I fail, perhaps the Goddess will find it in her heart to take me to her breast once more."

There was a look on Sister Carol's face that Friday had seen before, something more than concern. Friday pushed her confusion about Philippe and her fears for Tristan aside, reaching out to Sister Carol with her soul. What she found was regret, and shame. "Sister?"

The Sister folded her hands and bowed her head. "You were one of my finest pupils, Friday Woodcutter, and you were a boon to our temple, but you were never meant for the Earth Goddess. I blame myself; in my selfishness, I could not let you go."

Friday forced herself to remain calm enough to pose the question she did not want to ask. "Was the Goddess ever going to accept me?"

"Oh, Friday." The Sister took Friday's warm hand in her cool ones. The skin was callused, but soft with age. "We are all children of the Goddess. She will always love you, as She loves all her creatures. Earth is simply not your nature."

Simply? There was nothing simple about this. Of all the things racing through Friday's mind on this rescue mission, the true nature of her, well, nature was something she wasn't ready to add to the list. But . . . it made sense. All of Sister Carol's actions, her attitude toward Friday—it all fell into place.

She tilted her head and considered the Sister. If earth was not her element, then what was it? Not water; Friday felt as foreign on this ship as a bird in mud. Air? No, if that were the case, she would have felt an even stronger connection with Elisa. The only other element left was —

"Fire," Friday whispered. "There is fire in my nature."

Sister Carol sighed. "You can see why we were reluctant to send you to their temple for teaching."

Fire acolytes were not known for their modest dress or purity of soul. Even thinking about the things they taught at the Fire Temple set Friday's cheeks aflame with blush.

"Your gift, the empathy, it is based on passion. Your sensitivity to emotions, the deep connections you form with people, your sheer capacity for *love* — it is all based on the highest level of Fire Magic. It is Spirit Magic."

Friday turned to Conrad. Her squire had known it all along. He had seen the color of her magic with his gift, and in the sky tower she'd seen it, too. Elisa's magic had appeared pale blue as the wind, but Friday's had been red as blood. Red as fire. How had Conrad described it? *The essence of love itself.*

What a fool she was, to spend her whole life serving and planning a path to the wrong god! It seemed that Fate had stepped in with Tristan and saved her from another disappointment, but it still felt like a blow.

"Do not despair," Sister Carol said quickly. "You have not been forsaken. I would have told you before this, had there been a decent teacher in Arilland for you, but all the Spirit Guides walked high into the mountains long ago and disappeared with the dragons. Your mother felt it was best for you to remain with me, with the children, and concentrate on your skills as a seamstress."

Friday wasn't the least bit surprised that her mother had a hand in this deception. Mama had doomed her second child to death with a slip of the tongue, so Friday understood why she might have taken extra care in this matter. Considering the stigma surrounding the Fire disciplines, had Friday known of her true nature, she would have lost herself in misery and self-loathing. Her young life would have been very different, devoid of joy and hope. In Mama's place, Friday most likely would have done the same.

Sister Carol leaned in and placed a kiss on Friday's forehead. "In my humble — and slightly blasphemous — opinion, I believe your true nature transcends that of the elemental gods."

Friday eyed the Sister quizzically. "How exactly is that?"

"Your ability to find the silver lining. To see the best in everything. It is something each one of us strives for and few ever truly achieve. You, Friday Woodcutter, Princess of Arilland, are a guiding light all on your own."

Friday hugged the Sister tightly and thanked her for her kind words, but one lingering thought still niggled in the back of her mind. What would Tristan say when he discovered this? Would he be able to look at her the same way again?

And what on *earth* was she going to do about Philippe?

Without warning, the boat lurched to one side. Friday was glad to have been holding on to Sister Carol so that they both weren't tossed to the floor like the rest of the people in the hold. Cold seawater sprayed through the portholes. Friday felt the apprehension of her fellow passengers wash over her too.

"What is happening?" Sister Carol whispered, so as not to further alarm anyone.

"We'll go up on deck and assess the situation," Friday said calmly. "You'll see to everyone here?" Sister Carol nodded and immediately began ordering everyone to sit securely and calling for the wounded.

Friday and Conrad made their way through the confused people back to the deck. Philippe met them in the doorway with the pair of swans and hastily shoved the birds belowdecks. "Mr. Jolicoeur needs you," he said to Friday.

The spray up here was far more ferocious than it had been in the hold. The salt stung Friday's eyes, and her loose hair, now drenched, slapped against her face. Here and there, Peter and Velius were working to lash crewmen to whatever secure fixture they could find. It was a miracle that Friday and Conrad reached Mr. Jolicoeur without being swept overboard.

Mr. Jolicoeur had his hands on the wheel of the ship. The giant muscles beneath his black skin bulged with tension. Friday sensed that Mr. Jolicoeur was pouring every bit of his not-insubstantial sinew into keeping the ship from losing control. The *Seven's Seas'* first mate was a very large, very strong man—but the sea itself was larger. And stronger.

"Is it a storm?" Friday yelled to him.

"Yes and no," Mr. Jolicoeur said through gritted teeth. "Look." He could not release the wheel to point with his hands, but his eyes went white as he looked up. Above them, the sky was as perfect as a summer's day, clear and blue. A few fluffy, innocent clouds scattered across the horizon like lost sheep.

"Is it a monster?" asked Conrad.

Mr. Jolicoeur shook his head. He growled as the wheel slipped out of his hand for a moment and struggled to regain control. "I believe," he said, "that the sea which came to visit Arilland is once more taking its leave."

Her first mate was right. For all that the *Seven's Seas* was being buffeted on all sides, it was obvious that by and large they were moving swiftly eastward. Along the horizon, Friday began to see trees.

"The gift!" yelled Mr. Jolicoeur. "Use it now!"

Friday removed the bed knob from her pocket. At that moment, an enormous wave hit the side of the ship, ripping the brass bauble from her grasp. Spry Conrad leapt up to snatch the item out of the air, but his hands were too small, and it fell tumbling to the deck.

Friday and her squire gave chase, throwing themselves in the path of the ball as the ship rolled this way and that, ever diverting the bed knob out of their reach. They raced up the length of the ship to the bow and back down again, swerving right and left, dodging crewmen and flying sails and rogue waves. Finally, as the bauble was about to fly beyond the stern railing, the ship shifted once more and Friday pounced. Her left forearm landed painfully on the knob, but her right hand managed to swoop in and capture it before it had a chance to slip away again.

Mr. Humbug had told Friday to cup the ball in her hands and whisper to it, but Friday wasn't sure the gods would hear a whisper in this din. With the ball wedged between her hand and her forearm, Friday yelled, "Please take us to the Green Isles!"

The world beneath them roared. Friday managed to push the bed knob back into her pocket. Philippe fell to the deck beside her, grabbing Friday with one arm and the railing with the other. Friday held on for dear life. Beside her, Conrad did the same.

From their vantage point at the ship's stern, the three of them saw everything. And in the heat of that moment, with emotions running high all over the ship, Friday felt everything as well. She focused on her own fluttering heart, and Philippe's, in an attempt to keep from losing her grip on reality — or the railing.

Earth and water rose up behind and beneath them at the same time. In the waves of earth rose all the colors of autumn, gold and russet and green. Rolling hills of forests and orchards and meadows and field after field of crops re-laid themselves in their wake. In the waves of ocean crashed schools of fish and larger creatures that Friday had only ever read about in Wednesday's books. Dolphins and narwhales and Great Wyrms raced the ship to the sea — the proper sea, the one that had existed long before Friday's hotheaded sister had summoned it.

Friday felt the wood of the ship creak beneath her under the stress of . . . flying. They must have been flying. Friday couldn't tell for sure, but she doubted they were low enough to touch so much as a crest of the endless high waves of water and earth wrestling below. They would surely be ripped apart between the two forces, if they weren't ripped apart by the Four Winds. Did Philippe's patron gods care enough about him to bless a flying ship full of strangers? Friday trusted Papa's skill and the protective runes Peter had carved from stem to stern, but if the gods had meant for ships to fly, they would have invented mechanical wings.

Even if she had full control of her Fire nature, she wouldn't have been able to help the situation. The last thing any sailor wanted on his ship was a fire. Instead, Friday concentrated on what Sister Carol had said and found the beauty in the situation. She reached up to the seam where her needle hid and pressed the pad of her thumb against the tip. For the first time in her life, the sharp point pierced the skin.

Friday had not learned runes from Fairy Godmother Joy as Peter had, so she drew the most powerful symbol she knew: a circle. A circle was complete and never-ending. It represented family, a whole greater than the sum of its parts. Friday took the colorful image of the churning earth and water before her into her heart, and from there shared the amazing, impossible image with every person on the ship.

She could almost feel the collective intake of breath at the sight, the gasps of delight and awe. Tears were shed, and each mind wondered how to put it into words so that they might tell their children upon their return. Friday could do nothing about the strange forces at work beneath them, or the overall integrity of her father's creation, but with her power over emotions she managed to turn a ship of frightened strangers into a ship of confident dreamers in the space of a few heartbeats. This image, this shared experience, would bind them together forever like few other things in life would.

Like her bond with Tristan.

She felt Conrad's hand reach out and pat her ankle reassuringly. He knew what she was up to; he could probably see the color as she worked her magic. If the passengers of this ship had not been an army before, they were now.

Philippe pulled Friday to him, buried his head in her shoulder, and wept. She hugged him back, so that he knew he was not alone.

Faster and faster the ship flew, until there was nothing below them but calm, blue ocean. They raced the clouds in the sky and won. The wind dried her hair, tangling it mercilessly, and chilled her to the bone. She shut her eyes against the blast. Deep in her soul, she felt the people belowdecks huddle against one another for warmth.

She did not know how much longer the ship meant to fly — safely past the Troll Kingdom at least, she hoped — and so she tried to think warm thoughts. She brought to mind a sunny day in summer in a meadow full of dandelions. She recalled the hardest day of her chores when she worked up a sweat, and the fur-lined gloves Papa had given her last midwinter. What else was warm?

And then she remembered Tristan's kiss, their last kiss, deep in the dungeons when they had arrived at the end of the curse and there was the very real possibility that he would live no tomorrows as a human. Through their lips they shared what might have been one of Tristan's final breaths. The memory of it still brought a flush to her body and made her toes curl.

In her arms, Philippe went very still. On the decks beneath her, she could feel the crew sigh.

It occurred to Friday to be embarrassed for sharing such a moment, but all the people who had joined this crew knew exactly what they were in for, and why. If they had any lingering doubts that Friday's love for Tristan was less than true, those doubts had vanished.

Friday had not always considered herself to be equal among her siblings, but by the time the ship finally came to rest in the harbor, she felt she had finally lived up to the Woodcutter name. Philippe removed himself from her presence immediately. But she was still afraid to let go of the railing.

Beside her, Conrad slowly got to his feet. "Milady?" He held out his hand to her, and she let him help her stand. Before he did anything else, he bowed to her, as low as he might have to any king or queen. "It remains my honor to serve as your squire," he told her.

"Thank you," Friday said, for she was not sure what else might be appropriate in this moment. "Mr. Jolicoeur?" Friday asked tentatively.

The large man seemed to be frozen to the wheel. Friday rubbed her hands up his arms, willing his muscles to release. Finally, Mr. Jolicoeur exhaled, relaxed, and let go. "Thank you, my captain."

"You have steered us well," said Friday. "I think." In truth, she had no idea where they were. The three of them made their way to the bow of the ship, helping the crew to unbind themselves from masts and railings along the way.

The port where they had docked lay in ruins. She could make out no single edifice that still stood above the rubble.

"This is old devastation," said Mr. Jolicoeur.

"Mordant did this when he seized the throne," said Philippe. The armor of his anger had returned in full force.

"Why would anyone ruin a perfectly good kingdom?" asked Conrad. "Especially if you were the one who wanted to rule it?"

"Some men prefer to start fresh," answered Mr. Jolicoeur. "They want to remake their cities and castles to their own tastes."

"But nothing was remade here," said Friday. "Only destroyed."

Mr. Jolicoeur nodded. "That speaks to the temperament of the new ruler. One needs manpower to rebuild a fence, let alone a city. If the men have fled out of loyalty to the former king and queen, there is no one left to rebuild."

"There is another possibility," said Conrad.

Mr. Jolicoeur nodded. "Yes, but I don't like considering that one."

"What?" asked Friday. "What is the other possibility?"

"That the former citizens of our kingdom are all dead," said Philippe. "Just like my parents."

The idea was deplorable, but the likelihood was all too real. "Then we must hurry," she said, "before any of the other former citizens of Kassora join them." She looked at the docks, and then to Mr. Jolicoeur. "Can you lower us down?"

Mr. Jolicoeur considered the ramshackle structure. "It may fall to pieces at any moment."

Friday looked from Conrad to Philippe, who would still not meet her gaze. Velius and Peter would be furious that she had convinced her first mate to let her down ahead of them. "We're willing to take that chance."

"Very well. I will lower you three, but I will send the rest of the troops in by skiff."

Friday looped the rope around her waist and Conrad tangled his arm into it as well. "We will head up to the ridge there to see what we can find. Will you please tell my brother and the duke?"

Mr. Jolicoeur made a fist with his right hand and placed it over his left breast. "Yes, Captain."

"You are an amazing person, Mr. Jolicoeur." Friday made the large man bend down to her so that she could kiss him on the cheek in gratitude. Even beneath his dark skin, she could make out his blush.

As soon as her feet touched the crumbling dock, she knew where Tristan and his siblings had gone. She could taste their frustration and terror as if it still lingered in the dusty air. Philippe immediately broke into a run, heedless of the rotting wood that fell away beneath his boots. Conrad kept pace with Friday. When the terrain became too rocky, he ran in front of her to show her where she might safely put her feet without turning an ankle.

When they reached the ruins at the city's summit, Friday spotted the Fire Temple in the distance. Smoke rose from its many chimneys. Philippe tore down the hill, heedless of the wreckage in his path, and threw himself against the garish, peeling gold-leaf doors. In an instant, Friday was beside him.

She and Conrad gagged at the smell of new smoke and old death. Before them, a melee ensued. Elisa and the brothers fought with the red-coated guards. The Infidel held Tristan by the wings and looked ready to rip them out. And upon the dais she watched as Mordant's blade missed Christian before finding François.

"NO!" Philippe's cry from the doorway cut through the din. And for a moment, the room was theirs.

18

Benevolence

SHE'D GOTTEN THEIR MESSAGE.

Tristan's shoulders were a mass of pain from the Infidel's rough handling of his wings, and his brain had yet to process the horror he had just witnesses upon the dais, but as soon as his eyes alit on his beautiful beloved, every other thought flew from his mind. She had come. And somehow, she'd found Philippe along the way . . . and magically traversed half the world with him to rescue them. But not all of them.

It was too late for François.

At Philippe's cry, it seemed as if the whole room started screaming all at once. Elisa clawed at the guard who held her, desperately trying to reach François on the dais. Christian and the twins pulled at their own burning shackles while using the red-hot cuffs to fend off several more of Mordant's men. Tristan ripped himself from the Infidel's grasp, leaving the assassin with hands full of precious feathers. He spread his wings, despite the pain, and launched himself into the air as best he could. He flew far enough to make the dais, landing squarely on the chest of a now unconscious Gana. The iron cuffs round his wrists went cold once more. The candles in the sanctuary dimmed ever so slightly.

Mordant took his dagger out of François's body and slithered into the shadows. They would find him. He could not go far. Right now, Tristan's main concern was his youngest brother. Careful of his chains, he knelt and took François into his arms, hoping to say one last word to the brother who had kept their spirits up for so long.

"François," he wept. But though his baby brother's soul may have heard the word from the ether, his body would speak no more. A great river of blood flowed from the gaping hole in François's shirt, over Tristan's hands, and into the floor. Heedless of the mess, Tristan clasped his brother's lifeless body to his bare chest. He begged the Winds to escort François to a place of peace, in the arms of the gods he had always loved.

Behind him, Gana began to laugh. Her scaled serpent-bird glided happy circles in the air beside her.

"He was not the brother I had selected," she said from the blood-covered floor, "but I will happily consume his essence just the same."

Tristan realized that François's blood was creeping along

the bone maze in the floor, pouring down the runnels and decorating the runes there. The entire floor began to glow with a red light, and there was a buzzing in Tristan's ears.

Gana inhaled, taking the red light into her body. Tristan made to leap for the sorceress, but the iron shackles burned hot once more, stopping him in his tracks. Tristan seized the opportunity. He tore open François's shirt and rested his chains against the wound, effectively cauterizing it and stopping the flow of blood. The sorceress saw his ruse and the shackles burned even hotter, blistering his flesh and turning the iron to ash.

The cockatrice landed on François's head, smugly curling his tail around a throat that would no longer speak. Tristan raised a ruined arm to knock the animal away, but the cockatrice's eyes met his and held them. Its eyes seemed almost scaled, like its skin, swirling with reds and golds and subtle blues like the flame of a candle. Tristan managed to pull his eyes away before he became lost in them, but it was already too late. He had almost completely shifted his gaze back to the door before his body turned to stone.

Tristan's mind remained intact; he could still hear and smell and see everything around him, but he was helpless to do anything but witness their defeat.

"Shame on you, pet! I could have used that one too. Well, no matter. There is more than enough blood here to give me sustenance and defeat them all."

"Is that so?" Friday strode confidently to the altar, breathing in the same red light. Her hair was wild, a giant halo of messy curls standing up all around her head. Her gray eyes shone almost ice white in the candlelight. The rest of her — her skirt, her skin, her shoes — began to glow as red as the shackles.

"If you had the first clue as to what you were doing, little one," Gana said to Friday, "you would know that you can't fight fire with fire."

"That is as may be," said Friday. "Perhaps I can't defeat you. But we can certainly fight." She pointed a finger at the altar. The candlestick to Gana's left burst into flame, singeing the sleeve of her gown.

Gana bundled the cloth in her hand and extinguished the fire. "Well met, princess. I will enjoy adding your magic to mine. But first, let's play." The sorceress pointed as Friday had done.

Friday leapt to the left as several candlesticks were enveloped in one great burst. The conflagration was short lived, however. A gust of wind whistled through the broken windows and toppled the sticks over, guttering the candles.

"What the . . . ?"

"Good job, Elisa!" cried Bernard.

Elisa stepped forward and clasped hands with Friday, and her shackles fell to ashes. Now that the strength of François's blood had fully permeated the room, it enabled all *three* magic users in the vicinity. Tristan was so proud of both his sister and Friday in that moment; he only wished that François was still around to witness it. Or that he could take up arms and join them in turning the tide.

With all the magic in this room, couldn't someone free him from this stone prison?

Streaks of fire continued to cross from one side of the room to another. Candles exploded. His brothers fought the guards as best they could while still in chains — theirs had not fallen to pieces as Tristan's and Elisa's had. They fought with bones and candlesticks and sometimes their bare hands. Every time they seemed to have a guard pinned down, the Infidel overpowered the brothers, sometimes two at a time. Glass shattered above him, bouncing harmlessly off his skin as it fell.

From high above the skull-covered altar, two white swans descended from the skies. Tristan mentally cheered their arrival, as he could not do so out loud. Sebastien and Odette went straight for the cockatrice.

Tristan could not move his head to follow the scuffle, but judging by the hissing squawks and crunch of bones, the swans were winning. When there was nothing but silence, Sebastien and Odette waddled back into view. Heedless of the blood, they curled up next to François, on either side of his head, and rested their beaks lovingly across his neck.

Tristan blinked. It seemed his petrification was fading with the death of Gana's beast, but not nearly fast enough.

The front door burst open again, this time coming off its hinges entirely. Through the entrance poured a sizeable civilian army, led by Duke Velius and Friday's brother Peter. Every man and woman wore some piece of patchwork clothing, perhaps in tribute to his beloved. They fought with conviction, cutting down their enemies in almost no time at all. It was truly a sight to behold, and Tristan was sorry that he could not be part of it.

There was still Gana to be dealt with, however, and the

Infidel, who managed to hold back the patchwork tide with naught but his personal agility and two daggers. And Mordant was still hiding somewhere.

"MORDANT!" Philippe screamed for the vile usurper. The brothers scattered in every direction, each with a contingent of Friday's soldiers.

Velius added his fey magic to Friday's and Elisa's. The candles surrounding Gana all flew into the air at once, their flames now glowing a deep blue. They circled around her, trapping her on the altar. And when they attacked, they melted into her, burning her skin.

Gana took one more deep breath of the red light and as she exhaled, she screamed. Her body dissolved into smoke. So, too, did the body of the Infidel. The dark clouds mingled together and fled up through the chimneys and out to the sky.

Velius and Elisa released Friday, who ran down the center of the sanctuary toward the altar. Tristan stood stiffly, wings and body covered in blood from head to toe, and opened his arms to receive her embrace.

Mordant got to her first.

Somehow, the slimy red son of a snake had slithered into the shadows between the statues and hidden there, still as death, waiting for an opportunity. And he'd found it. Friday screamed, kicking and flailing. Tristan lunged forward, ready to take on Mordant with his bare hands. From the opposite side, Philippe closed in as well.

"BACK!" Mordant pressed his dagger into Friday's throat, deep enough for her to wince. Tristan and Philippe froze. They moved no closer, but they did not move any farther away, either. "Be still, witch." A drop of blood trickled down Friday's neck and she obeyed. "Everyone, drop your weapons."

There was the briefest of hesitations before Velius said, "Do as he asks."

Swords and daggers and pitchforks clattered to the stone floor. The twins tossed their bones aside. Elisa and Velius raised their empty hands. Tristan's body ached to overpower Mordant and set Friday free. Across from him, Philippe raised his eyebrows, urging him to do so. Perhaps, if they both moved at exactly the same time, they could overpower Mordant before he had a chance to hurt Friday.

Tristan shook his head and growled, at both his brother and himself. He couldn't take that chance.

"Step away from each other," Mordant said. Velius and Elisa complied.

"Tell us what it is you want," said Christian.

"I want the Green Isles," said Mordant.

Philippe seethed. "Death first."

Tristan took a step forward while Philippe had Mordant's attention, but Mordant spun himself and Friday back to Tristan; the blood from her neck began to stain her shirt above her heart. "I SAID, BACK!"

"Please," Friday begged without moving.

"I'm sure we can find you a vessel of some sort," Peter offered. "We could ensure your safe passage off the island if you promise never to return."

"NO," said Philippe.

"This is my kingdom!" cried Mordant. "Mine! I fought for it and won!"

"We fought back," said Rene.

"And you lost," said Bernard.

"Gaaaaaanaaaaaaa!" Mordant called repeatedly to his mistress, but she did not answer. He called to his gods, but they did not come to his aid. Finally, he began muttering to himself, nonsense words that Tristan couldn't make out.

He's lost more than this kingdom, thought Tristan. *He's lost his mind.* But his true love was in the arms of this madman. "Just tell us what you want."

Mordant stared at Tristan; his dark eyes were wild. He pulled Friday's head back by her hair with one hand, and with the other he stabbed his dagger deep into her belly.

"I want to see you watch her die."

The company surged forward again, but Mordant replaced his dagger at Friday's neck. "Come any closer and she dies more quickly. I have decided to grant you both enough time to say your goodbyes." Mordant smiled. "Let it be said: I was ever a ruler of grace and benevolence."

Tristan would never have called Mordant "benevolent." But he had to say something. "Friday . . ." he began, and then remembered that the last word he'd spoken to his brother had been his name.

"Do you love me?" Her voice was a gargled whisper of pain.

Tristan could feel his heart breaking into a thousand pieces. "You know I do."

"And do you . . ." She seemed to lose her breath. Tristan

was worried she'd lost more than that, but she inhaled a bit of the waning red light still emanating from the bones at her feet and some strength seemed to return. "Can you forgive me for what I am?"

Tristan spread his freakishly giant wings wide. "Only if you forgive what I am as well."

Friday's face remained pinched and serious. Suddenly, something occurred to Tristan. "I wish I could take your pain," he said to her.

"You can't," she whimpered. That same thought had occurred to her, but she wasn't able to convince her heart to complete such a task. This was why she'd sought his forgiveness. And he'd made a joke! Gods, he was a fool.

"I love you," he said, this time without embellishment. "And I forgive you."

A tear slipped down her cheek as she inhaled another deep breath of the red light and slowly reached up to touch the hand with which Mordant held the dagger at her neck. "Forgive me," Tristan heard her whisper again.

This time, it was Mordant who doubled over.

Friday spun out of his grasp and threw herself into Tristan's arms. The dagger dropped to the ground. Slowly, Mordant followed. "What have you done?" he gasped.

"It was you who sentenced yourself," said Velius. "You have died by your own hand."

But Mordant was dying too slowly for Philippe. Tristan's almost-twin picked his sword up off the floor, stepped forward, and stabbed Mordant directly in his heart.

Friday trembled in Tristan's arms. The pale skin beneath her torn shirt was unmarred, with not so much as a drop of blood or bruise to show that Mordant had touched her at all. Just as she had taken Tristan's nearly fatal wound from him when they'd first met, she'd returned to Mordant the wound he'd given her. It was a power Friday had only been able to access when her gifts had been amplified by someone else's magic.

Tristan's breath caught in his throat as he swallowed a sob. François would be proud to know that his death had saved Friday's life. Tristan tilted his head heavenward. Somewhere above them, with any luck, François knew.

Somewhere below them, Mordant drew his final breath on a bone-covered floor. All of them stood silent, patiently waiting for the usurper to die.

Well, all but one.

Applause broke out from behind the altar. From the shadows stepped a young, pale-skinned man with shoulder-length black hair and long, flowing black robes.

"Bravo!" the man cried, wiping an imaginary tear from his eye. "Bravo! That was wonderful." He strode up to Tristan and Friday and looked them over from head to toe. "I must say, you two are the most fabulous gift I've ever received." He took them both by the cheeks and kissed their foreheads.

"Who are you?" Tristan couldn't help but ask.

"Oh, must we ruin it?"

"He is Lord Death," said Velius.

Lord Death stuck his tongue out at the duke. "You always were a spoilsport."

"We were a gift?" Friday asked.

"From my wife!" Lord Death boasted. "She's a trickster, that one." He turned to Peter. "You remind me of her, a little."

"Your wife," Friday clarified.

"Of course!" He clapped his hands together again. "You know her better as Fate."

Friday's head settled back down on Tristan's chest in defeat.

"I'd like to have some words with your wife," said Tristan.

"Wouldn't we all?" said Lord Death. "Now, where were we?"

"You were explaining about gifts," prompted Bernard.

"Yes, thank you. Don't you see? Oh, it's a beautiful thing." Lord Death stepped back slightly to admire them as if they were a framed portrait. "An Angel of Feathers and an Angel of Fire."

At the mention of angels, two figures manifested out of the red light and smoke beside Lord Death. One was a man with wings of feathers. The other was a woman with wings of fire.

"You"—Lord Death pointed to the lifeless body of Mordant—"have been a naughty little boy."

From Mordant's body rose a shade with the same silhouette as the man lying prone at its feet. "You and your cohorts have trapped many a good soul in this edifice." Lord Death shook his finger at the cowering shade. "Tsk-tsk. And *you!*"

Lord Death moved to the altar, where a translucent image of François hovered above his body. "You are a hero, sir, and your legend will be spoken of for years to come." He bowed low to François.

"No."

They all turned to Philippe, who still stood over Mordant's soulless corpse. "It should be me," said Philippe. "Take me instead."

Lord Death shook his head. "That's not how it works, my brave warrior."

But Philippe would not be dissuaded. Leave it to his bull-headed brother to be the one to not back down from a god. "Oh no?" He crossed his arms over his chest. "Ask your wife."

Lord Death's brow furrowed. A moment later it smoothed, and the god smiled from ear to ear. "Well played, sir." With a snap of his fingers, Philippe collapsed.

"No!" Friday tore herself from Tristan's embrace and fell to her knees at Philippe's side. Elisa did the same, crying out his name over and over again.

Tristan heard a raspy cough. Behind him on the altar, a very pale François gingerly lifted himself out of a pool of drying blood. "What happened?"

"Your brother won a duel with a god, François," said Lord Death. "And now we must bid him *adieu*."

Humbly, Philippe's shade rose from the body on the ground. One by one, Philippe's shade met the eyes of everyone in that room. When he looked at Friday, she closed her eyes and put a hand to her lips. When his gaze fell to Christian, Philippe dropped to one ghostly knee and bowed his head in a pledge of fealty to the new ruler of Kassora. The rest of the room bowed with him.

Tristan could not keep his tears from falling, nor did he

want to. Philippe's form wavered until he blinked them away. Christian nodded with a hand on his heart, unable to force his insubstantial brother to rise. The Angel of Feathers took care of that for him, placing a gentle hand on Philippe's shoulder.

"I'm not sure I remember the last time I saw anything so touching," said Lord Death. "But, as brilliant as this has been, I'm afraid it's time to go."

"Thank you," said Tristan. He wasn't quite sure which part of his involvement he was thanking the god for, but it seemed the right thing to do.

Lord Death winked. "This isn't forever, my friend. We shall meet again."

Despite the overwhelming sadness of the occasion, Tristan caught himself smiling. "Undoubtedly."

It was the answer Philippe would have given.

"And you," Lord Death snapped back over his shoulder at Mordant's slimy shade.

The Angel of Fire looked entirely too pleased. The tall, pre-ternaturally beautiful woman strode majestically to the shade and lifted him up by his throat. Mordant wriggled and writhed in her gasp. She tossed her hair — sparks snapped in the air — and gave a low, knowing chortle that Tristan hoped he would never hear again.

With a wave of her free hand, every image of submissive fire-winged angels that had been painted inside the sanctuary charred black and smoldered.

"All wrong," said Lord Death. "We look forward to show-ing you what the Angels of Fire are really capable of." With that, the Angels of Feathers and Fire disappeared again, along with their charges.

A very large man in a patchwork shirt scooped Philippe's body up into his very large arms. No one made a move to touch Mordant. "We should be going," said the man.

"Thank you, Mr. Jolicoeur," said Friday. She bowed to the god. "And thank you, My Lord."

"I assure you, the pleasure was all mine." Lord Death reached up and pinched both their cheeks. "Wonderful!" he said, and then vanished into thin air.

Christian was the first one who dared speak. "Well, that was—"

"Wait!" yelled a voice, and in a snap, Lord Death had reappeared. "You really should leave now. I'll be taking all the souls in this building to the other side with me, and there won't be much left afterward."

"Yes, sir!" said Christian. With a salute, Lord Death disappeared once more. The floor began to shake, and what glass remained in the windows began to crack.

"I don't need to be told twice," said Peter. "Let's get out of here."

The swans were the first to flee. Velius stayed behind to make sure everyone had evacuated the Fire Temple before leaving himself. The second after he crossed the threshold, the gold plating aged to rust and the walls toppled in on themselves.

The remaining heirs of Kassora looked on in silence as the last building left standing in their kingdom was crumbled to dust by the hand of a god.

19

A Heart as Big as the Moon

IN THE END, it was Friday who gave Tristan his first flying lesson. She placed Mr. Humbug's brass ball into his cupped hands and bade him whisper the name of the port city Velius had told them. From there they would take the King's Road to Arilland, assuming it had returned once Saturday's magical ocean had fled. Mr. Jolicoeur had decided to remain with the ship. He assured Friday that he would see it safely into the hands of a good owner: his former captain, the Pirate Queen Thursday Woodcutter.

Christian, Elisa, François, and the twins remained on the Green Isles, though not in Kassora. Mr. Jolicoeur had sailed them to another island in the chain, and then another, until they discovered a group of former Kassorans who had run from

Mordant's forces and survived in hiding. When they told the people there of Mordant's defeat and his sorceress's exile, the people bowed to Christian and recognized him as King of the Green Isles.

Friday gave Christian her flag, so that the white swan upon the colorful background might stand for peace, unity, and re-membrance. He vowed that his people would remain in hiding no more, encouraging men, women, and children to spread the stories far and wide so that they knew it was safe to come home.

They did not include Lord Death in their recounting. No one would have believed it anyway.

King Christian gave Tristan and Friday his blessing, both to be together and to leave, with the condition that they postpone any sort of formal wedding until the Green Isles was ready to host a proper celebration. Standing side by side with ribbons wrapped around their entwined hands, they had agreed.

"Are you ready to fly without wings?" Friday asked him when she handed him the bauble.

"I've been flying since I met you," said Tristan, "my girl with a heart as big as the moon."

~~llee~~

Friday let Tristan be the one to tell Rumbold and Sunday the de-tails of Mordant's defeat. Rumbold congratulated them on their triumph and promised to send aid to the Green Isles as soon as possible. Sunday expressed their extreme sorrow at Philippe's loss, and ordered white candles lit in all the windows of the palace in his honor.

Friday and Tristan made their own pilgrimage to the top of the sky tower. They lit their own candle there and said a prayer to each of the Four Winds and all the Elemental Gods. Without Elisa's magic to keep the wind at bay, Friday used her own strength to maintain the candle's flame. The wax glowed a deep red while the stones below it glowed indigo. The flower petals they tossed were instantly caught up in the drafts and carried far, far away.

From the moment they'd set foot in Arilland, Friday had not been able to stop thinking of the towerhouse. Her home. She wasn't sure how to go back to her quiet life, the one she'd had before Saturday had torn the world in two, but she did miss it. Tristan promised to milk cows with her or cross-stitch in the queen's solar, whichever she preferred. Friday loved him for every word.

But first, of course, Sunday had to throw another ball.

Thankfully, Friday still had Monday's giant white chiffon gown in her rooms.

Tristan was another matter. "Perhaps you might be able to fashion another shirt for me?" he asked sweetly. "If you have the time, of course."

Friday kissed him on the cheek. "You know I will. Even if I have to cut my own dress in half for the material."

The shirt Tristan had worn while in the islands and all the way home had, in fact, been made of the extra patchwork skirts she'd brought with her on the voyage. She'd taken the time to unpick the hems, salvage the thread, and use it again to make a shirt for him that covered his body but still left his wings free to move. It had been a challenge. Even with the proper supplies, it still would have been a challenge of which her mentor would have been proud.

"I meant to ask, who was it that made your shirt for that first ball?" Friday would remember that ball — and that kiss — for the rest of her life, as would anyone who had journeyed with Friday on the *Seven's Seas*. She would also remember that strange, haphazard shirt he'd worn with all the buckles.

Tristan gave her a dazzling smile. "Did you like it?"

"It was . . ." What was the best way to be judicious? He looked so proud; Friday had seen the same smile often enough on Michael to recognize it. She didn't want to hurt his feelings. ". . . quite creative."

"I was similarly impressed. The guards' tailor whipped that up for me in almost no time flat."

"Who?" Friday had never heard of such a person. Since when did the guards have a tailor? Had one arrived with the refugees and not made himself known to her?

"He said his name was Grinny."

Friday couldn't help herself. She burst out laughing so hard she doubled over from the effort.

"What my eloquent sister is trying to tell you," Peter said helpfully, "is that Grinny Tram isn't the tailor. He's the hostler."

The look on Tristan's face was priceless. It sent Friday into paroxysms of laughter all over again.

"That shirt of yours was pretty much his equivalent of saddling a horse," said Peter. "Only upside down."

Tristan looked as if he was giving the matter serious thought. "It did look rather saddle-like, now that you mention it."

"And the *buckles!*" Friday giggled, tears springing to her eyes.

Peter slid his arm deftly over Tristan's wings and draped it around his shoulders. "Grinny's *true* talent is the creation of one seriously potent honey mead."

"You'll have to fetch me a dram sometime," said Tristan, "and we can toast my incredible fashion sense."

With that, Peter led Tristan off to the men's quarters, while Friday scrambled to fetch material and trimming for her new projects. She wanted to find him emerald green satin and gold buttons, if there were any left to be had in the palace. She could use the remnants to trim her own white dress. With any luck, the splash of color would tone down the overwhelming feeling that she was disguising herself as a cloud of fog.

She finished the shirt and had Conrad deliver it to Tristan's room while she finished her dress. In the remaining time, with her remaining fabric, she sewed a new green coat for Mr. Humbug. He deserved so much more; perhaps, in time, her family might one day truly repay him.

If the people of Arilland had been happy about the last fete, they were positively joyous now. Most of the refugees had gone home to their farms and families, but some had stayed, and were welcome. New alliances had formed. Customs and recipes had changed hands. Within a fortnight Arilland had become a hub of commerce, where men and women came to do business while they reunited with the friends they had made during their stay.

Best of all, the farmers had gone home to full harvests and more fertile ground than ever before. Cook's pantry burst at the seams with the surplus of fresh goods. She sent a great deal back to the Temple of the Goddess with Sister Carol. The orphans helped her manage everything — they were Sister Carol's army now. Friday missed them, John and Wendy and Michael most of all.

Sunday's ball was the first reunion of the Arilland refugees. Adults and children alike wore their finest finery — though it was not rare to see a patchwork item or two scattered proudly throughout the crowd. Goods were exchanged, as well as many, many gifts, so many that Friday was overwhelmed by the bounty. The air was filled with laughter and love and hope for the future. Friday let her heart rest in the ease as her hand rested in Tristan's.

His shirt looked amazing, though her gaze rarely strayed from the blue of his smiling eyes. One day, perhaps those eyes would not remind her of Philippe and all they had lost that day.

In the midst of the celebration, there was a fanfare. Sunday and Rumbold appeared at the top of the Grand Stair to address the crowd below.

"It is my great pleasure," said Rumbold, "to pay tribute tonight to a man to whom I, my family, and, dare I say, my country would not be whole without. Honored guests, let us please raise a toast to the esteemed Mr. Henry Humbug!"

There was another fanfare. Conrad brought Friday the green silk coat she'd made for Mr. Humbug. She clutched it nervously, wondering whether or not he would like it.

"Mr. Humbug, would you please step forward?"

The crowd fell silent. Everyone began looking this way and that, but the man was nowhere to be seen.

"Search the castle," she heard Rumbold whisper to his guards. "Be discreet."

The coat weighed heavy in her hands. Friday hoped nothing terrible had happened to Mr. Humbug—too many people in her life had disappeared under mysterious circumstances. Perhaps he had simply anticipated this moment and chose not to be called out in front of so many strangers . . . but somehow, Friday doubted that.

She bade Conrad return the coat to her rooms and leave it on her bed; she would give it to him in the morning, or find a way to send it to wherever he'd gone.

Sunday raised her glass and made a toast anyway. "To the absent man himself," she said. "And other absent friends."

"Hear, hear!" echoed the crowd, and the revelry resumed.

This time, Tristan tried his best not to let his new friends manipulate all of Friday's time. He begrudgingly allowed Peter to cut in and dance with her. Once. Papa attempted to ease Tristan's overdramatic suffering with a flagon of freshly brewed ale. Friday danced with Conrad and Rumbold and several others after that, so she assumed Papa's peace offering had been successful.

It was with great reluctance that Friday retired to her

rooms, still smiling and humming to no one while she danced herself down the hall. Conrad opened the door for her and she walked through dreamily — and then stopped.

"Conrad, where is the coat I made for Mr. Humbug?"

"I laid it on the bed," he told her. "Just like you asked."

Friday walked over to her bed. On top of the sheet where a coat might have once laid was a silver coin. It was not currency, but the kind of coin that couples threw in a well and wished on to keep their love forever. Beautifully inscribed on the coin was the word "Bliss."

"I will always wonder what happened to the donkey," said Conrad. "His name was Bobo."

Friday smiled into the magic of the moment. "Good night, Conrad."

"Good night, Friday."

Friday changed into her nightdress and slipped the silver coin under her pillow. With her heart full of happiness, she slept the most restful, dreamless sleep of her life. She was home. She was loved. And she would do great things.

With a family like the Woodcutters, it does not take a village to write a book.

It takes a kingdom.

Thanks to my beloved cousin, Jamie Feddersen (he would like me to tell you that he's my *favorite* cousin), a wildlife biologist for the Florida Fish and Wildlife Conservation Commission. Jamie was instrumental in that initial "swans or geese?" conversation.

Thanks to Dr. Theda Kontis, Dr. Dave Tunkel, and my other-favorite-cousin Alexandra, who whisked me away to a convention where I was neither a guest nor a star . . . just a niece and a cousin. You will never know how much that meant to me.

Fishy kisses to my Waterworld Mermaids: Carlene Love Flores, Dana Rodgers, Denny S. Bryce, Diana Belchase, Kerri Carpenter, Kimberly MacCarron, Masha Levinson, Pintip Dunn, and Susan Jeffery. My sanity thanks you.

A million thanks to Fairy Godeditor Reka Simonsen and everyone at Harcourt; my tireless publicist Jennifer Groves and her team; Christine Kettner; Julie Tibbott; Joan Lee; Emily Holden; Lisa DiSarro; Jessica Yodis; Daniel Nayeri, and Adah Nuchi.

As always, essential was the magic of my Fairy Godagent Deborah Warren; my Fairy Godfamily: Joe, Kassidy, and Ariell; my OF: Dad, Soteria, Cherie, and West; and my mother, Marcy Kontis, who read every chapter of this as I wrote it. Thank you, Mom, for cheering me on since elementary school.

And thank *you,* my friends and fans who are like family to me, for reading this series, and for sharing our love of fairy tales with the world. May you all live Interestingly Ever After.